No Matter
THE PRICE

DANIEL PARE

Black Rose Writing | Texas

ISBN: 978-1-68433-822-1
PUBLISHED BY BLACK ROSE WRITING
www.blackrosewriting.com

Printed in the United States of America
Suggested Retail Price (SRP) $19.95

No Matter the Price is printed in Jensen

*As a planet-friendly publisher, Black Rose Writing does its best to eliminate unnecessary waste to reduce paper usage and energy costs, while never compromising the reading experience. As a result, the final word count vs. page count may not meet common expectations.

For all the Parents…

No Matter
THE PRICE

Chapter 1

Karen looked around the waiting room and tried not to stare. She flipped the page of a magazine she didn't know the name of. The smaller patients, children ten and under, played with puzzles on a red plastic table in the corner near a fake fern that needed a dusting. Under the watchful eye of their protective parents, who instructed their wounded offspring to sit still in between offering words of encouragement, the kids interacted as if at a playground or a friend's house.

The eleven- and twelve-year-olds, along with a handful of early teens, focused on the screens of their video games with the precision of surgeons. They didn't move from their seats or acknowledge anyone around them. And the older teenagers, some of whom could drive, listened to music on their phones with rounded shoulders and low hanging heads. Most of the girls brushed back the hair that hid half of their faces. Many of the boys did the same.

The room had a mild scent of Novocain despite the former tenant vacating the premises a year earlier. Two of the walls were painted yellow with a blue checkered border and framed posters of cartoon characters served as decorations. The hardwood floor by the entrance curled around to a granite countertop where a pleasant older woman with the name tag BETSY resided. Ms. Betsy greeted everyone with a gap-toothed smile. Next to her, where patients signed in, was a plaque with a happy face that read EVERY DAY IS SPECIAL. AND SO ARE YOU!

Karen turned up her wrist and pulled back a white blouse. It was almost time. Her legs bounced, her mouth felt dry. She rubbed the dark swollen bags under her eyes, mindful not to rub too hard and smear off the bronze plastered makeup, when the rear door of the office swung open. She took a deep breath and stood as Jason emerged, flanked by his psychiatrist.

He wore a hoodie with the strings pulled tight and passed his mother in silence. His gaze was pointed at the floor. The doctor glanced at Karen, nodded slightly, and forced an uncomfortable smile that came across as such. Karen began to follow but stopped.

She spun around to ensure the stranger she once knew so well sat down and didn't wander off like the last time. With the car keys clenched in her hand, she walked past a young couple whispering among themselves. A bright hallway led her to an office with tan cushioned chairs and a plate glass window.

"Thank you for coming in today," Dr. Baker said. She took a seat behind an L-shaped desk. "I know it's awkward meeting at our children's office, but the renovation on the main building is almost complete."

Karen nodded.

"The results of Jason's blood work came back and the news is still positive from that standpoint. Nothing has changed in the last several months. All his numbers are within normal limits with the exception of his vitamin D, which is slightly low. Overall, your son is a physically healthy twenty-one-year-old man."

"Don't you mean boy?" Karen said. She fumbled through her purse for the two crisp one-hundred-dollar bills she withdrew from the bank, and placed them on the desk.

"Jason will be twenty-two next month. I don't consider that to be a boy anymore. Neither should you."

"Can I get a receipt?"

"We'll take care of that when you check out," Dr. Baker said, setting the money aside. "Are you still having some issues with the insurance company?"

"Our plan keeps getting more expensive and the deductible always goes up, never down. They're becoming more stringent on how much and what they will cover."—she shook her head—"But it doesn't matter. Coming here is worth it. It's important. It's worth it for Jason."

Dr. Baker rolled back in her chair and glanced at Jason Turner's chart. It was a thick chart. Too thick. "We've reached a delicate point," she began. "Progress with Jason has been slow, sometimes nonexistent. During the last few sessions it's become obvious he's regressed yet again. I've consulted with numerous colleagues on the subject and you know how many times we've altered his meds. I hate to admit it, but I think we're at an impasse."

"Then you need to try harder," Karen said, raising her voice. "It's my son we're talking about. And you told me yourself—he's a perfectly healthy twenty-one-year-old boy. There has to be something you can do."

"We haven't given up, I assure you. But we've been at this for the past five years and I wanted to be upfront. You deserve that. The results aren't there. I'm not sure they ever will be if the treatment continues here."—she stopped and forced the uncomfortable smile again—"I'm reluctant to mention this but . . . You may want to consider a change in treatment. A change in therapists."

Karen stepped away from her seat and walked to the window. She took in the view of a three-story building that contained a law firm and a chiropractor office with a smoothie shop on the corner. Strawberry banana, that was her favorite. Her stomach grumbled from not eating all day. She wondered if Jason might want to stop on the way home, then asked, "Can you tell me something, Dr. Baker?"

"Of course."

"What's going on with all these kids?"

"What do you mean?"

"I mean your waiting room is full of children who have serious psychological problems. I saw a little girl out there who couldn't have been more than six years old. What could be so wrong with a six-year old child they need to see a trained psychiatrist? What is it with all this depression and problems? Where did it come from?"

"Please, come sit down," Dr. Baker said. "It's a lot more complicated than it appears and our patients come to us for a variety of reasons. So let's not assume we know. Right now we need to focus on Jason."—she went and placed an arm around Karen, bringing her back to the chair—"You've seen firsthand how serious depression can be. While the symptoms are consistent, the duration and intensity can vary. Some people respond quickly to therapy, others take longer. The same with meds. Many people won't take them once they feel better or because of the side effects. With all that we know about the brain, there's still so much to uncover. As of now, though, Jason hasn't responded favorably to anything. I'm growing increasingly concerned."

"So that's it? You won't treat him anymore and we have to start over with somebody different?"—she sniffled and the tears welled up in her eyes—"Don't do this to us. He can still get better. My boy is not totally broken."

"I agree, and it's not that I don't want to treat him anymore. But I think a higher-level option should be explored. A more inclusive approach."—Dr. Baker removed a brochure from her desk and handed it to Karen along with a tissue—"I want you to keep an open mind. You and Larry should look this over. Seriously consider it."

The front page of the brochure was glossy and thick, constructed from a high-quality stock. There were pictures of horses in a pasture of rolling hills with a sunset behind them. Inside was a brief synopsis, highlighted in bullet points, which detailed what kind of therapy the facility specialized in.

It mentioned the above-average number of doctors on staff and provided columns of data to support their positive claims. Scattered throughout were testimonials of success stories from former patients, complete with photos and current levels of either occupation or education. Everyone smiled and appeared happy and strong. It contrasted the expression of Karen with her scrunched up forehead and tight thin lips.

"This place is in Virginia," Karen said. "That's on the opposite side of the country."

"It would be a five-hour flight is all."

"And it's a twenty-four-hour, seven days a week inpatient facility."

"That's the reason I brought it up. I believe this is what Jason needs to get better."

Karen folded the brochure and stuffed it into her purse. "How much does it cost? I didn't see any mention of the price."

"As you can probably imagine, it's not cheap. But they're considered to be the very best."

"How much?"

"The average expense runs twenty a month, give or take, depending on what's required. It's tailored to each individual specifically in conjunction with group methodology and they have the most experienced comprehensive—"

"Twenty thousand a month? For how long?"

"We recommend a minimum stay of at least four to six months."

A burst of incredulous laughter shot from Karen's chest. "Larry and I don't have that kind of money. We can barely afford coming here."

"I know it's a lot. But they have financing available with a few different credit plans. Maybe your insurance will cover at least a portion of it."

The women sat quietly after Karen put forth a few more objections and then relented. She closed her eyes and sighed. Having a child was never supposed to be like this. Kids that came from good homes who were showered with love and support weren't supposed to have major psychological problems impairing their lives. It wasn't fair. It didn't make any sense.

There was no logical or reasonable explanation for Jason's condition because as far as she knew, she'd done everything correct. She attended his activities, supported his interests, helped with homework, made nutritious meals, chaperoned field trips, and praised him with love. She pushed all her children to be good people with goals and aspirations. She reminded them how fortunate they were. But she didn't push too hard. She knew when to back off.

So how did this happen? Why? Where did she go wrong?

Karen never heard of serious, long-term depression in young people when she grew up. She couldn't even begin to understand it. Sure, everybody got the blues once in a while. That seemed normal. Who hadn't been sad at one time or another? Then life goes on and it passes. But to be sad for months and years on end at such a young age with . . .

She sank her head into her hands and dismissed the doctor who tried to intervene. Her mind drifted. She reminisced about precious random events taken for granted because as her little boy grew, things were only supposed to get better.

She thought of the time Jason came home covered in mud wearing his good church clothes after getting in a mud fight with the neighbor. Larry hosed him off in the backyard while she stayed in the house and laughed because he looked so damn cute. Or the time he ate his first whole cheeseburger from McDonald's and beamed with pride like he'd made a great discovery. In the sixth grade, Jason used the change in his piggy bank to buy a seashell necklace for her birthday and he did so of his own volition. Karen considered it one of the finest gifts ever received and still wore it proudly.

He was so happy and thoughtful and free back then. She couldn't recall the second or minute, the day or the month or the year, when the switch was flipped and the replacement of her son got underway. Where had he gone? Why wouldn't he come back?

"I'm sorry," Dr. Baker said. "But I have my next appointment."

Karen nodded and crumpled up the tissue.

"I wouldn't suggest the facility if I wasn't extremely concerned. I care about Jason too. He said some unsettling things today. It wasn't overt, but I could tell it was there, because they were some of the same precursors he said before the last time. Now, since we have the required paperwork from him giving you authorization when he signed . . . It's only been six months—"

"I don't want to talk about it."

"He needs a higher level of treatment, a full-time structured environment. Two days a week isn't enough. I understand what a challenge it can be to get him to attend group therapy and . . ."—Dr. Baker moved around to the front of the desk—"Why don't you think about the brochure and talk it over with Larry? Let's have a conference call about it next week."

Karen nodded again.

"Mother to mother, I feel for you, and we'll find a way to make this work. But as I mentioned before, please go see somebody yourself. Your mental health is important too."—she walked to the door and reached for the handle—"Take as much time as you want. I'll use Dr. Flagg's office for my next session. He's out sick today."

"Wait," Karen said. She approached the doctor and clasped onto her like a person drowning in the middle of a cold choppy sea. "Thank you. I know you're doing what you can, that you have our best interests at heart. Me and Larry, we appreciate it. We'll be in touch about the facility."

When the doctor left, Karen removed a phone from her purse and dialed a number. The call went straight to voicemail. She'd wait ten minutes then dial the number again. With her compact open and her lipstick out, she lingered in the office to redo her makeup and steady her nerves. Somehow her boy would be saved. He had to be. She needed to believe it could happen.

Jason sat in the exact same position when Karen returned to the waiting room. After getting a receipt at the checkout desk, she tapped him gently on the shoulder. He yawned several times and stood. Speechless, he fell in line and followed her to the car with his clothes too baggy and his bones too thin.

"You want to stop at the smoothie shop for lunch?" she asked. "We're right here."

Her question went unanswered.

"How about Arby's or that new pizza place near the house? You said how much you liked their sauce the last time we ate there."

The last time they ate there was ten months ago, when Jason had a *good* day.

He pulled his hat down low and blocked his eyes as they exited the parking lot. Within a few miles he buried his face in the window. She looked at him, strengthening her grip on the wheel. Karen wanted to have an in-depth conversation but knew she wouldn't get through. So many discouraging attempts had been made already. They turned left at the next traffic light and the drive home was a long one, a silent one.

CHAPTER 2

Larry Turner stretched out an arm while he balanced near the top rung of a thirty-foot ladder. The sun baked the back of his leathery neck. He flicked his wrist side to side, watching the white soaked bristles slide against the weathered planks of a four-bedroom Colonial. A wasp's nest was observed up in the eaves and he noted to bring a can of Raid with him after lunch.

"Yo, Mr. T.," Zach Smolinski shouted. He shut the door of a slightly dented but still in good shape gray Nissan Maxima. "Working kinda hard for being on vacation!"

"Shouldn't you be leaving for the long weekend?" added his twin brother Josh.

"Hold on guys, be right there," Larry said. He flashed a grin and welcomed any excuse to put the brush down for a minute. His fingers ached while descending the ladder and he wondered if the onset of arthritis began to creep in. Perhaps he was getting old. Perhaps he was just tired.

He stepped onto the lawn in his paint-stained sneakers when his cell phone rang. He knew who it was without checking and dreaded having to answer it. After a brief debate, the call went to voicemail.

"Gentlemen," he said, shaking hands firmly with each of the boys. "What brings you to this part of town on such a magnificent afternoon?"

"We're going for a swim at his girlfriend's house," Josh said, and shoved his brother in the arm. "If you can believe a dork like him could actually get one."—

he shoved him again—"We saw you on that ladder driving by and had to stop. It's the Fourth of July weekend. Don't you always head up to the cabin on Friday?"

Larry and his family hadn't visited the cabin in years and there was no indication of going anytime soon. It wasn't the same anymore. The ninth-grade science teacher at Morell Park High School opened a cooler and passed his former students chilled cans of diet soda. "It's a good day for a swim. No doubt about that. Enjoy these summers off before they're gone."

"Speaking of summers off," Zach said, "why are you painting Principal Smith's house?" He was the younger twin by fifteen minutes and stood a full inch taller than his six-foot seven brother.

Larry had known the Smolinski boys since they were eleven, when they moved down from Oregon. He was friends with their parents. The families even vacationed a few times together. He coached them in basketball through middle school and on into high school along with Jason. Before Jason quit.

"To the Morell Park Warriors," he said and cracked open his soda. He held up his drink in the air.

"To the Mighty Warriors," they repeated in unison.

He wiped his mouth after taking a sip and looked at the can with a smile. "I used to paint houses on my summers home from college. My dad got me the job. It's a great way to earn some extra money and you're not stuck inside all day. Doug, or Principal Smith as you know him, mentioned his house needed to be painted so I offered my services."

"Isn't having the summer off a perk for being a teacher in the first place?" Josh asked. "I saw Ms. Jenkins waiting tables last week when I went to the diner for breakfast."

Larry didn't want to mention that most of his co-workers had other jobs to supplement their meager salary or that he'd often wished a different career path had somehow grabbed him and bit him in the ass. So he towed the company line to put on a good spin. "You'll never get rich being a teacher, that's a given. But that's not why we do it. You can't put a price on shaping the future of our country."—he gulped some soda and it stung his throat, making his eyes water—"Speaking of money, either of you young lads interested in earning a few dollars? There's a lot of work left on this place and I have plenty more brushes in the truck."

They laughed like the offer was the most comical question they'd ever heard. Manual labor was not in the playbook for the Smolinski twins. It was as if they were allergic to it, and they said they couldn't remember the last time they took out the trash or mowed the lawn. The twins went on to explain how prolonging any real kind of work was a high priority because once they got older that's all they'd probably do; like every other adult. Besides, there were basketball camps to volunteer at, parties to attend, and girls to date.

Larry couldn't decide if the boys were part of the generation labeled *entitled* and *soft* or if they were flat out smarter than he was growing up. His cell phone rang and he switched it to vibrate, ignoring the call once again.

"How's Jason?" Zach asked, causing his brother to glare at him. "We haven't seen him in a long time. I heard he was going to community college down in the valley."

"He's mulling it over," Larry said. He cleared his throat the way he always did after telling a lie. When it came to his son, he cleared his throat quite often.

Jason Turner hadn't stepped foot onto any sort of academic campus since Larry pulled some heavy strings to get him to graduate from high school several years earlier. In fact, Jason never should've received his diploma at all. He went from an honors student and starting point guard on the basketball team during his junior year to a virtual dropout by the end of his senior campaign.

His academic slide coincided with a loss of interest in most activities, including socializing with family and friends. When Larry begged his boy to attend the graduation ceremony and make his mother proud, Jason opted to stay in bed with the curtains drawn instead. The framed piece of paper his father secured for him remained in the closet, buried among boxes of trophies and awards.

Community college? Larry thought. He took a final sip of soda then crushed the can and threw it in the bed of his pickup. *I could only dream.* He'd heard that rumor before in addition to Jason joined the military to fight in the Middle East, Jason traveled through South America on a motorcycle road trip, Jason was dead, Jason worked at a convenient store in Sacramento, and Jason went to Hollywood to become the next big actor. Larry had no idea how any of the stories got started but wished they'd stop.

He grinned at the young men and changed the subject—another area he excelled in when discussing his oldest child. "So, how are things going for you guys at college? I hope you're hitting the books as hard as you're hitting the court."

"I made the Dean's List last semester and this dummy over here earned a three point seven, or so he says," Zach said, flicking Josh's ear. "We got a good squad returning this fall and I have a real chance of starting at forward. With a little luck, we might even make the tournament. You should come down and see a game. You could bring Jason."

For the first time all day, Larry realized how hot it was. The air was stagnant, devoid of a breeze, and the sun smoldered high in a cloudless sky as the sweat clung to him like an itchy burlap bag. He stared at the house he'd painted for the past four weeks, his wraparound sunglasses protecting his eyes. He observed how much had been finished and was dismayed at the prospect of what still had to be done.

An odd feeling bubbled in his stomach, grew up through his throat, and assaulted his mind. He was happy for the boys standing before him with all their success; he truly was. But a combination of envy and disbelief engrossed him, bordering on anger.

They were leading the life his son was supposed to have, the life he envisioned since Jason's first baby steps. Jason should be the one going for a swim with friends on a hot afternoon. Jason should be the one who played basketball at a division one college and showcased his ability on TV. Jason should be the one getting asked to volunteer at basketball camps, to teach the young kids how to play. He was no doubt more talented than the twins and had a better jump shot with a quicker first step. He was captain of the team in only his sophomore year and if he kept improving, if he kept up his grades, if he . . .

"Hey Mr. T.," Zach said. He waved his arms in front of him. "You still with us?"

"Thanks for coming by," Larry said after scolding himself for being so petty. "But I need to get back to work."—he picked up a black can of wasp spray and shook it—"It's always nice talking with some of the best basketball players I've ever had the privilege to coach. Be sure and tell your folks I said hi."

"Don't work too hard, Mr. T. You're not as young as you used to be," Josh said with a smirk.

"I can still kick both your butts in a game of HORSE."

"You really think so?"

"Oh yeah. As long as there's no dunking and we only shoot free throws. How many times did I beat you guys in practice at the foul line? How many times did you have to run sprints?"

They threw up their hands in surrender. "You're a good foul shooter, we'll give you that. But . . ." Josh bent his arm and flexed a muscle, showing off a sculpted iron bicep.

Larry tapped himself on the side of the head. "This is what you need to work out the most. Now gentlemen, can you please explain to me the theory of plate tectonics?"

"That's our cue to leave, bro," Zach said. "He's starting with the science trivia."

"How many types of igneous rocks are there? What's the difference between evaporation and sublimation? Who was Michael Faraday and why is he important?"

The twins hopped in their car, leaving the diet sodas unopened behind. Josh rolled down the window and dangled his arm out the side. "Tell Jason we should shoot hoops some time at the park like we used to. Maybe hit the food truck scene in the city."

"Will do," Larry said and cleared his throat.

"We'll send a pair of tickets for a home game this year. You can be our own private scout and tell us where we need to improve."

Larry cupped his mouth and yelled, "Play hard!" to them like he did so often in practice as their car sped away. *They're good boys*, he thought. *They're good boys.*

The paper nest wobbled from the narrow stream of the spray. While the majority of inhabitants died on contact as advertised, he did suffer one painful sting on the arm and another on the leg.

His cell phone continued to vibrate so he unhooked it from his belt. He stared at the object harassing him and wanted to smash it with a hammer or chuck it into the woods. But he compromised instead. The ringer was adjusted to silent and it contrasted the period in his life when the calls were relished, when the allure of hope still had meaning.

After finishing the planks on the north side of the house, Larry set down his brush and turned around. A small patch of shade finally presented itself. He leaned back against the ladder admiring the view.

At almost three stories up, the suburb of Applewood Heights appeared larger and more spread out than when driving around. He saw the fire station, the elementary school, and a new convenience store that was under construction. He was proud to be part of the town for the last twenty years and never regretted moving there from the flat plains of Kansas. Larry loved the weather, loved the people, and loved living close to the mountains. But on that day, as most others, there was no longer any enjoyment.

He should've answered her calls without hesitation. Hearing what his wife had to say needed to be paramount. He should've reaffirmed that she wasn't alone in the great big bag of misery thrust upon them, and he should've shown his support. So he hit number two on the speed dial because who did he think he was kidding? There were no seconds or minutes or hours off from dealing with the situation; certainly not half the day. And besides, the calls would never stop.

"How'd it go today?" he asked when she picked up right away.

"Not good," Karen said. "Jason isn't . . ."

He listened half-heartedly, serving more as a sounding board than anything else. Larry had seen the movie hundreds of times and was familiar with the cast, the actor, the director, and the script. The ending always remained the same.

For the past five years, the news was never good or cheery, only varying degrees of bad. He knew the conversation would be replayed again and again on an endless reel in the bedroom, the kitchen, the living room, and the garage. It would be hashed over, dissected, analyzed, and scrutinized. As much as they tried, Karen and Larry had lost the ability to talk about anything else.

Twenty minutes later, he returned to painting and found himself hypnotized by the brushstrokes. The mindless simplicity of the repetitive process soothed him. It offered an escape to the unshakeable mindset that he failed as a parent, that he failed as a dad. Up and down. Side to side. Back and forth. Over and over. Regardless of the storm swirling about, Larry Turner, at that specific moment and at that specific time, felt some tiny measure of control.

He dipped his brush in the paint and marveled as the bristles worked their magic. They transformed something old and dusty to appear vibrant and new. Little did he know, before too long he'd try conducting some magic of his own. With his own flesh and blood.

Chapter 3

The empty paint cans were disposed of and the brushes rinsed off with a garden hose. He watered Karen's shrubs on one side of their garage, then her rose bed on the other. The temperature dipped into the eighties and cooled his sun-soaked skin as he organized his work supplies for the next day. Larry walked toward the house with another twelve hours on the jobsite behind him.

"Hello, I'm home," he announced. He entered through the living room and removed his shoes.

Melissa, his seventeen-year-old daughter, was propped against the base of the couch with a laptop open. "Hi Daddy," she said without taking her eyes off the screen.

He washed up in the bathroom and changed his shirt before going to the kitchen. A plate on the stovetop awaited. He removed the lid and leaned in close as the aroma of pork chops with mashed potatoes filled his nose. Larry grunted in pleasure like a caveman, knowing it didn't get better than a home-cooked meal when you were hungry.

He turned on the small TV mounted under the cabinets and poured himself a glass of milk. Melissa soon joined him at the table.

"Sarah went with some friends to go see a movie and Mom stepped out for a bit. I'm gonna take a shower and go chill in my room."

"Did Mom say when she'll be back?" he asked, scooping a forkful of potatoes.

"She won't be long. I think she like went to Starbucks for her caffeine fix, and you know, a change of scenery."

"What about Jason? Did you be sure to—"

"It's all good, Dad. I've been here since Mom left. No worries."

No worries, Larry thought, and chuckled to himself. *Yeah right.* There hadn't been *no worries* in the Turner house for quite some time.

The remaining scraps on his plate were devoured and he wanted seconds or possibly thirds. But there was nothing left. He rummaged through the pantry for a box of cookies, yawning as the long workday caught up. His fingers still ached and his knuckles felt like rusty hinges. Larry looked at the broken dishwasher they'd yet to replace and cranked on the faucet. There weren't many rules in the Turner house, but one was universal: He or she who cooks does not clean. The mantra was even printed and stuck to the fridge.

In the last few years, however, the rule ceased being enforced; both girls taking full advantage of it. Karen, an inherently tidy person but by no means a neat freak, had turned into a cleaning machine. She cleaned in the morning, she cleaned at night, and she cleaned when things weren't dirty. If a person left a cup or a bowl on the counter and spun around, it would not only be washed and dried, but also put away.

He stood in front of the sink with a blue sponge in hand when his wife arrived. A dish towel was slung over his shoulder. She came in across the back deck, through the screen door, and dropped her purse on the counter where it landed with a thud. The loose change jingled on the bottom.

"You doing alright?" he asked.

Karen shook her head no and he could feel her anxiety penetrate the air. Her eyes were red and puffy. They were always red and puffy. Larry rinsed a plate and knew what was coming but he waited. The continuation of their phone call from earlier was imminent.

"So, what do you think?" she finally said.

God how he hated that question. It was so unfair because the truth could never be told. How could he go about saying, "Well, my dear, I think I'd like to get in my truck and drive around aimlessly for the next few weeks and pretend to be somebody different."

What he said instead was, "Can I see it?"

He pulled the metal stopper from the sink and was confident the dishes would pass her high-level inspection. He wiped his hands with the towel. The sudsy water circled clockwise down the drain as the bubbles melted away.

Karen passed him the brochure from Dr. Baker's office she had jammed inside her purse. It was folded in half and something was written on top.

"Have you ever been to Virginia?" she asked. She took the towel from his shoulder and started to dry the silverware. "That's where the facility is located."

"No. But I always wanted to visit and hike in the Blue Ridge Mountains. It's pretty far away though. Is this place our only choice? Isn't there something closer?"

"The doctor said it's the absolute best, and that's what Jason deserves. This is what they recommend. Why go anywhere else? Don't you agree?"

Of course he agreed and they'd tried their hardest to provide it. Why would she ask him that? What more did she think he had left to give? Larry glanced at the cover of the brochure but needed his reading glasses. When he turned from Karen to retrieve them, he noticed the clock on the microwave. It was almost 9 p.m. His nightly check was due.

"Can we talk about this later?"—he pointed to the ceiling as a light thump echoed through his chest—"I can't focus on anything until I get this over with."

Their eyes briefly met and she squeezed his hand. He lowered his head. Nothing else could or needed to be said.

The Turners' house was built in the nineties on a small corner lot at the bottom of a hill. It had white vinyl siding with black shutters and came with a detached garage. Downstairs was tile. The upstairs was carpet. They had a gas fireplace that rarely got used and the house resembled most other homes in the generic development. A forty-foot oak tree shaded the front lawn.

Larry walked to the bottom of the staircase with a slow gait. His shirt felt suddenly tight. He stared at his socks and noticed a hole in one of them. *How has it gotten to this?* he asked. *How has our son gotten so far away from us?*

His left knee cracked as he kneeled on the steps and pressed his hands together. After a brief list of prayers and a soft, "Amen," he gave the sign of the cross. Gripping the bannister, he forced himself up. The thumping in his chest grew heavier—the echo became louder.

Jason's bedroom was the first one to the left near a double sink bathroom containing a laundry shoot and a linen closet. It was mostly dark as usual. The only light came from the glow of a green sheet that swayed from the air conditioner vent above it. Larry hit the switch on the wall and began his ascent. The scar from six months earlier was beside him.

After incident number one, the lock on Jason's door had been removed. It provided some measure of comfort for the Turners and allowed them access whenever they needed. Both Karen and Larry believed it to be the right thing to do as responsible parents. There'd be no more arguments through the wooden barrier in a state of wonder about what's going on inside and they wouldn't have to bang on the door demanding he let them in.

When that failed dismally and incident number two blew up in their faces, the family was rocked to the core. Karen then insisted the door come off completely. Larry agreed. Jason complained that it wasn't fair and invaded his privacy. But after what he'd put them through, their son had lost the right to any kind of privacy.

His mind seemed cloudier with every step and halfway up the stairway, he desperately wanted to retreat. What would he find? Could he handle seeing it again? Larry would've rather been anywhere else but didn't have a choice—he never had a choice. So he trudged forward like an ox strapped to a yoke, plowing a field of misery. When he finally reached the top, he paused.

It took him a minute to collect himself, to get prepared, and he noted how the fabric wore thin on the right side of the sheet where they pulled it back to enter. It was a cheap sheet after all, not a sturdy door. It should've lay flat on a bed somewhere covered with blankets instead of hanging limply from a doorjamb.

He hated the sheet and all it represented and fantasized about burning it in the fire pit. He even gave it a nickname, calling it the Berlin Wall. Larry realized the name made no sense whatsoever. The occupant inside was not trapped behind an Iron Curtain of the Soviet regime and could leave whenever he wanted. But the occupant chose not to. Because the occupant never left. Unless they made him.

"Jason? Is everything okay?" he asked and knocked on the wall outside.

No answer.

He counted off ten seconds, their agreed upon timeframe, and took a deep breath. He knocked louder. "Son, you alright in there? I'm gonna need to come in."

Eight seconds later, a meek voice responded with a single word: "Okay."

Larry bent over and grabbed his knees as the color in his face returned. He was about to leave but still didn't feel comfortable, so he stuck his head inside the room anyway. And when he saw Jason wrapped in a blanket staring at the bright screen of the TV, could see the whites of his eyes and confirm they were blinking—then, and only then, did he relax. He ducked from the room as fast as he'd ducked in. The thumping in his chest faded. The echo stopped. It never got any easier, and the next night he'd do it again.

He went downstairs to join his wife and they didn't talk right away when Larry crawled under the covers after showering. The married couple of twenty-five years became accustomed to their interactions of silence. Karen leaned against the headboard surrounded by a stack of pillows. She listened to music from the radio on her nightstand, lathering moisturizer on her legs.

He massaged his stiff, creaky hands. Some aspirin were needed to combat the pain but the bottle was in the truck, and the truck was in the driveway. He was tired. It was late. So he slipped on his reading glasses and picked up the brochure his wife had left on the bed. He folded it back along the opposite way of the crease. The first thing he saw was a note on top that read AT LEAST 100K. PROBABLY 150.

"How is he tonight?" Karen said.

"Alive. Breathing. Despondent . . . Pretty much the same."—he realized his tone was too sharp and softened it—"Sorry. It's been a long day. How about you?"

She turned off the radio and inched closer to him. "I don't even know where to begin. For Jason to go away to a facility, it's just . . . I'm not sure what we did to deserve this. Maybe we were bad people in a past life, did something terrible. It makes me want to scream. But at who? And now we have to start all over."—she settled onto his chest and clutched him around the waist—"I really thought he'd be better by now. At least a little."

He stroked her wavy, blond hair and kissed the top of her head. "It's gonna be okay," he said and clicked off the lamp. "Things will look better in the morning."

No more words were exchanged that night, both of them exhausted. They held each other in the dark as the crack in their family life widened, and the abyss grew deeper.

CHAPTER 4

When Larry woke at 6 a.m., his wife was gone. She slept on the couch in the living room that provided a clear view up the stairs. Karen snuck out there at least three times a week and he knew he couldn't stop her. They'd recently had discussions about expanding the alcove near the front door to create enough space for a bed.

He shaved, got dressed, and made toast for his wife. It was served on a wooden tray with a tall glass of juice and a hot mug of coffee.

"We'll talk later," he said, scurrying from the room. "I'll call you at lunch."

Working on a Saturday had a different feel, like you shouldn't be there. The natural inclination to move slower was inevitable. Larry accomplished little on the jobsite and spent most of the day studying the brochure as if there'd be an exam.

The name of the facility was Pine View Behavioral Center. It encompassed fifty acres of rural land on the outskirts of the Shenandoah Valley. Disclaimers were listed across the bottom of certain pages next to red asterisks stating *Results will vary* or *Many factors included*. Results will vary? That's not what he wanted to hear. Results guaranteed sounded a hell of a lot better, especially for the money.

The more Larry read, the less he was sure. The whole idea felt like his son was being shipped off to some kind of sanitarium. Maybe that's what Jason needed, maybe not. Maybe nobody, including himself, had any clue what the right thing to do was.

He left work early and drove to the park where he sat in his truck and observed. The basketball courts were full of high school kids scrimmaging as shirts and skins. Larry used to run the summer league before painting houses. He noticed Mark Williams only dribbled with his right hand while Quentin Reece faded to the left on his jump shot. He considered going over to instruct them and say hi to the coaches, but he remained seated with the windows rolled up and the AC on instead. And he watched. Because that's all Larry did anymore. He watched from afar, a spectator of life. He'd become a non-participant.

A text from Karen buzzed on his phone and it startled him. The brief hiatus he orchestrated from work ended with a reminder that Jason duty, or JD as they referred to it, needed to be coordinated. Since he and his wife were going out for dinner to discuss the finer points of expensive psychiatric treatment, somebody had to be home to keep an eye on their son. That meant one of the girls. Melissa got stuck the night before and sacrificed a concert at the amphitheater, so it was Sarah's turn to step up to the never-ending plate.

She protested when he called her and argued with him further when she begrudgingly came home. Larry expected it, having endured her backlash numerous times before. But after thirty minutes of venting, she caved. At least for him. He knew his oldest daughter and middle child would transfer her resentment onto Karen and blame her for everything. They fought constantly now and it bothered him. It never used to be like that.

He assured Sarah their evening away would consist of only a few brief hours before they returned, and he never got upset with his daughters when they complained about JD or expressed their angst toward the situation. He understood their plight. How many teenagers were required to stay home on a Saturday night and babysit their older brother from the scariest possible outcome?

The girls had been compassionate and understanding while being sucked into the vortex with everyone else. Larry appreciated that. But with each new stagnant day of no improvement and Jason's latest devastating setback, they too had reached a breaking point for self-survival.

Twenty bucks was the going rate for a large pepperoni pizza. He gave Sarah five more for the tip plus an extra ten-spot to make himself feel better. Smelling of cologne, he backed the minivan from the driveway.

Larry felt satisfied there was at least one area in their combustible lives which caused them no anxiety: where they were dining. The bistro near his school was his favorite and not only because they bestowed a five percent discount to all faculty members. It had spacious booths to accommodate his frame and the place was never too crowded, so it was easy to hear a conversation.

Karen ordered her usual black coffee, thick as mud, with a side of carrot cake. He splurged on a root beer float and the sandwich of the day.

"Excuse me, madam," he said in a British accent that sounded more like a Leprechaun, "you wouldn't happen to have a $100,000 I could borrow to help my troubled son?"

"You're doing the accent thing again, huh?"

He nodded in approvement of his attempted ice-breaker. It used to be so effective.

"I haven't merely a penny to spare," she said, her tone flat.

He changed countries, performed his best Jamaican and French impressions, but his plan to introduce some levity died a weak death. Karen sipped her coffee and stared at the paper placemat on the table. She scribbled numbers on the edge of it near the ads.

"We could apply for a loan," she said. "Get a home equity line on the house."

"We've already taken a second mortgage, remember?"

"There's always—"

"No," he said, and held up his hand to stop her. "It's not fair to the girls. What are we supposed to tell Sarah? Sorry, but you can't go to college next semester because we spent your entire college fund. Or what about Melissa? Should we tell her there's only enough money left in her account for one semester when she graduates?"

Karen picked at the cake, chewing like food revolted her. "You know, my parents never paid for my education. It's not unheard of. I'm not saying we shouldn't, but—"

"We started saving for each of the kids when they were a year old," he said. "Birthdays, holidays, special events. My father put in $2,000 apiece when they made their First Communion. Jason's savings have been long gone. We can't do this to the girls. We have to think of their future too."

She pushed away her plate and covered it with a napkin.

"You're right, you're right. I know you're right. We need to come up with something else then. Maybe something to sell."

He sipped his float, fidgeting with the straw. An elderly couple was spotted three booths away and they laughed and smiled as they ate. They appeared to enjoy their dining experience. He wished he had the courage to walk over and say, "Mind if I join you?"

Did they talk about a book or a funny movie? Did one of them tell a joke? Larry would've happily donated a finger or toe to sit with his wife and discuss something fun.

"What about the cabin?" Karen said.

"The cabin? For real?"

"Why not? We never use it anymore."

He squirmed in his seat. "I guess . . . we could get . . . I guess we could get maybe thirty or forty grand, if we're lucky. I'm sure it needs a lot of work from the last big storms."

"It's a good start. Don't you think?"

Yes, it was true, they'd talked about selling it once before, but Larry never thought it was serious. And yes, it was true, they hadn't been there as a family in several years. But he loved the cabin, loved all it represented.

He planned to take his grandkids there to hike and fish one day, to show the next generation of Turners the beauty of nature. Leaving the cabin to his children was supposed to be an integral part of establishing his legacy. Why should he be forced to sell it now? What was next? Everything they ever owned was a house.

They already cashed in their 401Ks and retirement savings. The medical bills were still sky-high. There were the trips to the hospital, some with extended stays, not to mention the ambulance rides, the medication, the diagnostic testing, the lab work, Karen's lost wages, and the continual specialized therapy sessions. Now Dr. Baker's treatment proposal could push them over the edge. Would the facility actually work and save Jason? Would it allow him to hold a job and function in society? Or would it all be for nothing and break them financially, tearing the family further apart? Where was the line he needed to draw? Where would he find a definition of what that line was?

"Larry?" she said. "Are you listening? How much more money could we get for the cabin if we fixed it?"

"What?"

"The cabin. How much if we fixed it?"

"I don't know. I'd have to go look."

"Let's put that down as an option. When do you think you can go?"

He shook his head, grinding his jaw. "Not sure. Maybe when I get done painting Doug's house I'll have some time."

Chills streaked down his spine as both shoulders tingled. The reality set in that he was sick of dealing with the situation, truly sick, at a level so deep he deplored himself. It could no longer be denied, and that made him sicker. Because he always strived to be a good dad.

A bus boy dropped a tray of drinks and they spilled on the floor. The liquid splashed across the side of their booth. Larry leaned over and tried to help the kid clean it up.

"It's okay sir," the bus boy said. "I'll take care of it. I didn't get any on you, did I?"

"No," Larry said. "Everything's fine."

And there it was. His two favorite words in the English language. If Larry Turner had a catchphrase or had to be remembered for something he said it would be, "Everything's fine."

People joked that when they buried him, the epitaph on his tombstone would read HERE LIES A MAN WHO THOUGHT EVERYTHING WAS ALWAYS FINE. Even those close to him could never quite get a read on the fifty-three-year-old man. It used to drive Karen nuts when he put up his, "Everything's fine," defense and wouldn't let anyone in. When Larry really got going, really wanted to suppress his emotions no matter what transpired around him, nothing could penetrate his Kevlar mindset.

Hey Larry, your shirt is on fire. Everything's fine.

Hey Larry, there's a nuclear war going on. Everything's fine.

Hey Larry, your son tried to kill himself. Everything's fine.

He removed a napkin from the canister and wiped the condensation that dripped down his glass. Karen made more notes on the placemat. They hadn't talked in ten minutes and her coffee refill was cold.

"Let's say we get forty for the cabin," she said. "We could probably get at least that if we fix it and I think ten to fifteen thousand seems realistic for my jewelry. I agree, no more dipping into the girls' college funds. That's off the list. But my brother is coming over tomorrow. Did I forget to tell you? I thought it'd be nice to have a barbeque for the Fourth."

"That's, uh . . . That's great. We haven't seen Nathan in a while."

"He said he'll bring fireworks. Everyone will be there, including the dog."

Larry ran a hand through his graying hair. He knew the only reason Karen requested the presence of her estranged brother was to ask for money they may never be able to repay. But it was fine. He'd conceded the notion of retirement. His destiny was to work in some capacity until his body or brain imploded, whichever came first.

Hey Larry, you're delving further into a black hole of debt. Everything's fine.

Hey Larry, Jason may never get better. Everything's fine.

Karen scooted to the edge of the booth and picked up her purse. "You didn't plan to work tomorrow, did you?"

"No," he said, and cleared his throat. "Not at all."

"It's late. We should go home to check on Jason."

Larry nodded and slid out behind her after finishing the remnants of his drink. He grinned at a parent he recognized and walked to the car.

Everything's fine.

CHAPTER 5

Karen and her brother were an odd pair of siblings who didn't look anything alike at all. There were no same colored eyes or familiar jawline, no matching noses or similar smiles. While she was thin for a woman in her fifties and rode the stationary bike in their house to stay that way, Nathan had a globe for a stomach and suffered from a condition he coined exercise-phobia. She liked to joke of being secretly adopted to account for their vast differences. He told people the same.

She rang out a mop after cleaning the kitchen and next on the list was to scrub the toilets. Karen didn't have many hobbies anymore. She hadn't designed costume jewelry or done scrapbooking in years. The neighborhood bake sale was a no-go, as was the Christmas carnival, and she stopped volunteering at the library altogether. Invitations for parties or weddings often remained sealed.

She didn't know how cleaning became her obsession. She preferred not to break down the causes or analyze the details. Why couldn't writing or glassblowing or something creative been chosen instead? But she had to admit it. She enjoyed cleaning. There were more pairs of dish gloves under the sink than could be counted. The one time the supermarket ran a BOGO, she shamelessly cleared them out.

Karen blew a strand of hair from her face and tucked it behind an ear. She watched from a window as Larry mowed the lawn, appreciating that he did so in a very specific manner. He was to go up and down the yard with the push-mower rather than utilize the square pattern he favored. Doing it the way she suggested produced a striped pattern reminiscent of a baseball stadium outfield.

She also appreciated that he hooked up the bagger so people wouldn't get grass clippings in their shoes. When Larry complained what an inconvenience it was because the bagger always got clogged, she reminded him what was at stake. Everything needed to be perfect for Nathan.

The Turners hadn't entertained in years but still knew the drill. She'd take care of the inside, which was never really dirty but needed to go from clean to super clean, while he'd take care of the outside that always looked nice as well. Karen made the girls pitch in by asking them to vacuum and pick up their rooms, but she immediately regretted it.

The teens spent more time arguing with her than working, as if they'd been requested to perform hard labor in a coal mine without water or food. Both daughters informed their mother they'd stick around briefly during the day for the obligatory photo ops and to let their parents brag on them a bit. But come nighttime, they were so out of there. Karen was okay with that. She felt thrilled they would stay at all.

"Is there enough gas for the barbeque?" she yelled to Larry through the screen door leading to the back deck.

"The tank is full and I cleaned the grates too. We should be all set."

She returned to the window with a chair and continued to watch him. *He's a good man*, she thought, and she was lucky to have him. He was lucky to have her too. While the goosebumps phase of their relationship was long gone, her love for him evolved into something far more profound and intricate.

They didn't talk as much or laugh as much or have sex as much, if at all. She missed having sex. It bothered her she'd lost interest but it wasn't entirely her fault. Larry had lost interest too. It wasn't just the orgasms she missed or the physical contact of kissing and touching. It was the after-party, when Larry would hold her and she'd feel young again, like when they first met in college.

They'd lie in bed naked confiding their dreams, sharing their ambitions. The future looked so bright. It seemed strange because she never thought it was possible, but the ordeal with Jason had somehow brought them closer on a different level. The fear and desperation they'd endured revealed neither of them possessed the strength to go it alone.

A complex codependency emerged and meshed within its fibers was the transformation of themselves, of their individuality. A new unit existed. Month by month they lost themselves further. But for all the Turners had been through, they'd somehow managed to avoid the one fatal trap so many couples fell into when a child like Jason presents themselves. They never pointed fingers or got caught in the blame game. Solidarity was their key. From the inception of his unraveling, the focus was always to help their son.

She watched Larry put the lawnmower in the garage. He wiped the sweat from his brow and picked up a basketball next to the weed eater. Like a Harlem Globetrotter, he spun it on the tip of his index finger with ease.

Jason had a mini basketball as his first favorite toy. By the age of four he could already dribble. By seven he was a good shooter, and by ten he was the best player on his youth team. He played basketball all year-round with no exceptions. When encouraged to try other sports, he scoffed. There'd be no soccer, football, baseball, golf, or tennis. Only basketball. That's all he ever wanted to play.

The father and son duo spent countless hours shooting hoops in the driveway, rain or shine. They battled intensely. One day when Jason was fourteen and the wisps of hair protruded from his chin, he beat his coach and best friend. That's when Karen suspected her little boy might be something special on the court, as Larry stood six-foot three and was a skilled player in his own right.

They weren't delusional parents or helicopter parents. Their son was in all probability not going to play in the NBA. And they didn't try to live vicariously through him to compensate for their own failures or shortcomings either. But the Turners believed in education as a bedrock for success and speculated Jason could earn a scholarship if he applied his talents.

Larry dribbled to the left on the cracked pavement of the driveway and jumped. He extended a hand above his head in a smooth arching motion and snapped his wrist. The ball rotated with a perfect soft backspin, landing through the net with a swish. He dribbled to the right and pulled up again. Another swish. A smile spread across his face. As she watched, Karen didn't see him as playing alone, but rather playing alongside her son.

The nostalgia of the happy memories flooded back and filled her with joy about what used to be, about what might have been. She could still hear the instructions Larry used to give, how he mixed in technical assistance with positive reinforcement and praise. When Jason started beating his father on a consistent basis, that's when the trash talk began.

"You're all mine today," Jason would say. "You've got no chance to stop me and you know it. First, I'm gonna hit a jump shot in your eye. Then I'll just go around you and dunk."

Larry always welcomed the challenge. He demanded his son play as hard as he could. Winning or losing wasn't the only point—that's what he tried to instill; it was all about the hard work and effort. They'd exchange high-fives after every game and have sodas on the deck where their conversations ranged from college to astronomy to fishing. Jason had a real competitive streak back then, a zeal to win. It made the surrender to his depression even harder to fathom.

Karen looked away from the window and dabbed her eyes as Larry kept shooting at the rusted hoop bolted to the garage. She understood he needed it— it was a form of therapy—and nothing did more for his emotional well-being than playing in that driveway. He continued for the next hour while she resumed sparkling the house until getting ready. When she brought out a glass of water, he chugged it, crunched on an ice cube, and handed it back.

"Thanks," he said. "How do you like the lawn?"

"Looks great. I think we need more chips. You mind running to the store?"

"Sure thing."

"And could you pick up some beer in case Nathan would like some?"

"What kind?" Larry wiped his mouth with the corner of his shirt.

"I don't know. Get something good. He likes those fancy dark beers."—she twirled in a circle, modeling her white shorts, blue top, and red shoes—"How do I look?"

"Very patriotic. Like a walking American flag. Our forefathers would be proud."

Karen grinned. "Nathan should be here in an hour. Can you ask Jason if he wants to go with you?"

"I would," Larry said, shifting his eyes around the yard. "You know I would. But I'm not up for dealing with it right now. Don't have the energy."

"I just thought . . . You don't ask anymore. I thought it might be nice if you asked, if he went along."

"Yeah, it would be nice. I'd love it. It'd be nice if we won the lottery too. Neither of those things are gonna happen though, are they?"

"We need to keep asking him to do things, Larry. Dr. Baker says it's important. We can't stop asking because you never know, maybe one day he'll surprise us."

"It would be the surprise of the century, I'll grant you that. But I don't think it'll happen and I'm sorry. Not today. Okay?"

"Well, then I'll try."

"I promise to ask another time. And I'll leave in thirty minutes, in case he says yes." He took one final shot at the hoop and closed the garage.

She went back in the house and adjusted her earrings in the hallway mirror before making it to the bottom of the stairs. With one foot on the first step, she rested her hand along a white bannister. A thin layer of dust was noticed. She thought it needed some Pledge. Karen scratched her chin, wondering if they had enough ketchup for the hamburgers. Did they have enough buns? Then she turned her attention to the baseboards. Were those scuff marks? Did she have any Swiffer pads left in the closet? They might need to be painted. Maybe Larry could do it before the guests arrived.

She continued finding innocuous items to nitpick until five minutes passed and she hadn't taken another step. It'd been a long time since she'd ventured to Jason's room to try and talk or ask him to do something. Her trips upstairs were mainly to bring him food, clean his room, do laundry, and get him to Dr. Baker's office. Making sure he was alive became the top, and in recent months, only priority.

Karen marched up the stairway and knocked on the wall. "Can I come in please?"

No answer.

She knocked again louder and pulled aside the sheet, coughing hard to announce her presence.

Jason lay in bed atop the covers with his back to her. He was slightly curled and donned a checkered pair of pajama bottoms and a brown T-shirt. He was either asleep, or pretended to sleep, which she knew he did very well. She kept her distance and asked the young man living in her son's room, "Your father is going to the store to get chips and beer for Uncle Nathan. You want to go along?"

"No," said an anemic voice.

"Are you sure? It may be good to get some fresh air and sunlight."

Silence.

Karen walked over to a barren desk and turned on a lamp. She folded a bath towel draped over a chair.

"Jason?"—she raised her voice a decibel above polite conversation—"Jason, I'm talking to you. I asked you a simple question."

"No."

"But maybe if—"

"I fucking said no," he snapped and covered his head with a pillow. "Why can't you just leave me the hell alone?"

Jason never used to swear in front of his parents and his manners were always well-maintained. Now he swore all the time. Dr. Baker said he had high stress with poor coping skills, that his brain wasn't fully developed. When he yelled at or insulted them, it was meant to be internally expressed against himself, not anyone else. But it still didn't make it any easier.

She brushed a hand over her shorts as if they were wrinkled and needed to be straightened. *Let it go*, she thought, recalling the reason she didn't journey up there any more other than to serve as a maid. Karen would become so upset with Jason, with his apathy and lifeless demeanor, she'd want to grab him and shake him until he woke up. She'd want to shake him into the past when he laughed and smiled, when he had the desire to be among the living.

And she never told anyone, not even Larry, but once, in a moment of weakness when despair overtook her and the supreme frustration could no longer be stomached, she did more than shake him. She hit him. She slapped him across the face, hard, stinging her hand. It scared her because she wanted to slap him again. That was the first time she'd ever struck a child, and within seconds she burst into tears.

Karen stood in the center of the room, unsure what to do or how long to stay. She looked at her son hiding under a pillow and was disheartened at his physique. Gone were the well-defined muscles he'd worked so hard for. His arms were now boyishly thin and his legs had been whittled down to toothpicks. Her former pride and joy seemed condemned to a hell on earth existence she couldn't explain or— much to her crushing soul—appear to be able to fix.

How could such a good kid, intelligent and talented with endless possibilities, be such a miserable zombie? How could his mind be broken so badly, and how did it break? A broken arm would heal and a broken leg would fuse back together. Even a broken heart would eventually mend. But a broken mind? She didn't know anymore. Her exhaustive research stopped offering clues and at times the task seemed impossible, like putting a scrambled egg back inside the shell.

She lifted an empty plate off the floor and turned to leave, dejected, when his voice surprised her.

"I didn't ask to be born, Karen. You and Larry need to know that."

Her neck stiffened and her throat felt tight. Why couldn't he stop uttering such viciously cruel statements? As much as a child may say that in a fit of anger when they're an adolescent, when they can't go to a popular R-rated movie or spend the night at a friend's house, they never really meant it. Jason was almost twenty-two. She knew he meant every word.

She stepped toward the doorway and said, "If you change your mind about the store, your father is leaving soon." She was about to add, only as a source of feeling compelled, "And why don't you come down later to visit Uncle Nathan? He's bringing the dog and he's going to have fireworks." But Karen didn't say that. The truth was, she hoped Jason stayed in his room and didn't make an appearance. Having people witness the spectacle of what he'd become was too painful, too embarrassing.

She felt terrible thinking that way and a voice chirped inside her head before she reached the bottom of the stairs. *If only you'd done things different. If only you were a better mother.* She knew it was irrational, that it wasn't her fault. But day in and day out, Karen Turner bore the burden of a relentless parade of guilt.

Chapter 6

"So then he was finally discovered after nearly a week in the woods," Nathan said. He emptied his brown ale with an aggressive pull of the bottle and immediately popped open another. "Can you imagine the ordeal?"

"Wow, that's amazing," Karen said, mashing a melted charred marshmallow onto a graham cracker. "Where was he again?"

They sat around a cast stone fire pit as the sun set. A slight breeze blew across the lawn. The smoke took turns getting pushed into everyone's eyes when the wind changed directions and Nathan's wife, along with their small kids, went inside to watch a movie. Long, thin sticks found under a patch of trees were used to make s'mores. When the tips burned up and became brittle, they snapped them off and tossed them onto the coals.

"He was up in Yellowstone," Nathan said. "Him and his friends were doing an off-route trail, very remote. Not the traditional touristy stuff most people do. It was supposed to be a weekend trip only. An early spring snowstorm came out of nowhere and they all got separated. The other three guys were never found, but Edgar, that lucky bastard, he somehow managed to survive."

Larry poked a log in the fire and stared into the flames. He stifled a yawn. Listening to his brother-in-law speak was a mundane event, like waiting in line at the grocery store. The man talked non-stop. Some people said it was part of his charm and while Larry enjoyed his company, Nathan was the type of person best taken in spurts.

"Have you spoken to him since the rescue?" Karen asked. "Is he alright?"

"He has some scars on his face from the frostbite," Nathan said. "They also had to amputate a few of his toes. But at least he didn't lose any fingers."—he took another chug from his bottle—"What can you expect, though? Don't get me wrong, I love the guy like a brother. But going off the trail is pretty stupid if you ask me. That's Edgar, always looking to show off."

"How do you know him?" Larry said. Karen instructed him earlier to act interested in whatever her brother said and partake in the conversation at all costs. Dead air was not allowed. So he leaned forward in earnest with a plastic smile.

"We met in college."—Nathan winked at Karen—"Best eight weeks of my life, right, Sis?"

The two of them laughed.

"Edgar help me land my first job in sales. It was commission only selling insurance. He taught me the ropes, took me under his wing. I owe him. Last week, he called me out of the blue. That's how I found out about his hiking fiasco. I haven't seen him in a while. He gets me on the phone, and after telling his story, he gets a little . . . weird. Says he misses our friendship. That we all need to be better people and stop taking life for granted, that it's all about family. It made me uncomfortable. We don't talk about shit like that. It's usually sports or business. He acted different, like a changed man. I've never heard him be so humble."

The neighbor behind the Turners' house launched a Roman candle into the air and children ran around waving sparklers. Firecrackers went off up and down the street, sounding like gunfire. Larry suggested they light their own fireworks as darkness set in but got drowned out by Nathan. The more Karen's brother drank, the worse his chattiness became. Beer number five drained from his bottle like there was a hole in it.

"I want everyone to be honest," Nathan continued. "Come on, raise a hand. Do you think you would have survived in that predicament? The weather, the terrain, the hunger. Not to mention the animals trying to eat you. Yellowstone is over 3,000 square miles. You're nothing but a needle in a damn haystack and nobody is finding your ass unless you crawl out on your own."

Karen shook her head. "No, not me. I need a blanket when the air conditioner is too low. I probably would've froze to death."

"And you, Larry?" he asked.

"The cold doesn't bother me and I can go for a while without food. Unless I fell off the side of the mountain or broke something, I'm sure I'd find a way back."—he looked at his wife—"I've got too much to live for."

Larry stood up to stretch and stacked more wood by the fire. He recalled the numerous times he hiked growing up while on vacations with his dad. They'd been to Glacier National Park, Mount Rainier, and twice explored the majesty of Yosemite. He understood the ease in which a person or party could get lost in the wild when their bearings got confused and everything appeared the same.

People panic. Irrational thoughts get triggered. Normally intelligent hikers started doing dumb things. They'd wander off the trail in search of shortcuts, get split up from the group, or make hasty decisions based on a hunch. Without proper planning, disaster could happen quickly. Add in a fast-moving storm or a serious injury, and it was almost a certainty.

"I'd like to think I would've survived," Nathan said. He peeled at the label of his bottle. "That as a man, I have the courage to persevere through a tragedy. I know I'm not the definition of fitness, but it takes more than that. Something inside you has to want life at all costs. I guess you'd never really know until being forced into that kind of situation, like Edgar."

"I bet you would've made it," Karen said with a smile. "When you put your mind to it, nothing can stop you. You're stronger than you think."

Larry rolled his eyes and threw another log on the flames.

Nathan Brolidge never acquired the book smarts or the academic credentials used to traditionally measure and define intelligence. He was smart in his own kind of way—in a practical way. Good with people and blessed with common sense, he had confidence in whatever he did. Telling stories came natural to him. There wasn't a person he wouldn't talk to, about almost anything, and he had a large network of friends.

As for Karen and him, they had once been close. But following the long, drawn-out death of their mother from Alzheimer's, they somehow drifted apart. It was slow at first, then sudden, neither of them really knowing how or why until enough time passed where it became the norm.

Nathan had small hands, a loud voice, and a thick head of hair he loved to tout. He was a salesman by trade who took command of every room. It didn't matter if a person was Albert Einstein or a rodeo clown; a good salesman would always make a lot of money. A great one would make enough so family members have to suck up all night after not seeing them in years and grovel for a loan.

"They still don't know how he did it," Nathan said. "They say it's a miracle he didn't die. I believe that. To top it off, they're gonna put his story on TV."—he shook his head—"I told you he was a lucky bastard. It's one of those true life shows about people beating the odds. This Tuesday it'll air. And while not usually my cup of tea, I've been telling everyone about it like I was an executive producer. I'm actually kind of excited. I've never seen anyone on TV I knew before."

"Sounds fascinating," Karen said, wiping some chocolate from her lips.

"Sure does," Larry added .

"Me and Edgar used to be tight. I was the best man at his wedding. Since I'm trying to lend him my support on this, I wanted to ask if you'll tune in to watch his show. You know, as a favor to me."

"Of course," Karen said and nodded. "We'd love to. Right, Larry?"

"Wouldn't miss it." He sat back down when a gray, pudgy dog named Milo jumped onto his lap and started licking his hand. The wind gusted and he squinted as the campfire blew toward his face.

"Anyway," Nathan said. "Enough of my babble. It's great to see you again."—he turned to Larry—"What's new in the world of science, my good friend? What's the latest discovery guaranteed to change all of our lives for the better?"

Larry yawned, tasting smoke in his mouth. "I could tell you about the large Hadron particle accelerator or the latest study of climate change I read in *Popular Science*. But I'm really just a teacher, Nathan. And a basketball coach."

He yawned again and didn't mean to be rude, but it was past his normal bedtime. He drank the rest of his diet cola and pointed to a rectangular box of colorful fireworks wrapped in plastic.

"I think it's time we set those off. I made a spot over there near the picnic table and laid down some bricks."

"Great idea," Karen said. She swallowed the last bite of another s'more. "Nathan, before we get started, do you have a second? I want you to see something in the kitchen."

"Always have time for you," he said, standing up, a little off-balance. "I've gotta take a leak anyway." He snapped his fingers and the dog fell by his side, eager to please his master.

They strolled toward the house arm in arm, brother and sister, playing the game called *siblings* with unabashed and convincing delight. As they walked across the grass, Larry overheard her say, "It's so great of you to come down like this. You look fantastic. Have you lost some weight?"

"Are you trying to flatter me?" Nathan asked, patting his flabby stomach. He laughed and launched into a story about a new diet he'd discovered that worked in sync with his cravings for cupcakes. Karen acted enthralled, overly interested, and had she been on the big screen would have been nominated for an Oscar; on the small screen an Emmy.

The things parents do for their kids. The sacrifices they make.

Chapter 7

Larry never arrived at Principal Smith's house the next day to paint. He didn't drink any beer all night and there was no chance for a hangover, but his lack of sleep almost felt like one.

Nathan held court in the Turners' backyard until four in the morning, when the fire burned out and the hot coals faded to ash. His wife permitted him to stay as long as he wanted and said, "How often do you get a chance to visit your sister?" He detailed one story after the other, repeating the saga of his friend's wilderness debacle ad nauseam.

At one point Larry wanted to say, "We get it, Nathan. The rescue was incredible. It's the most remarkable thing I've ever heard. Now would you kindly please leave so I can go to bed?"

What came out of his mouth instead was, "Great. Wonderful. You're kidding? He didn't. Really?" along with a bunch of enthusiastic, "Uh-huhs," and nods of the head. He understood the social norms and rules of proper etiquette. You cannot ask someone for a large chunk of money then request them to leave. No sir. Nathan owned the night. And he knew it. The audience would stay put. They'd sit or stand, clap and applaud, throughout however many acts the man on the stage deemed necessary.

Birds chirped outside their bedroom as Karen and Larry stood side by side in the bathroom brushing their teeth, spitting foam in the sink in a not so cute manner. They'd showered to remove the stench of campfire smoke and Karen threw their clothes in the washer. Tired but awake, the married couple hadn't pulled an all-nighter in years. The last time they saw the sun rise was a trip to the cabin when the kids were little. They laid on blankets and watched a meteor shower, gazing at the Milky Way and the infinite number of stars.

"By the end of the week," Karen said with a smile. She stretched out in bed and snuggled under the covers. "We'll have the money from Nathan by the end of the week."

"How much?"

"I asked for thirty and he agreed to twenty-five."

"It was that simple?"

"Nothing is ever simple with him. As always, he wanted to negotiate."

"What does that mean?"

"It means we're going to have to pay a tiny bit of interest. But just a little."

Larry turned over, his eyes meeting hers. "Your own brother is charging us interest? What is he, a bank?"

"Nathan said he'd have to move some money around from one of his accounts that was performing really well. He's serious about his portfolio. That's his thing now. He doesn't mind helping but said he can't afford any kind of loss. I think he's saving up to buy a boat."

"How much will it be?"

"Prime plus a point."

You can always count on family, Larry thought, shaking his head. "Did you tell him what it's for?"

"Of course not"—Karen reached over and turned off her lamp—"I didn't want to get into it. As far as he knows, Jason is enrolled in culinary school and works long hours at a restaurant. I said the money was for Melissa because she got into Harvard."

"Harvard? When did she get into Harvard? She'll be so excited. I thought she was considering Yale. What about Oxford?"—he laughed aloud—"So just to be clear, is she no longer attending a state school?"

"I know, I got a little carried away. But I don't like to lie in the first place, and I'm not very good at it. The next thing I knew, I blurted stuff out and couldn't stop."

"How did the whole culinary thing come about? That's a new one. Couldn't you have picked something more believable? I'm sure Nathan saw right through it."

"I got the money, alright?"—she jerked the blanket to her side of the bed—"You weren't there. But I got it done, and you have no idea how difficult that was."

"Karen, I'm not suggesting . . . I'm just saying it's—"

"We can use the twenty-five thousand to get Jason out to Pine View and handle the rest of the bills as they come in. I already checked with our insurance. It's not going to be covered. We kind of figured that anyway. I'll start gathering my jewelry so you need to square up the cabin."

"Hey," he said, caressing her hand. "Maybe we should slow it down. Things are moving way too fast. Are you sure about this? I know how much you love your jewelry."

"It's only stuff, Larry. Material items. It can always be replaced. Don't you remember what you preach to everyone about stuff?"

He returned to his side of the bed and turned off his own lamp. "I'd rather do stuff than have stuff."

"Exactly. And doing stuff like helping Jason is far more important to me than having stuff like jewelry."

"Does that stuff include your wedding band and engagement ring?"

The room went silent. He fluffed his pillow and stole back some of the covers. It took him seven months of working an extra job during the school year to save up for her oval cut diamond. It took another few months for him to gather the nerve to propose. Her wedding band was engraved, which cost him more. It read: My heart is yours.

Karen reached over and set her alarm. "How long do you think before we can unload the cabin?"

This is crazy, he thought. *What's happening?*

"It's not even on the market yet, so I haven't the slightest. Since we're getting some money from Nathan, don't we have more time? Jason's entire treatment doesn't need to be paid up front."

"Time is something we're up against," she said. "Before we know it, the bills from Pine View will come tumbling in and they'll need to be paid in full. No exception. Because there can't be any hiccups with this. It could be his last chance to redeem some kind of life, and it could be our last chance for him to come back to us."

Larry closed his eyes and thought of a response but didn't feel up for an argument. Karen was right. Their situation required more money, but at what cost? Maybe they could sell one of their cars instead. Maybe both of them. But the cabin? Were they really going to do it?

They lay on their sides and he faced one wall while she faced the other. A sliver of orange sunlight poked through the curtains onto the bedspread. The ceiling fan spun overhead. He considered getting dressed for work, to forgo any sleep. Maybe with enough strong coffee or Red Bull he could do it. Every hour he wasn't in motion slopping a paint brush on somebody's house equated to losing money. If possible, Larry would have squeezed in a second job for the summer, or even a third.

"I know this is hard," she said, and slid in behind him. "I'd never ask you to do this if we had any other choice. But we don't. Which means we have to do everything in our power to help him. Otherwise, how will we be able to live with ourselves as parents?"—she rested her head on his arm—"It's not about us anymore. It's not about us at all."

Isn't it about us a little? Don't we have the right to some kind of life? We're middle-aged. There are years ahead. What about the girls? What if we lose the house?

That's what he almost said. Almost. But he knew that would be combative.

"You know I love you, right?" she said.

"Yes. And I love you too."

He stared at the wall until sleep came for him and he needn't stare any longer.

Hey Larry, you're on the precipice of losing it all. Everything's fine.

Karen was already gone when he arose. She'd left a note on the fridge that the laundry was done, she'd picked up the yard, cleaned the kitchen, checked on Jason, put dinner in the Crock-Pot, and was headed to work for a few hours. His wife had the energy of a thirty-year old. He marveled at her. Lounging in bed for the first time since incident number two, Larry reflected on what she'd said. He couldn't fall back asleep.

Was there any other way?

CHAPTER

Karen stopped working full-time the day after Jason's first incident that damaged her in a way she never imagined possible. A new reality had been shackled to her mind, a new jagged fear stabbed into her heart. Like any normal parent, she was ill-equipped to handle it.

She was the one who found him the first time around. It was a fluke really, when Karen returned home from work shortly after arriving because she forgot her cell phone in the kitchen. Jason's car was parked in the driveway and it surprised her. He should've been at work too. At the urging, and often times badgering, of his parents to do something rather than lie around his room all day and sleep or play video games, he accepted a part-time job they arranged for him.

Dr. Baker supported the decision and an action plan was created. Jason started out with ten, then fifteen, and increased his way to twenty hours per week stocking shelves at a pet supply store. It wasn't college or any type of promising career. It certainly wasn't what the Turners envisioned when their firstborn scored a 1,200 on the SATs in the tenth grade. But his deteriorating condition continued to reset the bar lower and lower.

The house was quiet when she walked in it that morning. Nothing appeared out of the ordinary. Sarah left a half-full glass of juice on the table, and the sink was stacked with breakfast dishes. Karen turned off the coffee pot and grabbed her cell phone to check it for messages. She thought Jason may have called in sick or the pet store closed for some reason. Then she headed upstairs to investigate.

"Jason?" she yelled and knocked on his door, receiving no response. "Jason, are you here?" She knocked again before entering, but the room was empty. So she snooped.

It wasn't the first time she'd looked around without his permission. The desk drawers contained nothing useful nor did the nightstand, the closet, or the area under the bed. She fired up his computer and glanced out the window before turning her attention to the garbage. That's when Karen became unnerved.

Mixed in among the potato chip wrappers, soda cans, and a blackened banana peel, she discovered three small empty bottles of vodka. Jason took after both parents and wasn't a drinker. He said he didn't care for the taste of alcohol or the impairment of drugs. His abstinence was a rare bright spot the Turners needn't worry.

Karen paced about the room and tried to configure the puzzle pieces, wondering how her son could obtain any liquor since he was underage. She thought about calling Larry, but he was in class. Her search of Jason's computer proved fruitless as the password had been changed. She then thought about the pet store. Should the manager be contacted to see if he showed? The number was downstairs on the side of the fridge and as she went into the hallway to get it, the bathroom door caught her eye.

It wasn't open all the way like usual, but it wasn't fully closed either. She approached it and pushed, but the door didn't budge. "Jason?" she said, pushing harder. Something blocked the entrance.

Adrenaline injected into her blood stream and her pupils dilated. She called his name again, stepping back. Karen ran toward the door and launched her body against it like a battering ram. The door moved a little. She rammed it over and over, harder, grunting. Her shoulder throbbed. When enough space was created she wedged her head inside the frame. What she saw, she wished she hadn't.

Butted up next to the door was a black high-top sneaker attached to her son. He was sprawled on the floor unconscious with prescription bottles near him and white tablets scattered everywhere. The opening scene of her nightmarish movie was underway.

A scream caught in her throat as she slithered inside. She pounced on Jason. His lips were closed and she pulled them apart. Karen stuck her fingers in his mouth and could barely control her shaky hands when she searched for pills, checking under his tongue and along the gumline. There was nothing.

She leapt to the sink and cranked on the faucet. She threw handfuls of water on him, yelling his name frantically. She threw more water. More yelling. The floor got slippery. She couldn't think. She dove beside Jason and shook him. Then another shake. She begged and pleaded. A harder shake. And when he gave the slightest groan, her mind exploded and the tears streamed down her cheeks. She shook him again and screamed for him to wake up. He groaned a little more.

The 911 operator told her to speak slower as she screeched into the phone their home address and what had happened. She cradled Jason, rocking him. Both of their clothes were wet. Karen brushed aside the hair from his forehead and planted a kiss. His skin was pale, clammy. She listened for more groans. His pulse was weak. She squeezed him tighter when the sirens roared down the street.

The fire department came, the ambulance came, the police came, Larry came, the neighbors came, the girls came. Everyone watched Jason get wheeled away in a stretcher with an oxygen mask strapped to his face and the EMTs hovered above him.

Karen trembled for hours afterward—she couldn't stop crying. She hounded the doctors for information, then the nurses. When she was informed her son would live and suffered no permanent damage, she collapsed into a chair, exhausted. The depth of her relief could not be explained. There weren't any words. But she also knew their lives had been changed irrevocably. Something inside her was lost in that bathroom. Something she would never get back.

From that day forward there'd be no peace of mind again. The incident would loom in the back of her brain, stalking like a predator. Finding her son half-dead was burned into her memory. What if she didn't leave her phone at the house that morning? What if she didn't go back to retrieve it?

The questions propelled Karen to become paranoid, morphing her into a hyper-vigilant parent. She didn't feel safe letting Jason out of her sight for quite some time. Not for a second. Not for a minute. The comfort of safety was gone.

As the tension in the house mounted, as nobody knew how to act or what to say, she wondered if Jason lay dead upstairs every time he didn't make a peep for hours. Should she check on him? Call an ambulance? Should they install an intercom? Or a camera?

She found herself hanging around the base of the stairs with greater frequency, arms folded, looking up. Sometimes she climbed halfway, then retreated. Other times she made it to the top and knocked on his door. The mental strain of living that way began to manifest itself physically.

An ulcer—Karen developed that quickly—and not far behind was the inevitable hypertension. Her headaches increased in both frequency and duration, and the fine lines around her eyes deepened. The tumultuous relationship she had with sleep grew even worse. She once described her anxiety-plagued mindset to Larry, one of the rare moments she was honest with herself in front of him.

"I feel like I'm walking through a haunted house," she said. "It's dark and I can't see. My hands are in front of me, searching for something to hold onto, but nothing's there. I walk slowly and shuffle my feet, and I'm scared. I expect the floor to drop out or something to grab me. I know as long as I'm in that house I'm gonna be scared, but I'm powerless to stop it. I can't leave. The windows are boarded and the doors are solid concrete. So I move forward in the dark and there's no turning back. The house won't let me. The only choice I have is to manage the fear the best I can because it won't go away."

That's why she needed to return to work, she'd told him. It helped her move forward through the haunted house, to maybe believe one day there'd be an escape. Five months after finding Jason in the bathroom, she went back to her job on a limited basis.

Chapter 9

Karen thrived working as a curator for a museum in the city. It was no doubt one of her great passions in life. She loved to talk about art and show people the innovative nature of the human spirit. After her sophomore year in college, she realized the lack of artistic talent in herself. Yet she still wanted to make a career out of being around it. She adored sculptures, from the David of Michelangelo to The Kiss of Rodin, and had a fondness for canvasses from Matisse to Picasso.

At first, she hired a sitter to help out with Jason, although she preferred the term *helper*. Interviews were held and background checks conducted, much to the confusion of the applicants who weren't quite sure what the job entailed. But the process didn't last long.

She never got comfortable with either the helper or the expense. Karen needed someone she could trust to keep the matter private. That reduced the number of people to four, and the concept of *Jason duty* was born.

JD was to be a deterrent. She believed a suicide attempt would be far less likely if another person was inside the house. A schedule was developed in an effort to be fair and she covered the majority of shifts, working mostly in the late afternoon. But there were plenty of arguments among the girls for different time slots and frequent last-minute dashes back home so the next person could get to work or school or a social activity.

While at the house, Karen constantly read articles online about depression in young people. She searched for causes and connections, hoping to stumble upon a solution. With safety in mind, every precaution was taken for Jason's well-being. All pills were banished from their residence, including the vitamins, and the medicine cabinets were bare. The lock on his bedroom door was removed as was the lock in bathroom.

Often bored, she called Larry. Her efforts to follow up and communicate with her daughters increasingly went to voicemail. But regardless of what Karen did, she always had an ear tuned into Jason's room like a momma bird guarding a delicate egg.

That's why the second incident only six months prior and two short years removed from the attempted overdose almost crippled her. It was on Larry's watch. She never once insinuated it was his fault as it easily could've been on her shift or one of the girls. How can you monitor a grown person all day, every day, unless they're locked in a cell or strapped to a bed?

The Turners had endured two close calls, two horrific incidents. After brief periods of slight improvement from Jason and a fragment of taunting hope, the inevitable disappointment of a backslide always followed. Incident number three circled about the house, waiting. It permeated the walls with a nervous energy and suffocated everyone. Unless something changed drastically, Karen knew she'd be unable to stop it.

At times she couldn't control her mind and succumbed to the darkness of fear. She speculated how incident number three would ultimately unfold. Would they find Jason on the bathroom floor overdosed once more? Or would they find him with his wrists slashed open instead, a puddle of blood around him, his body rigid and blue? Perhaps his bloated corpse would be discovered face down in the neighbor's pool or he'd be slumped in the corner of the garage with a plastic bag wrapped over his head. Maybe he'd storm from the house to lunge before a bus or a train, or maybe he'd swan dive from the highest building in town.

Perhaps the hardest thing to watch would be Jason starve himself into the afterlife, withering into dust at the tempo of a slow leaky faucet. She hated herself for thinking these things. It only added to the guilt. Because as scary and macabre and disturbing as they were, the thoughts were based in reality.

Karen cried daily, stopped asking *Why me?* to the Good Lord, and withdrew from the church altogether. She moved through life in a detached bubble, like she had blinders on. She and the girls had grown further apart, not closer as one would have expected. While she was still a good mom and a good wife and a good person, a little piece of her died further each day and there was no way to hide it.

Larry begged her to attend therapy and talk with someone. She was also encouraged to do so by the friends she had before freezing them out. Karen acquiesced, going twice, but she never gave into the process.

"I don't have the time," she'd say. "Maybe next week I'll try again when I'm not so busy. I have a lot on my plate right now."

Her excuses made no sense.

Larry would counter with, "You need to make time. I want you to be around with us and not fall over in a heap one day. The girls need us both. Stop being stubborn and let people help you."

"I don't want to incur the expense," she'd argue. "I'd rather use the money for therapy to help Jason."

"The group I go to is free," he reminded her. "You aren't alone. Others have been through this before. I've asked you to come with me like a million times. And you did, you came once and met my friends Chip and Pauline. But you never came back. I can't figure out why."

"I don't want to be around those kinds of people. Misery may love company, but I want no part."

"Those kinds of people? What's that supposed to mean? Who do you think we are?"

"That's not what I meant and you know it."

Karen despised being around *those* kinds of people, unwilling to acknowledge that she was one of them. She didn't believe anybody could relate to what she was going through. Her boy was not broken. Any day now he'd wake from his slumber and snap out of the funk. It wasn't supposed to be this way.

He'd walk downstairs with his beautiful smile and ask what was for dinner, his eyes clear and bright, his hair spiked with gel. She'd be overjoyed to feed him, elated with his voracious appetite. They'd eat together as a family and watch a movie before Jason would venture out to the park with friends.

She'd been to every single basketball game her boy ever played in and she missed sitting in the stands with the other parents, feeling the love and adoration thrown her son's way. She missed it when Larry coached him from the sidelines.

Those were the memories Karen reveled in the most, and it pained her there'd be no more.

An abduction had taken place, the robbery of her child, and it happened right in front of her. She was unable to stop it. She didn't know what to do. So she agonized in silence, bewildered, a disillusioned parent unable to fathom her predicament.

Chapter 10

Larry dozed off in a beige cloth recliner with his head twisted to one side, his mouth slightly agape. A trickle of drool dangled from his bottom lip. He'd climbed up and down the ladder at a heightened pace that day, painting faster than usual, and took a short lunch. A deal had been cut with Karen and after missing a full day's work because of Nathan's lengthy stay at the barbeque, he needed to make up for lost time.

"I have to be able to think," he'd told her, not wanting to discuss the sale of the cabin any further. "Let me see if there's something else I can come up with, maybe some other way we can do this."

He guaranteed his wife to be finished painting Principal Smith's house by the end of the following week. It would allow them to receive a check they counted on, and he could also line up another job. When that was done, he promised her whatever she wanted.

His self-imposed deadline was impulsive and shortsighted. It only gave him nine days to finish the painting and would require working like a beast to do so. But something had to be done to provide a degree of breathing room and buy himself some time, to stall Karen and get her off his back.

The cabin debate exhausted Larry and he felt weary from standing his ground—something he rarely did anymore. He wished it was all a big game, like when he coached, and when things weren't going his way—when his Morell Park Warriors were getting hammered on the boards or not getting stops on defense—

he could signal the referee for a timeout. If he could just get the clock to stop ticking, he thought. But it wasn't a game, and nobody was playing.

They'd purchased the cabin soon after getting married when Larry cashed in some savings bonds and sold an old motorcycle he no longer rode. Owning a place in the woods had been a dream of his since college. It was his father's dream too.

Papa Turner, an avid hiker and outdoors enthusiast who passed on long ago, provided a helping loan on the cabin. He forgave the loan when the deal was completed and explained it was a gift. But Larry still wanted to repay him, on the principle of pride. He'd leave money in his house or sneak it into his car, and they often vied for a restaurant check like they were going to fight. He always wanted to take care of the man who took such good care of him.

After six years of payments to the bank, the cabin was paid in full. The debt-free asset was a rare commodity for the Turners, a rare thing for most people they knew. And Larry was to head up to this asset he loved in a little over a week with no other way around it.

Once there, he would assess the damages from the last few years of neglect and calculate the cost to repair it. He also considered spending an extra day to canoe and fish. Only then would it be determined if the cabin was truly going on the market or not. Only then, he, Larry Wendell Turner—teacher, coach, father, husband, and part-time house painter—would deem the appropriateness of allowing his beloved structure to be sold.

But he wasn't fooling anyone, certainly not himself. He knew the cabin would be sold immediately. There was no plan B. The decision to sell had already been made without him deciding it, dictated by their impending situation. He simply wanted to hold onto it for as long as he could, to savor the trip for a final goodbye. He wanted one more endearing moment with the memory of his dad.

"Here," Karen said to him when she entered the living room. She held a bowl of popcorn in her hand. "I thought you might want a snack."

He looked at the delightful surprise thrust on his lap and sat up. The smell of warm butter streamed toward him. "What's the occasion?"

"It's Tuesday. Don't you remember?"

He shrugged. "Remember what?"

"We told Nathan we'd watch the show."

"About his friend in the woods? I know we said we'd watch it, but come on, what else were we supposed to say?"

"I gave him my word and may I remind you, he's giving us money."

"Lending us money," he corrected her, then thought, *and charging us stinking interest.* "I planned on watching a movie. *Goodfellas* is coming on cable."

"Number one: You were sleeping. You were actually snoring pretty loud. Number two: How many times have you seen that movie? Come on, we'll eat a little popcorn and watch the show. How bad could it be?"

"It definitely won't be as good as my movie."

"You want me to get you a drink?"

He rubbed his eyes like a tired child. "Can you put ice in it, please?"

She nodded and picked up the remote that'd fallen on the floor. She set it on the armrest. "I already checked the guide. It's on channel eighty-six."

Larry had seen survival shows about the wilderness many times before, and during a brief period in his television viewing life he enjoyed them. But how many times could he watch them since they're almost always the same?

The story went along the lines of a lone guy or a naïve couple makes a stupid decision to go for a hike in a remote terrain with only a small bottle of water and a pack of gum. They pay zero attention to their surroundings and don't have a map or a compass. They either forget to charge their battery or there's no coverage for their cell phone.

Darkness comes, the cold sets in, and they're in trouble. They get further lost by walking in the wrong direction. Days pass. Maybe a week. They almost die. A miraculous rescue comes about somehow and they get saved. They cry. Roll the credits.

Karen told him to be quiet and shushed him as the narrator eased into the introduction with an authoritative baritone voice. *What's the big deal?* Larry thought. He only tried to tell her about his day. Why was the narrator so dramatic anyway? It wasn't like this guy was so much different from all the other people. It wasn't like he was the President or an actor or somebody famous. He was just Nathan's friend.

His full name was Edgar James Suarez, a forty-nine-year-old father of four from Long Beach, California. He was the director of sales for a national insurance company. His personal claim to fame before getting lost in Yellowstone was when he climbed Mount Kilimanjaro back in 1993 and surfed the big waves of Hawaii as a teen.

The first thing Larry noticed was how gaunt the man appeared. The sides of his face looked compressed, accentuating his high cheek-bones. His neck was as round as a cornstalk and perhaps as long, and he had a pointy nose that tipped up at the end like a ski jump. He was tall, a good six feet or so, with scrawny shoulders. His slender hands were folded neatly on his lap.

Larry shifted in the recliner. He sat up straighter and crammed his mouth full of popcorn. Nathan's friend reminded him of Jason.

Chapter 11

Edgar Suarez spoke in a high-pitched voice, borderline nasally. The tears gathered in his eyes the instant the camera zoomed in on him. He sat in a director's style chair with his legs crossed, and beads of sweat were already present on his forehead. At times he stammered. While the ordeal took place five months earlier, discussing it forced him to stop and collect himself several times, for which he apologized afterward.

But it wasn't all bad, he explained. As he continued to talk about his battle with the snowstorm and getting separated from his friends, of how he spent almost a week alone in freezing temperatures without fire, food, and very little water, he seemed to recall the traumatic experience with a sense of reverie.

"I feel so lucky to be alive," Edgar said. He removed a gold rope necklace from under his shirt and kissed a cross. "My wife always says things happen for a reason. I'm embarrassed to admit, but I never used to believe that. It seemed silly. But she's right. You see, I . . . I was doing well in life. I had a great job and a nice family. I earned good money. But I also worked all the time and spent less time with my kids. I had no spirituality. I felt depressed at times and didn't know why."—a large tear dripped down his cheek—"Sometimes I used work as an excuse not to come home. I lied about things. I'm not proud of that, but it's true. I was turning into a person I never thought I would be. I was turning into my dad—how he was with us, pulling away."—a rush of big tears—"My father committed suicide when I was twenty.

The camera zoomed in on Edgar further and the music intensified. Larry's eyes narrowed as he leaned forward.

"He shot himself in the barn behind our house. They found him on a pile of hay. He never even left a note to say goodbye. No explanation. No nothing. Just gone. I was away at college. My mom—I don't think she ever got over it. It messed me up pretty good too. It's tough for me to say this, to admit my weakness. But I want to be honest. I always do now. The thought of taking my own life had entered my mind before. It seemed—the older I got, the thoughts—they'd pop in there without my control. They say that kind of thing can run in families.

"I never believed I'd ever do it—to abandon my kids like my dad. But then again, I really couldn't say for sure. But now I do. I know 150 percent. Never ever would I do that. You see, for some reason I felt sorry for myself and believed I was owed something. God owed me something. Life owed me something. I was supposed to be given more gifts than I already had. I really thought I was special back then . . . But not in a good way. I was greedy.

Karen sniffled and wiped her nose while Larry sat so close to the edge of the recliner he was about to fall off. He turned up the volume on the TV until the speakers crackled.

"That's why I believe this happened to me. To wake me up. God tapped me on the shoulder in that wilderness and said, 'Edgar, stop being ungrateful. It's time to do something good.' So I did. And I have. I realized I wanted to live. I want to live as long as I can. Now each day I'm filled with a new joy and appreciation for my family, my friends, and my job . . . For my life. I've never been happier. In a strange way, I wish this happened to me many years ago, when I was younger. I wish this could be a way to give people some kind of relief. A form of therapy, so to speak. To change their perspective. Because some people need it."—he kissed his cross again—"I know for sure that I was one of them."

The interview continued and Edgar talked about survivor's guilt, his new physical ailments, and why they made the fateful decision to hike off the trail.

There were the cut-ins of photos displaying the size and scope of Yellowstone and video re-creations of the weather conditions. When asked if there was ever a movie made about his ordeal and he could pick the actor to play him, Edgar stated his answer would be Leonardo DiCaprio.

Then he added, "I guess every guy wants to be played by Leonardo. But he would need some serious makeup since I am much older and not as good looking." That was the only light moment in the interview. Then it was over.

"Amazing," Karen said, wiping her nose again. She crumpled a tissue. "Nathan was right. What a story."

Larry was silent. He stared at the TV as if in a trance, his brain in hyper-drive. He could feel the neurons buzzing. Edgar Suarez once thought of killing himself and now he couldn't be happier. The man was alive. He wanted to live. Getting lost in the woods and almost dying served as a wake-up call. The disaster was viewed as a form of therapy, a positive curative experience. The words continue to ring in Larry's head. *The man wanted to live.*

"Hey, you over there," Karen said. She threw a piece of popcorn at him. "You okay? Can you lower the volume now?"

He tried to smile but his face felt tight. "Everything's fine," he said, raking a hand through his hair. He stood and passed her the remote.

"Where you going?" she asked. "Let's watch a movie together after I check on Jason. Anything you want for sitting through the show with me."

"I got a stomachache," he said, and cleared his throat. "I have to get up for work. I'm going to sleep."

"Are you sure? Is there anything I can get you?"

He ignored her questions and dashed to the bedroom where he dropped to the floor. He stretched out an arm under the bed and searched until his fingers reached a clear plastic bin with a blue lid. The words TAPES-JASON were written on the side in marker. The bin was a collection of videos Larry made when his son first started playing basketball.

He had boxes of tapes for each of the kids—Sarah on the soccer field, Melissa on the softball diamond. Neither of the girls stuck with sports and found other interests, but there was tape after tape of Jason on the hardwood.

Larry dug through the box until finding the one with the error on it, the one where the lever on the tripod broke and the camera accidentally zoomed in on the ground. He'd captured sixty minutes of gymnasium floor footage before realizing the problem to salvage the end of the game.

The VCR was stored in the closet under a bag of old shoes and a pile of board games. The bulky antique was in surprisingly good condition. After he hooked it up and set the clock, then the timer, he popped in the tape. The recording was to begin at midnight.

Throughout the airing of Edgar Suarez's interview, the network advertised that the program would be rebroadcast in its entirety again. Larry picked up the brochure from Pine View on top of the nightstand and read it cover to cover one last time. He focused on what Karen had written.

AT LEAST 100K. PROBABLY 150.

He thought of his daughters, of how much they meant, and he thought about the undying love for his wife. He didn't want to lose any of them. As always, he thought of Jason and didn't want to lose him either. But did he wait too long?

"Can I do this?" he said, scarcely above a whisper. "Can it really be done?"

His hands shook and his legs felt weak when he went into the bathroom, his idea carrying the weight of an anchor. He leaned over the sink and splashed water on his face. He considered young Edgar, what the boy endured. Larry tried to remember the events that took place when he was that age. How would he have dealt with life knowing one of his parents were dead? Would he have stayed focused in school or gotten into trouble? Would he have still settled down or wandered about?

He lifted his head and water dripped from his chin. Larry stared in the mirror. Every day he resembled his father a little bit more. At times he talked to the spirit of his dad and asked for advice, expecting the man staring back to answer. He missed him just as much now as the day he suddenly passed, and the scar he suffered never shrank or faded away. Fathers and sons, what they do for each other, and in some cases, to each other.

With a towel wrapped around his neck, he walked to the dresser and put on his sleep pants. Larry had been lucky to have a great dad. He'd once been lucky to have a great son too. Returning Jason to greatness wasn't on the agenda because after all he'd seen, he didn't believe it was possible. Getting him healthy and whole, to be a productive member of society and take care of himself—that had to be the purpose. Perhaps it couldn't be done, but he realized he needed to try. On his own terms. The future of his family depended on it.

Thank you Nathan, he said to himself. *Thank you Edgar Suarez.*

He turned on the TV and hopped under the sheets. Larry punched in channel eighty-six, waiting for the show to begin. His mind continued to race and he couldn't stop it. But he didn't want to. Come morning, he'd reach out to his friends and make the call. The line he wasn't sure existed was about to be crossed.

CHAPTER 12

The bagel grew stale. She ripped off a piece of her carb-loaded breakfast and tossed it to the pigeons. The fattest one bobbed over to grab the food first. Taxis raced by as the sidewalks became congested and while she only worked five blocks away, Karen never much ventured to that part of the city. Next to her was a purse, the biggest she had. She wore a large pair of sunglasses and a baseball hat. Every few minutes she touched the purse to make sure it was still there.

The temperature was already warm and by noon it'd be blistering. The forecast called for another sustained heatwave well into the hundreds. Across the street was a row of narrow storefronts shielded with metal gates and rife with graffiti. She eyed one storefront in particular called Billy G's Pawn, established circa 1998.

An elderly man waited out front with a duffle bag by his feet. He leaned against the wall and smoked a cigar near a woman who hosed down the sidewalk. Karen had her suspicions about the place but relied on her research. Billy G's Pawn allegedly gave the highest payout in the area. At least that's what the reviews said.

She slid down the bench to a shady spot and wondered how much she'd get for her effort. Having never set foot inside a pawn shop before, her expectations were unclear. It was astonishing how a lifetime of acquiring jewelry for birthdays, anniversaries, holidays, and special events could all fit so neatly in one bag. She didn't know why, but she thought there'd be more.

This was for Jason, she reminded herself. And she owed it. Nothing was to be spared, including the cheap stuff that would only bring pennies on the dollar. She'd contemplated asking the girls what they could contribute, perhaps a necklace that hadn't been worn or a bracelet they'd forgotten about. But then she thought better of it. Her daughters already teetered toward complete isolation.

Karen glanced at her watch, unclasping the strap. She dropped it into the purse as the gate guarding the pawn shop rolled up and a neon OPEN sign flashed. The last chunk of bagel was thrown to the birds and she extended her left hand in the air, rotating it. The nail polish was chipped, the color faded. Another brown spot emerged on her skin seemingly from nowhere. She sighed, then looked at her ring finger. The diamond sparkled brilliantly in the sunlight. She sighed again.

Only one last thing remained before traipsing across the street and she dreaded it. She never thought it would get to this. Jason should have been better by now. The bagel churned in her stomach, mixing with the nerves and her fears and the uncertainty. She felt sick. A vow was made that at some point in the future, she'd get them back. But pragmatism preceded sentiment—that's how she consoled herself. Sometimes a mother has to do what needs to be done. And Larry needed to understand that.

They were tight, super tight. She twisted, pulled, and twisted some more. The metal and skin bonded into a solitary unit over the decades and she suspected they wouldn't come off that easily. She reached into her pocket and retrieved a bottle of lotion. The creamy white substance was squirted onto her finger and rubbed all around it. Using a tissue, she gripped the rings, and twisted again. Karen felt a slight movement. She pulled hard toward the barrier of a stubborn knuckle and grimaced.

She twisted and pulled, twisted and pulled, twisted and pulled. Her finger burned as the blood rushed to her face. She gnashed her teeth and yanked harder, groaning. People who walked by gawked at her. But she didn't care. She was prepared to rip the digit clean off her hand if necessary.

With her finger on the verge of being shredded and the skin about to peel, Karen pulled hard one last time. She shrieked. When the wedding band finally slid off followed by her engagement ring, she squeezed them. Her eyes watered. Her body trembled. The trauma of the event weakened her.

She'd never taken them off before. Not once in twenty-five years. Not when she did the dishes and not when she went to bed. Not when she swam, not when she showered, and not when she made meatloaf for her family or kneaded pizza dough on the counter. And she used to make pizza often. It used to be Jason's favorite.

"My mom makes the best pizza ever," he boasted to people starting in the fourth grade. "You should try it."

If she ran a business he'd have been the perfect spokesman and she always regretted not getting him into commercials. Karen and Larry didn't know where his obsession came from. They too enjoyed the occasional pie, but their son was a literal pizza-head. That's all he ever wanted to eat.

"Jason, what do you want for dinner?" she'd ask him.

"Pizza. Your pizza."

"What do you want for breakfast?"

"Pizza. Your pizza."

"How about a snack?"

"Pizza. Your pizza."

"You're going to turn into a pizza, little boy."

He'd giggle. "That's okay with me."

He ate pizza hot or cold, thick or thin, plain or loaded with toppings. By the time high school began, he said, "Mom, you should open up your own pizza place. We could do it together. Be co-owners."

"Nah," she said smiling. "You'd eat all the profits and we'd go broke."

Jason used to have friends over all the time when he was younger. Karen would feed everyone until they were full then send them home with leftovers. She loved it when the house was packed with people, when the laughter and energy soaked into every room.

She eventually showed him how to make the dough from scratch, by himself, and how to simmer the sauce to perfection. Both recipes were copied from her favorite chef on TV. The thing that surprised her most was that he was good at it. He took a real interest in cooking. When mother and son were in the kitchen, just the two of them, it was their thing; their special time together.

At the end of his freshman year, he tried to convince his parents that a brick fired oven in the kitchen was a necessity. A case was presented for all the wonderful items he could make in addition to pizza, such as calzones and Stromboli. By the time he was a sophomore, he became serious about one day opening a pizza shop. He took a small business class as one of his electives and decided on a company name. He even designed the logo.

Then poof, it suddenly stopped. Like a puff of smoke or a magician's trick, the interest he expressed disappeared. Karen couldn't remember the last time she'd eaten a slice of pizza. It didn't taste the same anymore.

She felt naked without the rings on her finger and her hand seemed so light, as if it could float away high into the clouds and never return. If she wasn't careful, her entire body would be next. *They're only some rings*, she thought, attempting to fool herself. She touched the indent circling her skin. But they weren't just *some* rings. They were *the* rings. Those were the rings girls dream of and the ones women wore with pride.

Her mascara was smudged and the eyeliner streaked down her face. She wiped her cheeks and told herself to breathe. *Stick to the plan*, she thought. A taxi beeped, the pigeons cooed, a bus squealed, and as more people walked in front of her talking on their phones, Karen decided it was time. She couldn't procrastinate all day. She took a deep breath and was about to proceed when somebody approached her from the side.

"Karen, is that you?"

She shoved the rings in her pocket as if they'd been stolen and prepared to flee the crime scene. She tried to knock the shakiness from her voice. "Yes, I'm Mrs. Turner."

"I thought so. You had your head down and I wasn't sure at first but . . . It's been quite some time."

Karen stood and hung the purse over her shoulder. "Have we met?"

"Have we met? It's me, Sally. Our boys played together. My son is Darren. Darren Covington."

"Sally, how are you?" she said, and gave the woman she hadn't seen in years a perfunctory hug. "It's so bright out here this morning and there's a harsh glare. Please forgive me."—she then stepped aside—"It was nice seeing you again, but I have to go."

"Are you alright? You seem a bit . . . I don't know . . . lost."

"Oh no, no, no. I don't work that far from here. I'm actually taking a break, trying to get in my morning walk."

"If you're hungry there's a pastry shop around the corner. We could catch up. I work about a block away, over on Gibson Street, so I go there all the time. I can't believe I haven't seen you over here before doing your cute little exercise. Do you have time for a cup of tea?"

Karen paused. She recalled that Sally, like her, was one of the mothers who volunteered to provide orange slices for the players at halftime during home games. She'd also heard that Darren, a skinny hard-working boy who came off the bench only when the game turned in a blowout, attended college on an academic scholarship.

"I should get back to the museum," she said. "I've been gone too long already."

"How is the museum anyway? I haven't been there in forever. My husband and I were just saying how we really should go. Do they have any interesting new exhibits?"

In a different life, prior to incident number one, Karen would've delighted in explaining the van Gogh's they received on loan or the young artist from Japan who had an opening soon. She would've escorted Sally over there herself and gave a personal tour, maybe throw in a complimentary souvenir from the gift shop. But that person ceased to exist. Now there was only awkwardness as Sally glanced at the old bank behind Karen's shoulder that'd been converted into apartments and Karen stared at the intruder's feet.

"How's Jason?" Sally asked, her voice lighter and softer than before. "I am so sorry to hear about what happened."

Karen knew the question was coming because the question *always* came. She chastised herself for not being curt and leaving right away. She studied the woman's face beyond the crow's feet or the wrinkles or the mole on her cheek. A sympathetic urge was detected just below the surface. It waited to erupt in a condescending comment or a patronizing hug—as if Jason were already dead.

The hollow catchphrases of, "If you ever want to talk," or "Call me anytime," would soon follow, punctuated by an emphatic, "I mean it." And there was no doubt Sally wanted to know how things were really going. She wanted to spread the news to everyone and use it as a measuring stick with her own children. But the woman standing next to her already knew Jason's condition. Because everybody did. It was impossible to keep secret.

So why did they bother to ask? Why be so cruel? Couldn't anybody understand the question was like a gut punch, mean spirited and vile? Couldn't they see how she struggled with it? She wanted to hold up a sign or pass out a leaflet that said, "If anything changes for the good with my son, on the positive side, I'll let the world know. Until then, be quiet and leave us alone."

She looked again at Sally and it was more than the sorrow or misfortune cast her way that was bothersome. Karen detested how every person she spoke with felt the need to be overly nice, to go above genuine concern and speak carefully and slowly, to treat her like a wounded puppy. She wasn't a bad parent. Her kid was still alive. And they would fix him. She wasn't a bad mom. She was a good mom. She wanted to scream it through a megaphone. She wanted . . .

Sally handed her a business card. "If you ever want to talk, call me anytime."—she pulled Karen into an embrace then stepped back and clutched her hand—"I mean it."

"It's good to see you again," Karen lied. She abruptly turned and marched up the street. She heard, "Call me anytime," shouted at her and kept on walking. Sally's card was thrown in the garbage and she crossed Billy G's Pawn off the list. She'd head to a different shop on the other side of town, maybe in a different city or state, where the likelihood of bumping into anyone she knew was remote.

CHAPTER

"Hi Pauline, it's Larry," he said from the cordless phone in his bedroom. "Sorry to bother you so early."

It was dark outside and Karen had already left for the morning. She beat him out of the house and mentioned she had errands to run or something about driving to a pawn shop in the city. He couldn't tell, still in the shower, but soon got dressed. He headed to Melissa's room and roused her. His daughter was informed he was off to work and she had JD until Karen got back.

Each member of the family had cell phones, but the Turners were one of the few people left who continued to use a landline. A cordless phone was in everyone's bedroom and there was one in the living room, one in the kitchen, and one mounted on the wall outside Jason's curtain. Karen insisted they have them in case there was a problem with their cell phones and they couldn't get a signal or somebody lost them—in case 911 needed to be called for incident number three.

"It's alright," Pauline said. "You know I don't sleep. I'm watching one of my knitting shows."

"Are you and Chip going to the meeting tonight?"

"Don't we always?" Her voice was deep and raspy, sultry when she was younger, now sounding masculine as she aged toward sixty. "I hope you plan on coming as well. We haven't seen you around the last few weeks."

"I know. Been busy with the painting."

"Everybody's busy, honey. Excuses are a dime a dozen. Nobody wants to be there, but we have to."

Larry nodded in agreement. "You think we could meet up afterward for a bite to eat?"

He heard the spark of a lighter followed by an inhale and knew she'd lit one of her extra-long cigarettes. "We can go to that dive bar a few blocks from the church. They serve food all night. I'll ask Mary and Shannon to join us too. They're new to the group. They adopted a little girl back in the day who's now fourteen. Has them worried sick. And you know stinky ole Rick Madsen will want to come along, I'm sure. The worst breath ever on a man, I swear to the Lord above."

"I was hoping some place a bit more private. Just the three of us. Like we used to."

"What's going on, Larry? You want me to wake up Chip to come get you?"

"It can wait until tonight. Everything's fine."

She cackled a laugh. "As fine as we're gonna be."

"That's our slogan."

"Listen, I'll take some chili out of the freezer and we'll have a late supper. I'll meet up with the other folks next time."

"Great. See you at seven."

"Anytime, sweetie."

Larry arrived fifteen minutes late to the meeting and hated to do so. But when he got home from work, Karen was gone. She ran to the grocery store for an ingredient to make dinner, and both girls tried bolting from the house the minute he stepped through the door. There'd been a mix-up in the scheduling.

He demanded one of them stick around until their mother returned. While JD could be inconvenient at times, it was important. After all, they were his sisters and part of the family, and they needed to pitch in, and blah blah blah blah blah. He'd given that lecture before and assumed it fell on deaf ears. He knew Melissa and Sarah were good-natured kids who loved their brother. They wanted to help but were scared. Everyone was.

Both daughters cried for a week straight after incident number one and missed several days of school. They were still so young and idolized Jason. He was the star of the family. They asked their parents repeatedly why he would do something like that. How could he? What was wrong with him? Was there a chance he may do it again? Solid answers were unable to be provided.

Life as everyone experienced it had changed, and from the moment incident number one occurred, the girls refused to use the bathroom upstairs for anything. They were petrified of what they may find—that's what they told Larry. He understood their trepidation and spent money not in the budget on the construction of their own private bathroom further down the hallway where the bonus room resided. Each of the girls had their own key and kept the door locked.

He also understood that had it been one of his daughters who found Jason that morning sprawled on the floor unconscious and surrounded by pills, things would've been so much worse. It could've scarred the girls eternally and dragged them into the realm of therapy themselves. Maybe they needed therapy anyway. Maybe the entire human race needed therapy.

And if the living situation for Melissa and Sarah wasn't bad enough, they also had to endure the repercussions at school. Some of the kids were tough on them. They made fun of Jason. Other kids they'd been friendly with avoided the girls altogether because they didn't know what to say. So did a handful of teachers.

Larry was aware about all of it. He had connections in the school system. But the girls rarely spoke of their difficulties to him or Karen anymore. There were the whispers, the pointing, the comments on social media, the gossiping behind their backs. Through no fault of their own, the spotlight shined brightly on them. Fair or not, they were the ones who had to suffer with it.

After incident number two in which Jason kicked up his death wish several notches, the girls stopped going in his room altogether. They became distant. There were no more surprise treats from the bakery or supplying the latest school gossip. They didn't watch funny videos online with him anymore.

It was hard for Larry to witness, to see his once lively daughters shut down and become reclusive. But how could he blame them? Their big brother morphed into somebody they didn't know, didn't want to know. It seemed like nobody knew Jason any longer.

The only interaction they still had with him was to stand outside the curtain and wait for a response when calling his name. That's what being on JD meant for them now. Those were the instructions. Observe and report. If he didn't answer within a minute, they were to immediately dial 911 then go outside. No exceptions. Larry couldn't stress that enough.

What he asked of the girls was a great deal to handle and forced them to mature quickly. He worried about the influence. Would it tarnish the innocence of their youth? How would they remember their childhood? But as confusing and uncomfortable as their home life might be, he couldn't have been prouder of their resiliency. They were stronger than he thought, stronger than they knew.

"Group hug," Larry said. He interrupted an argument over who had to stay when he left, and threw his arms around them. "How about a selfie?"

"You're so corny, Dad," Melissa said.

"Like a total dork," Sarah added.

He grinned. "That may be the case. But I want you to know how much your mother and I love you, that you're special. Life without you would be unbearable. I'm sorry for everything that's happened." He heaped more compliments upon them and gave another hug. As they continued to harass him for being uncool he noticed them trying to contain a smile.

He grabbed his keys and handed them twenty dollars apiece. "Be careful," he said before walking to his truck. Then it occurred to him. He never asked where they were going. He'd forgotten. His lack of questioning was becoming commonplace. Perhaps the girls were genuinely being relegated to the background, or perhaps Larry knew the reply to his inquiry would be, "Out." They were going out. And they were getting out.

Sarah planned to transfer schools next semester to a college in Texas. She'd take the train by herself and announced she was not returning home for the holidays. While it was true that Melissa would attend a state college after graduation and not the aforementioned Harvard, the campus was located as far from the house as possible. In the meantime, both of them stayed with their friends whenever they could.

Will my daughters ever come back? Larry thought when he pulled from the driveway. *Are they already gone forever?*

CHAPTER 14

He snagged a seat in the back of a room set off the main hallway of St. Peter's Church. The room was used primarily for Bible study, Sunday school classes, and an AA meeting every Wednesday afternoon. It was filled with grief-stricken parents, many of whom lost a child to the mysteries of the mind, many others in a state of limbo praying it would never happen. Gray plastic tables were arranged in a U-shape surrounded by metal chairs. The underlying smell of incense was strong.

Larry spotted Pauline and Chip all the way up front, as usual. They were permanent fixtures at the meeting, like they had something to prove, and always held hands. Russell Eckels was at the podium, sniffling hard after every sentence. His youngest daughter tried to commit suicide while away at college and overdosed on opioids. She survived, but suffered a toxic brain injury. She would never be the same.

Kerry Stinson was the next speaker. Her twenty-three-year-old son's car went off an embankment into a lake. There were no skid marks or any indications he tried to stop. He'd been threatening to harm himself and his death left more questions than answers. She didn't know if she could go on. Charlie Ross's teenage son lost thirty pounds since being diagnosed with depression and barely ate, while Sue Power's daughter wouldn't stop eating and refused to take her meds. Neither parent knew what to do.

When the hour passed, Elizabeth and James Tuttle, the support group founders, led everyone in a group prayer. The meeting concluded with an announcement that a 5K race was coming up to raise awareness for depression in children and young adults.

Larry met Pauline in the foyer near a marble fountain of holy water and a stack of church newsletters. He was greeted with a friendly peck on the cheek. A pat on the shoulder from Chip soon followed. Each person inside those walls had it rough and it was a club nobody ever wanted to be indoctrinated to. But there were degrees of misery in life. Little doubt remained that Chip and Pauline Waltzer had it much worse than everyone else.

Six years prior, their only child Wesley committed suicide. It was tragic, like so many parents had seen their children end their lives too early. But adding to the torment was that Wesley, as the story went, walked into high school one cold overcast morning during his sophomore year with no books or backpack. And there was no evidence he ever made it to his locker. Instead, the hallway cameras showed he went straight to the cafeteria where some of his classmates ate breakfast. A witness told police Wesley stood in the doorway and just stared at everyone, getting bumped into.

Some of the survivors said he yelled something when he pulled out a gun. Others said he didn't say a word. The .45 caliber handgun tucked in his jacket was legally registered to Chip. Wesley stole it and had an extra clip. Three students were killed along with a teacher. Four other students were seriously injured, one of whom was paralyzed.

When the police surrounded Wesley he barricaded himself behind an overturned table in a corner. There was a brief standoff and exchange of words before he shot himself. Chip was out of town for work. Pauline couldn't get there fast enough.

"Great meetin'," Chip said. "Glad to see you made it. Where the hell you been, partner?"

"I already spoke to him about not coming around lately," Pauline said.

Larry shook his head. "Been painting so much I haven't made it a priority to be here. You can really feel the difference when you come back around. It's surprising how quickly we forget."

"This is our medicine," Pauline said. "If we all know one thing, it's that you can't stop taking your meds."

Chip worked the room for a bit, hugging people, being hugged—especially by the newbies. He wore a scuffed pair of cowboy boots and a sleeveless shirt. A tattoo on his arm read WESLEY PATRICK WALTZER, RIP. Underneath it was a picture of his boy's face, the black ink crisp on Chip's pale skin. He had it touched up every year.

Pauline wrapped her arm around Larry as they strolled outside into the warm night air. She smoked a cigarette and while he hated the smell of it, he kept his mouth shut. She was a short woman, thin as a rail, with a white streak parted down the center of her hair like she'd been electrocuted. He always wondered why she dyed it that way.

She worked from home as an appointment setter for a real estate company and was the breadwinner of the family. Since their son's death, Chip struggled to hold a job. He retired early after twenty-three years as a crane operator.

The Waltzers moved to the west coast when the blowback of their son's tragedy turned them into pariahs, infecting them as toxic. Local residents demanded they leave town. They were shunned. After receiving multiple death threats and having their house repeatedly vandalized, Pauline and Chip capitulated. All their possessions were either sold or donated, and they bought an RV. Canada was their initial destination.

They explored the beauty and vastness north of the border, their car in tow, and had no maps or GPS. Getting lost was not a concern. But after a few years of wandering the road and a brief stay in Alaska, they settled in California. The campground in Applewood Heights was now their home.

It approached ten o'clock when they reached the RV. Larry furnished the tape and the VCR he'd stashed in the truck and set in on the counter. He tapped his fingers like they should read his mind.

"What the hell's up with that old thing?" Chip asked. "We gettin' ready for an episode of *Antiques Roadshow* or somethin'?"

Larry knew he may have been the only person left in America who owned and operated a VCR. One of his many projects was to convert Jason's basketball videos to DVD. He still watched the tapes from time to time and fawned over his son's athletic ability. But his viewing sessions were becoming less frequent.

"I'm assuming you don't have a VCR?" he said.

Chip glanced at him then headed to the couch. Pauline removed the cover of a pot and stirred the contents inside with a wooden spoon.

"Didn't think so. Glad I brought it with me."—he walked over to the TV and fumbled with the cords before pushing in the tape—"You need to see this."

The three of them sat in the cozy living room and ate bowls of turkey chili with dollops of sour cream on top. They watched the story of Edgar Suarez fight for his life and survive in Yellowstone National Park.

"What do you think?" Larry asked when it was finished.

"Am I missing something, sweetie?" Pauline said. "You wanted to meet back here, in private, to show us this? What in God's name for?"

Larry rose and motioned to the screen. "Didn't you see those tears, the pain he'd overcome? Those were the tears of a man so happy to be alive it's completely transformed his life. He didn't want to die in the wilderness, so he fought. He fought hard. Against all odds he never gave up, and it changed him."

"That's typical in those situations," Pauline said. "It's only natural for people to fight to stay alive. They don't wanna die. He did what everybody would do, including me and you. It ain't nothing special." She picked up her knitting needles and a roll of yarn.

"Exactly," Larry said. "People don't want to die. It's counterintuitive to our species." He pressed the rewind button and the VCR made a clunky sound as the tape sped backward. "I can't believe I never thought of this before."

Chip, silent for the last thirty minutes, blurted out, "You gotta be careful in the woods. When I used to hunt . . . When I used to use those damn evil things. It's just . . . You gotta be careful in the woods." He wiped a tear from his eye and went to the stove, scooping another helping of his wife's famous meal. The once prolific hunter and gun aficionado sold all his shotguns, rifles, and pistols immediately following his son's death. It wasn't difficult to imagine why he never wanted to see another firearm again.

Larry continued: "And because it's not natural and people don't want to die, they fight. But sometimes they need to be put in a position to fight. The ultimate fight. The right conditions are required to transport them into a set of dire circumstances. With their backs against the wall, it'll reveal their true character. They need to see what they're capable of. Edgar Suarez said he was happier than ever, in a better place mentally, even though some toes are gone and he has scars on his face. And he wouldn't have found that mental state of evolution unless he got lost in the woods. His near-death experience saved him."

"Not sure I'm following you, honey," Pauline said, setting her needles aside. "What does this have to do with anything?"

"Jason. This has to do with Jason."

"How so?" Chip asked. He snapped back into the conversation like nothing happened.

Larry looked between them, his hands on his hips. He nibbled his lower lip for a moment, then singled out Chip. "I want you to help me kidnap my son."

Chapter 15

The RV went quiet. The sound of wind chimes clattered in the breeze as a diesel truck pulled from the campground, humming its distinctive low growl. Chip took off his baseball cap for the first time all night and rubbed his chin. His bald head reflected in the overhead lighting. Pauline looked at her husband as Larry stood before them like a pathetic salesman who'd made a bad pitch and didn't have a chance of securing a deal.

"What in the hell is this man talkin' about?" Chip said, squinting.

Pauline shrugged. "I think he's been away from the meetings too long and is getting lost inside his own head. Larry, sit down, honey. You want me to get you something? You want one of Chip's pills to relax?"

Larry unfolded the brochure from Dr. Baker's office and handed it over. "I know, it sounds crazy. It's hard to believe those words came from my mouth. But this is where I'm at. And that place there, that's where the doctors want to send Jason. If we go through with it, I think it's gonna break us as a family."

"Why would it break you as a family?" Pauline said as her eyes skimmed the first page. "Seems like some kind of treatment facility."

"Because I don't think it'll work."

She passed the brochure to Chip, who scanned the pages, flipping back and forth. "At least a hundred thousand. Probably one-fifty."—he looked at Larry— "Is that the price?"

"Approximately."

"And that's where they want to send Jason?"

"Uh-huh."

"So what the hell does this have to do with kidnappin' your son?"

"You're scaring me, sweetie," Pauline said. "Come, sit down. You can spend the night if you want. I'll make up the couch. Do you want me to call Karen, tell her you're gonna stay?"

"I get it," Larry said. He shifted his weight from foot to foot and wanted to pace, but there was nowhere to go. "I thought you may say that. Who wouldn't? That's why I wanted to meet back here in person. You're the only people I can trust about this. You guys are the only ones who may actually understand."

"Talk to me," Chip said, patting the cushion next to him. "Sit on down like my wife just said and let's see if we can work this out together."—he pointed to his friend's head—"What you got clatterin' around up there?"

Larry took a deep breath and dragged a hand over his face. He returned to the couch as instructed. "We're broke."

"How broke?"

"Broke, broke. Karen and I don't have any money and we can't afford to send Jason there. On top of that, our debt is out of control. If we go through with this, it'll be the final straw for our finances. We'll probably—no, definitely—lose the house. We're three mortgage payments behind already. We've raided the girls' college funds to the point of embarrassment and Melissa doesn't know it, but by the time she graduates she won't—"

"But this is your son," Pauline said sharply. "It's your blood, Larry, your only boy."

"If I thought it'd work, to send Jason across the country, then I'd feel different. Maybe I'd be on board with this Hail Mary miracle Karen is hoping for. But from what I can tell, it seems like the doctors don't know what to do with him because he's getting worse again, not better. It's never ever fucking better."

Crossing his arms, he leaned back. "It's obvious they're out of options. I'm not sure if *they* even believe it'll work. But I guess that's their solution, to lock him in a looney bin. Because that's what it really is. You can try and sugarcoat it, but that's the truth. What kind of life is that for a person, for my son? Who knows how long he'll be in there? It's not living, that's for sure. It's just enduring. Enduring more and more pain. When it's all said and done, Karen and I will be back to where we started, only worse."

"Why don't you think it'll work?" Chip asked, flipping through the brochure again. "Looks pretty good to me. Get a listen to this: 'The doctors at Pine View are committed to an all-inclusive comprehensive treatment plan structured with the latest theories and technologies in the behavior modification stratum to progress past traditional methodologies.'"

"Sounds impressive," Pauline said.

"Sure does," Chip added. "You may wanna give it a chance before doin' somethin' stupid."

"Sounds impressive?" Larry said. "Do you know what any of that means? Because I don't. Nobody knows Jason better than me, or at least I used to. Karen says he isn't broken. But I'm beginning to believe otherwise. I'm starting to suspect that somewhere along the way a malfunction occurred in his brain. The wires got crossed. What else could explain it? He was fine, progressing normally, and then he wasn't. I don't know how or why this happened, but I'm pretty sure it can't be fixed through more and more talking."

"How can you say that?" Pauline asked. She picked up the needles and knitted faster than before.

"Because I'm living it. Every day. For the past five years. Karen and I are psychologically jailed, in our own home, by our own son. That's a fact. We're like prisoners of the moment, yet the moment never ends. We're afraid to say anything wrong to set him off, but we don't know what wrong means anymore. Neither of us wants to be responsible in case he does something, so we've become these timid parents who tiptoe around on eggshells. I hate to acknowledge this, but I don't want to be there most of the time. It's terrifying. But I have to be. For Karen. For the girls."

He paused and gazed at the floor. "You know we need a babysitter in the house, right? Twenty-four seven. Not to change a diaper or feed in infant, but to check on Jason and make sure he's alive. Do you have any idea how sad that is? Or humiliating? It breaks my heart. But it's other stuff too. Simple stuff that grinds on you. If I want to take an aspirin because my hands hurt, I have to go to my truck to get them because pills aren't allowed in the house. And the knives. Well, they're all locked in a kitchen drawer with a padlock. Every one of them, including the butter knives."

He raised his voice, looking up. "Do you know how ridiculous that is when you want to make a sandwich? I forgot the combination last week so I just dipped my finger in the mayonnaise jar. Gross, I know, but I did it. I mean, if Jason wants to shave, I have to stand there and watch, then take back the razor when he's done. And Chip, you need to see my garage. You'll never see anything so organized in your life. Everything I thought he could use to hurt himself has been locked up or sold. But how can you make everything safe when Jason is a grown man? Do I have to use bubble wrap?"—he kept getting louder and felt his cheeks getting red—"How can we baby proof an entire house when the baby is old enough to buy beer now?"

"It's okay," Chip said in a calming tone. "Let it out, partner."

Larry pinched the bridge of his nose and exhaled, trying to combat another stress-induced headache. His eyes were saggy from the fatigue of life and his weather-beaten face had too many lines for a man of his age. "Every time I walk up those stairs and have to see that hideous curtain, to pull it aside and discover if my son is still breathing, it's the most frightening experience I've ever had. It turns me inside out. I feel like I'm playing Russian roulette and my mind gets shattered into a million pieces."

He immediately regretted the *mind shattering* statement or any reference to guns, given Wesley's death, and was about to apologize when Chip said, "There's no shame in cryin' here. We're friends."

"That's the thing that gets me. I haven't cried in months. And it pisses me off because I should cry. I want to. I need to. But the tears won't come anymore. I know it'd make me feel better because my son is gone. It's like Jason packed a bag in the middle of the night and snuck out his bedroom window. I'm not sure when, but he did, and he left some mutated version of himself behind. Although me and Karen jump up and down and wave our arms, he keeps walking further away. Reason and logic have failed us. Deep in my heart, I think the only way to get him back is for something drastic to happen. Talking and analyzing and taking pills hasn't worked. It's not gonna work, as far as I'm concerned."—he exhaled loudly—"I apologize for springing this on you. You probably think I'm the one who should be committed."

Pauline glanced at Chip. She was about to speak when he shook his head to stop her. He retrieved a bottle of water from the fridge and handed it to his friend. "How does the whole kidnappin' thing fit in? Where would you take him? What would you do?"

Larry unscrewed the cap and took a sip. "I believe Jason needs to be put in a situation to decide once and for all what he wants to do. As a father, I'm responsible to provide that opportunity. He either digs down deep and finds some spark of life left inside, however small, or . . . I want to change him by creating an environment like Edgar Suarez was thrust into. I think it's his only chance. Maybe ours too. The only alternative is to let him go."

"Let him go?" Chip asked, raising his eyebrows. "You mean like let him go, go?"

"Yes. Let him do what he wants."

Chip reached over and placed a hand to Larry's forehead. "This is some heavy shit, partner. You runnin' a fever or somethin'?"

"I'm fine, and it's fine. Karen can't straddle this fence anymore. The strain is killing her. She's aged a decade in the last year alone and I have too. We're losing the girls if they haven't been lost already. As a family, we're sinking deeper into the sea every day. Something has to be done. And I'm not talking about sending my boy off to a mental asylum for a last gasp fix. Because this is about Jason. To see him, living with that torment between his ears, it destroys me. He has no idea what's happened to him or why. This cruel disease eating his brain may not have a cure. But I think I can fix him, or at least try—"

"I'm not sure I wanna hear any more of this," Pauline said, standing. "I don't like your speech, Larry. It's ignorant. This is your goddamn son you're talking about. He ain't some experiment. All this craziness about wires and kidnapping, it's making my brain hurt."—she moved around her tray table near Chip—"I'll finish my knitting in the bedroom. You boys don't stay up too late."—she turned and stood above Larry—"Get this nonsense out of your system. Understand, sweetie? Because that's what it is. Nothing but nonsense. It's a bad idea and no good will come of it. The only thing to do is surrender it to the Lord. Let *His* will be done. Next time I see you, I don't want to hear any more about it. You got that?"

He nodded and she patted his shoulder.

"Good. Say hi to Karen for us. And you best be at the meeting next week. And the week after that. Sounds like you need them more than ever." As she walked to the bedroom, Pauline shouted, "Don't stray too far inside your own head, Larry. It's not where you wanna be."

They sat quietly and stared at the TV with no picture on it. Chip nudged Larry's knee. "We'll get you fixed up. Don't worry about her. Probably just thinkin' about Wes, second guessin' all we ever done. You can be sure she'll leave the door wide open listenin' to every word we say. It's nice out tonight. Wanna go for a drive?"

Larry looked at a clock in the kitchen that was shaped like a sunflower. It was almost midnight. He had to wake up extra early to paint and needed some sleep. "Can we talk about this again?"

"I'm here for you any time, and it's always good to talk. Just don't do anythin' stupid. I repeat, do not be stupid."

"Thanks for the chili. But I have to go."—he leaned close to Chip's ear—"My window for this thing is pretty narrow. If it goes down, it'll go down fast. Time seems to be running out, for everyone."

"I kinda gathered that."

"I don't see a choice here anymore. I think I can do this. And I think I'm gonna. But I could sure use some help."

When Larry reached the door, Chip said, "Hey, what about your crappy old VCR and that tape?"

"Keep it for now. Watch it one more time, for me."

"You bet, partner."

Larry drove home on autopilot and wondered if he'd made a mistake confiding in them. How had a lifetime of doing the right thing led him there?

CHAPTER 16

The phone was pressed firmly against her ear with Larry on the other end, the line silent. She'd contacted him precisely at 2 p.m. for their pre-arranged conference call. They'd been on hold for fifteen minutes and waited to get patched through when the receptionist chimed in.

"I'm sorry, but Dr. Baker is running slightly behind schedule today." Ten minutes later she interrupted again with, "Do you want to call back later, Mrs. Turner, or maybe tomorrow?"

"No," Karen said. She slouched in the kitchen chair and twirled a pencil between her fingers. "We'll wait."

And wait they did. For twenty more minutes. She could sense Larry's growing annoyance and heard him mumble under his breath. He also released a few heavy sighs. She felt bad knowing how hard he worked to finish the job and get up to the cabin as planned. But he'd never say a word or complain. She loved him for that. Her husband did everything with their son in mind; with her as well.

She put the phone on speaker and her ear was warm as she jotted some notes on a scratch pad next to a calendar. The calendar—a Christmas present from Sarah—had photos of beaches from around the world. There were lines crossed out, lines added, and arrows pointing to and connecting different days.

Jason's departure date was still unclear, but the loan from Nathan would cover the deposit and at least get him out there. In addition, Karen's jewelry proceeds of $12,000 should satisfy the first wave of bills. She'd gone to two separate pawn shops in a different part of the city to get the best deal. As for their plane tickets, her hotel stay, and the incidentals incurred upon traveling, she planned to use what was left on their credit cards. But the date—she was anxious to learn the date.

The coffee pot finished brewing and the TV played softly in the background. She never watched much TV during the day but it was always on, the noise serving as a form of company. It made her feel like she wasn't alone. Because most of the time she was alone. All alone.

The girls were gone, off to school or to spend time with friends or anywhere else they could be, and Larry worked constantly. Jason stayed in his room. He rarely appeared downstairs anymore while Karen meandered about the house trying to keep busy.

She topped off her mug with a fresh hot pour and caught a glimpse of herself in the decorative mirror on the wall near the fridge—an arts and crafts project Melissa made in the seventh grade. She smiled and stretched her lips apart. The yellowish stains on her teeth had become evident.

Perhaps she should drink her coffee through a straw or attach it to an IV. She thought about switching toothpastes to a brand with more whitening power, then touched underneath her eyes. She pushed on the dark skin that was always a little swollen. Karen retrieved the compact from her purse to apply some makeup and returned to the table. The calendar was surveyed again.

While she had a mild fear of flying on a plane for five long hours at 36,000 feet, there was no way they could send Jason to Virginia by himself. Since Larry had to work because they needed the money, the responsibility to deliver their son to Pine View fell on her. That's how she felt most of the time—like the responsibility of everything fell on her.

The receptionist's voice came on the line: "Alright, Mrs. Turner, the doctor just finished her session and will be on the phone momentarily. I'm so sorry for the delay."

"No worries," Karen said and took the phone off speaker. She doodled on the notepad, wondering what the treatment facility would be like. She'd visited their website countless times and speculated how the staff would not only treat but interact with her boy.

Would they check on Jason every few hours like her and the girls and Larry did? Would they be compassionate and understanding? Would they allow a TV in his room? If not, it could be a problem. He enjoyed TV and watched it all the time. She may need to speak with a manager about that. And what about the food? Would it be healthy and nutritious? Would it be seasoned properly but without too much salt? He didn't care for too much salt. Would they have pizza on the menu? If so, would Jason like it?

She looked forward to meeting the other patients and hoped they'd welcome her son. Maybe Jason could make a friend. Then she questioned the bed. Would it be soft, but not too soft? Maybe she should buy a foam egg crate to put on top of the mattress. She took a sip from her mug and wondered how much an egg crate or a TV would cost when a new thought leaped into her mind. It struck her nerves like a thunderbolt.

What if Jason doesn't want to go? What if he refuses? How would they get him out there? Would they have to drag him by force or drug him up to be shipped like a FedEx package? She was embarrassed that she never considered the idea before. How could she have had such an oversight? It was a distinct possibility and highly probable. Did she expect Jason to meet her at the bottom of the stairs with a suitcase and a smile, like the time they sent him away to basketball camp in the sixth grade, and say, "I'm ready for my awesome trip, Mom."?

There'd be no way to bribe him with money or a car or an extravagant vacation. How could you bribe somebody who didn't care about himself, didn't care about anything? Jason was, after all, a legal adult, twenty-one years of age, almost twenty-two, who hadn't made an actual threat to harm himself again—just implied it strongly to his therapist. She put her head in her hands. Why did everything have to be so difficult?

After incident number one, in which they coerced him into signing power of attorney for his own good and protection, he tried to rationalize what happened with the overdose. At first he blamed his knee. He claimed he had tendonitis from years of playing basketball and that's why the sleeping pills were taken along with the pain meds; for a solid night's sleep. He simply took too many by mistake. Karen brought him to the orthopedist six weeks earlier when he first mentioned the mystery pain. The knee was perfectly fine.

Jason then said he misread the labels and got confused; it was a math error. But nobody ingests that many pills accidentally. She pushed back on all his excuses as they made no sense and questioned him further about the bottles of vodka she'd found in his trash. Karen wouldn't let it go.

Finally, after she and Larry stayed in his room for hours and refused to leave, after they said how much they loved him and wanted to help, he confessed. Yes, he tried to take his own life. All three of them wept. It was the hardest thing she ever heard.

The doctors who initially performed the examination determined the dosages he took probably wouldn't have killed him. But another hour spent on the bathroom floor without medical attention could've caused irreversible damage to his organs. He'd been spared the agony. He got lucky. They asked if it was the first time her son cried out for help, and sadly, Karen shook her head no. She'd already seen his cry for help. It was called cutting.

During his senior year of high school, Jason began to cut himself. When Karen and Larry discovered it they immediately brought him to therapy. The cuts were mostly on his legs, on the meaty part of his thighs, and could easily be covered with shorts or pants. Some of the cuts resembled a scratch while others were deep, spanning the entire width of his leg. It wasn't until doing his laundry that Karen noticed.

Each of the kids were required to do their own laundry starting in the eighth grade as part of the Turners' plan to teach self-reliability. But when Jason got sick for a couple of days and was bedridden, she decided to do it for him. While loading the washer, she saw dark stains on his sheets but didn't think much of it. It could've been anything. The boy was messy and always ate in bed. Maybe it was food or spilled soda. Maybe it was urine or . . .

She then saw similar stains on his underwear, shorts, and pants. When asked about it, Jason said he dropped a pair of scissors and nicked his leg. But the wound was bandaged right away and he would definitely be more careful. No cause for concern. Mind your business, Karen.

Her motherly instincts told her otherwise. Three days later she snuck in his room and poked through the hamper only to find more bloody clothes, more bloody sheets. When confronted again, he acted indignant.

"How dare you go through my stuff?" he said. "I never asked you to do my stupid laundry."

"Don't change the subject. What's going on?"

"I don't know. I can't say. Get out and leave me alone."

She didn't give up though and grilled him further. During an intense argument with a bombardment of rapid-fire questions where she followed him all over the house, he eventually broke down. He admitted his self-mutilation. He didn't remember how it started or exactly what caused it, but cutting provided him some relief. It made him feel better. He couldn't articulate why. It just did.

Karen and Larry were horrified, unable to comprehend why anybody would want to cut their own body. From then on, every knife and sharp object in the house was locked up or disposed of. Perhaps she overreacted, she didn't know. But what was she supposed to do? A mother's job was to protect her children, and the issue of cutting wasn't something she'd been prepared for.

But it didn't matter what the Turners did or didn't do. Cutting became the least of their problems. Jason changed directions on everyone and introduced a new level of fear to the family when he unveiled the anguish of incident number two.

Chapter 17

It was Larry who found him the second time around. Karen was selfishly relieved about that. Physically, she didn't know if she possessed the strength to perform like her husband did. It may have taken her too long to get inside and by then it would've been far too late. Mentally, what else could she say? She was glad not to see it. She felt sick thinking how the story unfolded, of how Larry explained the details of finding their son.

"I got home from practice later than usual. J.C. Cook, our starting center, had car trouble and needed a jump. When I walked in the door Sarah was gone and Melissa did her homework in the living room. She waited for me to arrive so she could go over to Sammy's. I ate dinner and watched *Wheel of Fortune*. I had some tests to grade, and that's when I heard the banging.

"At first, I couldn't tell where the noise came from. It was soft, like somebody tacking up a picture. I didn't pay it much attention and thought it was one of the neighbors. After working such a long day maybe it was in my head. But then I heard it again, only louder. I went to the front of the house, where it became much louder. I looked up the stairs. It seemed to be coming from Jason's room. *What the?* That's what I thought. It was so out of place. I went and knocked on his door and he told me to go away. I heard him crying. Music played. Then there was more banging, right in my face.

"I turned the knob and shook the door but it was locked. The banging got louder, faster. It sounded like nails being driven into wood. I knocked harder. I kicked the door. I demanded he let me in. Jason screamed at me to go away. I kicked it again and pushed, and it felt like something had been moved in front of it. When I looked down, I noticed there was no light coming from under his door. I figured he'd moved the dresser. Then I realized what the banging was. He nailed the door shut from inside.

"We argued back and forth and he kept screaming but I couldn't make out what he said. He became incoherent. I sprinted downstairs to get my cell phone and dialed 911. When I got back upstairs, we argued for another minute. I felt if I could just keep him talking until the ambulance arrived he'd be okay. I wanted to keep him engaged. There was more banging. Then he let out a final scream like I've never heard . . . And I'll never forget . . . And then it was quiet.

"I called his name but got no response, so I ran to the garage for a sledgehammer. It seemed to take forever, like my feet were in cement. When I finally broke through it was hard to believe what I saw. It didn't seem real. I mean, you hear about things like that, like an out of body experience, but still. My son was in front of me with a rope around his neck, hanging from the chin-up bar I installed during his freshman year. His legs dangled and his body kind of spun, like a human piñata. His face turned blue and I thought he was dead. My heart almost stopped. For a second, my brain froze. I went and got a knife in the kitchen and I wished I'd gotten it before when I grabbed the sledgehammer. But never in a million years did I believe he'd do something like that. I knew Jason had problems but you just don't think your son is gonna wake up one day and hang himself in the house he grew up in.

"As I sliced the rope his leg started spasming. I took that as a good sign. His body fought for life. When I finally cut him free we tumbled backward off the desk chair and he landed on me. I smacked my head hard on the floor, which under any other circumstance, would've dazed me. I held him in my arms until the EMTs arrived a few minutes later. I can't even describe what a godawful experience that was. Holding my dying son as if he were a baby. The life draining from his body.

"I was so scared, I didn't know what to do. Just pure panic. He was barely breathing. The EMTs somehow managed to save him and those guys are my heroes. They're incredible. I can still see the image of Jason hanging from that chin-up bar and I don't know if it'll ever go away. It's hard to believe what happened, that I was able to get him down . . . And there's no chance I could do it again."

Jason tried to explain why incident number two took place and apologized several times to his parents. He said he didn't want to die but wanted to end the despair, to make it all stop.

They kept him in the hospital for a while before he was transferred to a mental health center. Then he was eventually released. He had a large scab on his neck from the rope burn and there were conversations about whether it would leave a scar.

Karen would've preferred to have kept him locked up indefinitely because at least she'd know he was safe. She didn't want him back at the house. She was frightened to have him home. Her son was 0-2 in killing himself and the Turners knew they had dodged two bullets. They also knew he would not go 0-3.

"Karen, Larry, my sincerest apologies for the lengthy delay," Dr. Baker said when she joined the call. "It's been extremely busy today. Thank you for your patience."

"It's quite alright," Karen said. "We completely understand."

"Nice to have you on the call with us, Larry. It's been a while since we last spoke. How are you?"

"Fine, fine. Busy. But I'm fine."

"Good. So, let's get started."

Karen wasted no time and jumped right in. "We have enough money for the initial deposit and can leave as soon as possible. I've been in touch with Pine View and you were right, we'll be able to finance the rest. It won't be easy and it could take us forever to pay off, but we'll manage. We just need your office to fax in the referral and send the rest of the paperwork."

"Exactly," Dr. Baker said. "The process has become quite streamlined. I'll take care of everything on my end this afternoon. I'm so glad you're going through with this and I think after six to eight months, perhaps a year, you could see some significant improvement in Jason. He might—"

"Excuse me," Larry said. "I think I lost you there for a second. Did you say a year?"

"This isn't an overnight fix and we can't put a definitive time-stamp on it. Are you both in agreement with that? That's one of the reasons for this call. I don't think it *will* be that long, but I wanted to be clear. It's a distinct realization of what may be required to achieve the necessary results."

"We're okay with that," Karen said. "Whatever it takes. Absolutely whatever it takes."

"And you, Larry?"

He cleared his throat. "It's fine. Everything's fine."

"Aright then. Karen, I'll send you a medical records release that we need you to sign."

"I'll pick it up," she said. "Let me call one of the girls to come home. I can drive over and take care of it now."

She took a big chug of coffee as her legs bounced and she tried to think three moves ahead like a chess player. She was so used to being alone, her thoughts were spoken aloud. "I'll call the girls, get one of them here, swing by the office, sign the forms, and I'll overnight a check for the deposit. But I have to get gas first and we need snacks for Jason. When I get back, I'll make dinner and throw in a load of laundry. Maybe begin to pack."

"It seems like you're on top of it," Dr. Baker said. "I'll leave everything at the front desk. Please call me for any assistance."

"I do have one quick question," Karen said. "It recently occurred to me and, I hate to even mention it. What if for some reason Jason doesn't want to go? I know he won't *want* to go, but what if we can't get him to cooperate?"

"Our goal is a smooth transition from your residence in a non-confrontational manner. Let's hope that takes place. We have precedence on our side, and you have the legal paperwork. Since we believe Jason may be at risk to harm himself again, there are things that can be done for his protection. I'd be willing to speak with him if you'd like. The facility he's going to, they can also accommodate an extraction if necessary."

Extraction? Karen thought. She didn't like the sound of that.

"But I don't want to get ahead of ourselves," Dr. Baker said. "Let's take it—"

"So if he doesn't want to go or won't leave his room, which he won't, we basically have to what, kidnap him to get him out there? Is that what you're saying?" Larry asked.

"Don't be absurd," Karen said, her tone scolding. "Larry, please."

"I'm only trying to clarify."

"Dr. Baker, I don't want to get sidetracked with all this. I'm sorry I brought it up and I apologize for my husband's inappropriate comment. We'll get Jason out there, believe me. I'll make it happen."

"You can drop him off next Friday, Karen. That gives you about a week. You'll get a tour of the facility and meet some of the staff, gradually spending less and less time there until leaving. They've found that helps with the initial transition of the younger patients. I think you're doing the right thing here, for both of you. And of course, for Jason . . . Larry, you've been pretty quiet. You have any further questions?"

"Everything's fine," he said in a monotone voice. "Everything's fine."

Karen admonished her husband the second Dr. Baker hung up. He apologized several times and said he didn't mean to be rude, but his emotions got the better of him. He swore it wouldn't happen again.

She spent the rest of the day traipsing about suburbia and coordinated her efforts to take care of the details, to be a good mom. They were trying to fix her son and she was happy about that, as happy as any parent in her situation could be. But spinning in the back of her mind was the troublesome reality of how they would get him to the facility.

It astounded her that she never considered this pivotal question before. In all her zeal to help, she'd forgotten about Jason himself. She'd lost sight that he was an actual person who could refuse to do things. He wasn't eight years old anymore, he couldn't be ordered around. They were fortunate he still agreed to attend therapy, albeit with a great deal of effort and coaxing. It saddened her the way she objectified him and reduced him to a label. At times she spoke about him, in front of him, as if he weren't there; as if he were an aging parent who'd lost their independence.

A new kind of guilt swept over her. She tried to be positive they were moving in the right direction and prayed Jason would go peacefully without the use of force. Karen then realized she was praying and stopped. She'd given up on God, given up on prayers. But old habits were hard to break.

Chapter 18

His shorts had splotches of fresh paint on them and his shirt was still sweaty. But the instant he opened the door, Karen ushered him toward the stairs anyway. She said he could clean up later when they were finished because the conversation needed to be had immediately. That's why he'd been summoned home early. And after their phone call with Dr. Baker the previous day, Larry wasn't surprised. He knew his wife wanted to find out if Jason would go to Pine View willingly. He was curious too.

The skin on her forehead was scrunched up tight, the worry in her voice was recognized. He understood that at times their son intimidated her and he agreed to whatever she said. Karen would do most of the talking. His job was to show support.

He leaned against the doorway of Jason's room with the sheet draped over his back. A hand rested on her shoulder. He gave a slight squeeze to remind her he was there—that she'd be alright. His lips tasted salty and dry, and he wished they could do this later so he could return to work. He wished it didn't need to be done at all.

The blinds were closed and the curtains drawn. No posters or pictures hung on the walls of any kind. The room was devoid of energy and had a sterile feel, like the person who stayed there had recently moved in or was passing through town on a brief stay. A noise machine rested on the nightstand, producing the sound of ocean waves. The time on the alarm clock had yet to be adjusted for daylight savings in the spring.

Karen called to Jason repeatedly with her hands clasped in front of her. As Larry expected, she received no answer. Their son's ability to tune people out and ignore them was staggering. She walked over and shook his foot lightly to wake him, to announce the exchange of words was forthcoming. It took several minutes of prodding for him to roll over so they could see his face.

He yawned, scratching his neck. Pale skin and hollow eyes gave him the resemblance of a strung-out junkie or someone in the midst of a hunger strike. But he took no drugs, at least not the illegal kind. And while his food intake became austere, he continued to still eat.

Jason pulled himself up against the headboard slowly like he'd been wrapped in heavy chains and sometimes Larry thought his son had to be acting. Could anybody be that lethargic, especially a young person? Jason turned in their direction and didn't look *at* them, but *above* them. He stared off into the space near the corner of his desk.

Karen glanced back at Larry and he nodded, reaffirming their tough decision. She sat gingerly on the side of the bed. When she glanced at her husband again he waved her on to continue. After biting her nails, she fidgeted with her hair, then reached over and turned off the noise machine. She explained to Jason he was leaving soon for Virginia and she was coming along.

"I'm not going," he said. He picked at a cold sore in the crevice of his mouth. "I know you made me sign those stupid forms so you can do whatever you want with me. But I won't go. I'll tear them up. They were signed under false pretense, when I was vulnerable. When I get around to it, I'll hire an attorney." His voice sounded strong, contrasting his appearance.

"Why won't you go?" Karen asked. "Don't you want to get better?"

Larry remained silent, watching the drama unfold. He took mental notes and configured the plan in his head. Jason seemed thinner and weaker than he recalled but he hadn't seen much of him during the daylight in quite some time. He hadn't seen much of his son physically at all in months.

When he checked on Jason it was usually nighttime and the room was mostly dark. The only light came from the glow of a TV where he'd see nothing but a body wrapped under a sheet with a head on a pillow. It was refreshing to see his boy sit up and reminded Larry how tall he was, what a great basketball player he once had been. The task of removing him should not be an issue, with or without the help of Chip.

"I know what's going on," Jason said. "Do you think I'm stupid?"

"Stupid? Of course we don't think you're stupid," Karen said. "Nobody ever said you were stupid. Because you're not. You're not stupid. You're smart. So smart. So very, very smart. Your father and I think you're incredibly smart. Really smart. We always tell everyone you're the smartest person in the family. Please remember how smart you are. You're so smart—"

"Karen," Larry said. He motioned for her to relax.

She paused and moved closer to Jason. "Why do you think something's going on?"

He didn't answer right away and his eyes remained fixed on the wall. "I have a curtain where a door should be. A curtain you put up so I wouldn't have any privacy. Do you know how emasculating that is? No, I'm sure you don't. I can hear everything through that stupid thing. I hear it when you watch TV or make dinner or scheme about what needs to be done next. I even hear it when you're outside my room, waiting to come bother me like I'm a little kid. So don't patronize me, Karen. I know about getting sent to some nut house where I can be around people even more screwed up than me."

"Why do you think it's a—"

"I'm not fucking going. Get that through your heads. And you can't fucking make me."

Larry was taken aback. It was more words than he'd heard from Jason in the last ten weeks combined. While the words were harsh, the delivery was soft and gentle, coming across as ironic. He didn't approve of the swearing but took it as a positive sign that his son spoke to them at all. It felt great to hear Jason talk again and not get a one-word answer. There was no greater punishment for him than being ostracized from his child's life and treated as a stranger they wanted nothing to do with.

Jason communicated—that was a good thing—and the cussing proved he might have something left inside him after all. Perhaps there was a glimmer of anger lying below the surface that could be used to resurrect him. Larry stepped further inside the room and placed a hand on his wife's shoulder again. He thought his idea stood more of a chance than ever.

Karen cried, not heavy sobs, but small steady tears flowed down her cheeks like she'd chopped an onion. She stretched out an arm and touched Jason's face. "Don't you want to get better? Don't you want to come back to us?"

He pulled away and burrowed under the covers. "I didn't ask for any of this. Both of you brought it on me with your selfishness. Because it's all about you, isn't it? About what you want. And it's your fault for bringing me into this world. How many times do I have to ask you to leave me alone? Can't you get that through your skulls? Just leave me the hell alone."

"We only want the best for you, to be healthy," Karen said. "Can't you see how much we love you?" She moved from the bed and withdrew into Larry's chest.

"I fucking hate you guys. Alright? Does that make you feel better? Will that make it easier to forget about me? Because that's all I want. To be forgotten. Like I never existed. Because this is never gonna end. But you won't let me, even after you did this to me. And I'm the one who has to live with it. You have no idea what it's like. Because you're normal. And I'm not. I know I'm not. So does everybody else. And I can't help it."

Jason looked at them with a scowl. "It's always dark and cloudy, even when it's bright. Nothing brings me joy. But you can't understand that. So how can I get you to stop trying to help and remove me from your memory? Do I need to call you more names? Will that work? I don't want to, you know I don't, but you're gonna make me, aren't you? You're always making me do shit. You're gonna force me to be mean. Fine. I'll give you what you want then. Karen, you're a bitch. A miserable smothering bitch of a mother. And Larry, you're an asshole. A stupid high school teacher asshole who has to paint houses in the summer because you suck at everything. You're both assholes. Are you happy?"—he closed his eyes and curled himself into a ball—"That's enough."

Larry wasn't surprised and had heard those damaging statements to a certain degree many times before. But they did have a little more sting than usual. He knew the person responsible for saying them was not the son he loved and adored, the son who'd volunteered alongside him at Habitat for Humanity on many weekends, the son who talked about the importance of getting involved in Big Brothers, Big Sisters; to give back to the community.

Jason used to always remember Karen's birthday and would cook her a meal, whatever she wanted. He duplicated the effort for each of his sisters. He did charity work for the homeless and was concerned about the environment. His participation in fundraisers at school was a common event. By everyone's standards he was a nice young man and a sweet kid with a promising future. Expectations of him were high. But that was eons ago, when he was a different person, when he cared about people and life; when he cared about himself.

Dr. Baker surmised that the negativity hurled at them was an attempt to push his parents away because of low self-esteem and intense self-loathing. She said his disrespectful behavior wasn't unusual for patients who suffered from mental issues, particularly in adolescents and young adults. There could be the additional perils of stealing and threats of physical aggression. They attack the people they love the most because they themselves hurt.

Some days Larry agreed with the doctor and others he didn't know what to think. It was hard to make sense of all the buzzwords, the labels, the coddling, the political correctness, the uncertainty, and the frustration of it all. Some days he thought maybe all Jason needed was a swift kick in the butt and to stop being so babied. Maybe they should have spanked him more as a child, made him do more chores. Maybe they should have been stricter or more disciplined. But that didn't make sense either, and it wasn't their style or belief.

The Turners had three children all raised in the same caring environment. Two of them turned out fine. The answer, unfortunately, was that there was no answer. That was the maddening part. Larry was just as miffed and confused as everyone else who tried and listened but didn't understand the disease of mental illness or the complexity of Jason's disorder. How did it come about? Why did it progress? How come it won't go away? It seemed so convoluted and defeating—it baffled the Turners. He wasn't sure if even the greatest scholars in the field could explain why.

He put his arm around his wife and whisked her from the room. When they'd reached downstairs he kissed the side of her head and whispered, "It's gonna be alright."

His resolve to save their son grew even stronger.

CHAPTER 19

Karen went straight to bed after dinner with a glass of ginger ale and a heating pad. She hardly ate, stating that her stomach was upset, and she had to lie down. It was still light outside as Larry scraped her plate in the trash and finished the dishes. He tidied up the kitchen before walking across the back lawn that led to his shed.

He bought the shed in his early forties when having summers off from school actually meant being on vacation. Larry had time to do stuff back then. He hiked and played golf, tried to go for morning bike rides before it got hot. The family traveled to the cabin every other weekend and he embarked on new hobbies like woodworking.

He enjoyed woodworking and once considered becoming a carpenter. But the more tools he collected, the more space he needed. The garage was a cluttered mess with all the kids' toys as Karen refused to discard anything. There wasn't enough room to fit their vehicles inside, let alone a bandsaw or a lathe. Since the concept of putting loud and potentially dangerous equipment in the house wasn't a realistic option, he came up with the idea for a shed.

It was green with a red pitched roof and he bought it on clearance from a building supply store going out of business. His wife joked it resembled an ugly aluminum Christmas tree. He couldn't disagree. One of the corners was cracked from getting hit by the lawnmower and soon after buying it the colors began to fade.

The shed was used often at first. He built a foot stool for Sarah to reach the cupboards and a coffee table they still had in the living room. He even made a doghouse for the dog they talked about but never got. Over the last five years, however, his presence in the shed lessened. It turned into nothing more than a storage unit where he rarely made an appearance. Spare time, a former luxury, had become extinct for him.

His every waking moment involved either being a teacher, a coach, a painter or dealing with JD. And JD had turned into a twenty-four-hour seven days a week proceeding. The system Karen developed, though noble, began to crumble as both girls recently slacked off on the rules. They appeared burnt out. The task of monitoring Jason became an increasingly difficult challenge to navigate.

Melissa was young enough to be kept in line with a stern lecture and a heavy dose of guilt, although her violations were getting more frequent. But Sarah was by far the biggest repeat offender. She'd sneak off with friends to the movies or the mall and leave her brother unattended. The rebellion against the insanity of her home life was obvious.

The Turners tried grounding her but she was too old and they threatened to stop paying her car insurance. But she didn't care. Sarah said she didn't want a car anyway, that it was a piece of junk, and she stopped driving it out of spite. So they sold it. After begging for her help and assigning fewer shifts, they promised that a solution would soon come about. Her behavior only deteriorated.

When it came to JD, Larry didn't know who was more paranoid about the possibility of incident number three: him or Karen. It was a no-win situation. They were scared to be in the house of what he may do, of finding him dead. But they were also petrified of being away from the house and somebody else bearing the trauma of finding him dead.

Larry keyed into the shed and opened a small window covered in cobwebs. He turned on a fan to alleviate the mustiness. The radio was tuned to a country-western station and he sat in a cracked leather bar stool, leaning against the work bench. If he was a drinker, it would've been the perfect place to drink. The same held true if he smoked. He opened a notebook and glanced around, taking inventory of the supplies he had and detailing the ones still needed.

There was a thick roll of duct tape already on a hook in the garage, so he checked that off the list first. He saw three small tents near a sleeping bag, a portable Coleman stove, and several lightweight pots to cook and boil water. A backpack was found beneath a case of empty soda bottles, the others having been lent to a fellow teacher who never returned them. He discovered multiple cans of near empty bug spray and a citronella candle that hadn't been lit. The waterproof matches were nowhere to be found. The same with the knives. Larry then remembered giving all the knives away in a panic when they found Jason cutting.

The microbial water filter had a hole in the tube and he could've sworn there were packets of dehydrated food somewhere. He had a first-aid kit, a bottle of hydrogen peroxide, and a roll of mosquito netting. The rest of the supplies would be purchased in the morning from a sporting goods store, but there was one item in particular he dreaded buying. Because a hostage cannot see their captor's face— especially this hostage. He wondered where they even sold something like that.

Above a shelf littered with sports magazines and old newspapers hung a calendar he received every year from his insurance agent. Larry studied the upcoming days. Dr. Baker said Jason could arrive at Pine View the following Friday. It was only a week away. That's all the time he had left for everything.

He knew the conversation from a few hours earlier was inconsequential. Whether Jason wanted to go, didn't want to go, clung to his bed in protest, cried, flipped out or screamed; it didn't matter. Karen would get their son to Virginia if she had to walk him there by herself barefoot in a snow storm and drag him by the hair the entire way. She pretty much said so at dinner, the few times she spoke.

His wife would never give up. She was relentless in helping their child, and he loved that about her. But he wouldn't give up either. His entire family was at stake and it had been confirmed what he already knew: Jason would not go to Pine View willingly. Jason would not go anywhere willingly. Outside force would be required. And Larry was the one who planned to provide it.

His cell phone vibrated against a hammer and he snatched it up.

"Alright," Chip said. "You got my ear. But as of now, that's all you got."

Chapter 20

They met at Coconuts Ice Cream Café. It was an unusual spot for grown men to meet, and it seemed a dark smoky bar or a busy restaurant would've been more appropriate. But the place had the best ice cream in town and since Larry didn't drink, Chip gave up booze, and they'd both eaten dinner, Coconuts Café it was.

They ordered thick handspun milkshakes and wandered over to a pond with a boardwalk around it and a fountain in the middle. Under the orange glow of the surrounding lights, people fed pieces of their cones to the eager wildlife. It was hot despite the sun having set. The café remained packed as it approached 9:30 p.m. on a weeknight.

When they were halfway across the pond and somewhat alone, Chip said, "My wife ripped into you pretty good this mornin'. She's pissed as hell for what you said last night, and I could tell she'd been stewin'. But I watched the tape you left again anyway. Watched it quite a few times. I gotta admit, you were right. Helluva story, partner, helluva story. It's a miracle that Edgar guy survived. So between the tape and what you said, it got me to thinkin' about Wes. Stirred up a lot of stuff. Well, a lot more stuff than usual."—he stopped and turned to Larry—"I'd a done anythin' to save my boy, anythin' at all. It breaks me up maybe I didn't do enough. Maybe me and Pauline failed him as parents . . . I'm willin' to listen to what you got."

"Glad you said that. Because I could use the support."

"What's this big plan of yours?"

"It's pretty simple," Larry said. He poked his straw up and down to loosen the shake. "We take him and bring him into the woods. Then, we let him go."

Chip narrowed his eyes and stepped back. "That's it? That's what you had in mind?"

"That's it."

"Your big plan is takin' Jason out in the woods and droppin' him off. Where the hell is he supposed to go?"

"I hoped—"

"And you think that's gonna somehow fix him? Shit, Larry, I thought you had somethin' better. Thought you were serious. I drove over here for this?"

Larry's face warmed. He was pretty sure his plan had a solid chance to work. But the other part, the part he struggled with and told him he was crazy, had serious reservations. What if everything went disastrously wrong? What if there were unforeseen consequences? He had to admit, when the idea was said aloud, it sounded ridiculous. "We don't just take off and grab a burger or start fishing. We don't leave and go home."

"Then what do we do?"

"We watch him. We follow him. We make sure he's okay and doesn't get hurt, but we see what he does, how he reacts. And we make sure he doesn't see us."

"What if he does nothin'? What if nothin' happens at all?"

"Then I'll know for sure that he failed the test. But Edgar Suarez didn't fail the test, and I don't think Jason will either."

"Failin' a test because you didn't take it and failin' because you tried and didn't pass are different."

"How about this?" Larry said. "If he lays down in the woods and resorts to the fetal position, waiting for death to take him, then I'll know he is 100 percent gone into another world already. Only his shell has been left behind. I'll know he isn't even gonna take the test in the first place, and I'll know his desire to die is greater than our ability to save him. But I don't think that'll happen. It's one thing being home when you have heat and AC and food and a nice bed. It's another when you're lost in the dark and hungry."

"It's a scare tactic then, a type of catch and release."

"I guess you could say that. Because that's what happened to Edgar Suarez. The primal fear he experienced brought something to the surface of his mind. It triggered something inside him. Now it's time for that trigger to be activated in Jason."—Larry lowered his voice as a family of four walked past them. The kids giggled and played. One of the parents chased their child from behind—"If he decides to lay down and give up, we'll get him out of there. We'll bring him back home. Then I'll know for sure."

They walked toward a wooden bench next to a garbage can and sat down.

"If that happens, you'll be back to where you are now," Chip said. "Only worse if he finds out it was you. Seems pretty risky for a plan that's most likely to fail. What're you gonna tell him anyway when you take him? If it's a kidnappin', some kind of ransom should be mentioned. But who'd want to kidnap him? You guys don't have any money. Do you plan—"

"I get it. It's stupid and desperate and illogical. That can't be denied. There's no explanation from a rational point of view. But none of this makes any sense in the first place. Does it make sense this would happen to Jason and ruin his life? To ruin our life? All I can say is I'm trying. That's all I've got."

Larry finished the remnants of his shake and crushed the container, then tossed it in the trash. They silently watched the line of customers at the ice cream window that didn't seem to shrink. He noticed the younger people in line, the ones around Jason's age. He saw a cute couple holding hands and sneak a few kisses. A group of guys goofed around and laughed, one of them swiping the others hat. It was normal behavior for normal kids. He wanted nothing more than his son to be a part of it.

"I gotta be honest," Chip said. "This plan sounds lousy. No offense. I mean, it's commendable, what you're tryin' to do. But what are you expectin' out in those woods? A Jesus moment? A religious experience with God?"

"A spiritual awakening would be nice. The Lord works in mysterious ways and I pray for Jason all the time. If he happens to find God out there or has a divine intervention, that'd be the best-case scenario. Miracles occur every day."

"Maybe you should think this through a tad more. If somethin' goes wrong and he dies, you'd be lookin' at jail time. If I help, me too."

"I don't know what you want to hear. But my gut is telling me this is the right thing to do."

"What if your gut be wrong?"

Larry raised his voice. "Dammit, Chip. Of all people, I'd thought you'd be the one who'd understand. Are you telling me you wouldn't have tried anything to save Wes? Anything at all? Regardless of how stupid or crazy it seemed? Because I think you would've. And had I been there, I would've helped, no questions asked. This is it for me. Don't you get it? This has to be it for everyone. I can't do this anymore. Either I get my son back or we let him do what he wants. At least that way I can mourn him and we'll have some kind of closure in our life. Jason can be remembered for who he used to be, for the beautiful son me and Karen raised. Not what we're dealing with now. Only then can I move forward and the same with my family . . . He either lives or dies, no more in between."

Chip removed a prescription bottle from his pocket. He unscrewed the lid, put a few white pills in his mouth, and jerked his head back. "There is no movin' forward when you lose him for good. You need to know that. It's like gettin' old— you can't explain it 'til you get there. And you can't go back, even when you try. Not a day goes by I don't think about Wes. I know what he did was heinous. There's no excuse. But I think about him constantly, and I think about those other kids too. I think about those other poor families . . .

"It was my gun at the school. That makes it a million times worse. I stopped lockin' the safe because I didn't think I had to anymore. How dumb was that? He liked to shoot, we both did, and we enjoyed goin' to the range together. I wasn't worried about Wes shootin' himself by mistake or firin' the gun by accident. He showed responsibility. I taught him about safety, the proper way. Made him take a class. I didn't ever think he'd do somethin' like that, could never imagine. It's just . . . The anger it would take. The self-hatred . . . When they told me what happened, the first thing I said was, "Not my son. My boy would never do that." Isn't that what all parents probably say? The power of denial. Because they're part of us. In a way, we had somethin' to do with it."

"Chip, you don't need to go down this path and—"

"You started this. Gettin' me all riled up. Now let me finish."

Larry nodded.

"Not sure how me and Pauline missed the signs. We had some issues, but nothin' that would break us apart. We both worked a lot, chasin' stuff we didn't need. And we didn't know what to make of his spats of sadness or his actin' out sometimes. He seemed, I don't know, kind of off-kilter. Guess I stuck my head in the sand, took a few jobs out of state that paid plenty. Tried my best to come home weekends or when I could. At the time, Pauline was crankin' as a realtor. She even won realtor of the year and got a huge bonus. The truth is, I guess we weren't home enough. Didn't spend enough time with him to see what was goin' on. Now . . . I'd give my life just to spend a minute with him."—he laughed a sad, desperate laugh, short and disbelieving. His shoulders slumped and the line between his eyes deepened—"But we had a helluva nice house and three cars in the driveway."

"You're a good man, Chip. And Pauline is a good woman. It's not your fault and you're not alone."—Larry got up and stepped in the direction of the parking lot—"Come on, let's go."

"Every year I return," Chip said, wiping his nose with the sleeve of his shirt. "On the exact day of the shootin', I go visit his grave to make sure it's fixed up real nice. Put down fresh flowers and a cross. I don't wanna leave. Wanna just lay near him and sleep. Then I go to the graves of those other poor kids and that teacher. I put flowers on them all and beg for their forgiveness. I beg the Lord too. But words ain't enough sometimes. Maybe some things in life can't be forgiven."—he removed a hanky from his back pocket and blew his nose—"Used to make anonymous donations to the families but realized it don't mean a lick how much I give or what I say. It's over. And you can't go back. You just can't go back."

"Come on, pal."

"Listen to me, Larry . . . I want you to really listen. It's the truth now. There's no goin' back when he's gone. Understand? Ain't no goin' back."

"That's why I'm doing this. To get him back."

Chip stood. "I got nothin' more to lose in this life, nothin' left to take. Me and Pauline, we're fragments of who we were. We occupy that RV like a couple of ghosts, and the only time we leave is to hit up a meetin' or go get groceries."—he took a deep breath—"If I can help someway in this stupid plan of yours, maybe I can help myself too. Who knows? But I'm with you, partner."

"Are you sure?"

"You bet. But there is one thing. We get caught, I'm hangin' you out to dry." Chip smiled, his eyes glossy.

"I wouldn't have it any other way."

They hugged briefly, and patted each other on the back.

"We go Monday," Larry said. "That gives you the weekend if you change your mind. You think you'll be ready?"

"What the hell else I got to do?"

They walked toward the parking lot, the therapy session over, two lost men in search of answers they'd never comprehend.

CHAPTER 21

The next day, Karen was in full research mode on the computer. She sat on the couch with her legs crossed and the laptop open, contemplating the best way to get Jason to Pine View. Her eyes felt strained. Every few minutes she glanced up the stairs at the wavering green curtain without realizing it.

A train or a plane—that was the debate. Perhaps a bus. Transporting her son would be a monumental challenge and each possible solution contained some type of problem. *Why does the facility have to be so far away?* she thought, resisting the urge to slam the computer shut.

The easiest and most logical scenario was to strap Jason in the minivan and drive the forty-seven hours to Virginia by herself. Larry could help secure him in the car, and once inside, a restraining contraption of some sort could be devised. But driving presented numerous obstacles—the bathroom breaks and fuel stops alone cause for concern because of all the opportunities to escape. Karen would've wagered the thirty-seven dollars in her purse that Jason took off and ran the first time he was unbuckled from the car.

She then reconsidered. It was more likely her son would sit on a curb or the ground and refuse to get back in, creating a scene when she tried. The logistics of driving were also problematic. A second driver was needed to reduce the overall travel time, avoid hotel costs, and provide relief by working in shifts.

A short list of candidates popped in her head. The first name she thought of was Mrs. Westcott, their neighbor four houses down. They used to be good friends and Karen leaned on the older woman often when the unraveling began. But the answer was an emphatic no. Mrs. Westcott was a gossiper who told too many people the Turners' business and betrayed Karen's request for privacy.

Maybe Nathan could come along? The notion vacated her mind before being processed and she was surprised it came to her at all. Nathan was much too annoying to be trapped in a car with, and besides, wouldn't he ask about his money? Hadn't she already lied about Melissa and Harvard and Jason going to culinary school? It couldn't possibly all be explained.

Perhaps the woman she met in the city near the pawn shop would like to go? What was her name again? Shelly? Samantha? She knew it started with an S and that the woman had a mole on her cheek and worked downtown. After all, she'd told Karen to call if anything was needed—and she meant it. But her business card laid buried in the trash somewhere, probably at the landfill. It seemed quite the imposition when she couldn't even remember the person's name.

Karen cracked her neck, then her knuckles. She didn't want to involve any co-workers and had isolated or dismissed all her friends. The short inventory of people she knew or interacted with was complete. *What if the girls came along?*

Maybe she could spin it as something cool, a cross-country adventure to bond the Turner women and provide a memorable experience they'd draw on forever. On the way back home they could do things the girls always wanted. Sarah talked about visiting Sedona while Melissa was partial to the Grand Canyon. Their time together would heal the wounded relationship and bridge the chasm that separated them.

"How dare you, Karen?" she said aloud. To embroil her daughters further into the mayhem of what was guaranteed to be a miserable scenario was the most selfish, unfair thing a parent could do. She pushed away the laptop and kicked a pillow onto the floor. Her attempt to contain the situation from escalating had failed. An extraction—how she hated that word—would be necessary.

She wanted to cry but didn't, and was impressed when Pine View answered her call so readily on a weekend. Karen walked to the bathroom and locked the door. She lowered her voice so Jason couldn't hear. "I need help with getting my son to your facility. I'm not sure what to do. Please, this has to be gentle and discreet."

Not to worry, they told her. The staff at Pine View were pros, they were specialists. This type of thing happened all the time. Every detail would be attended to, including the plane tickets and her hotel stay. And the Turners' bill would grow that much larger.

Karen jumped in the shower, mindful not to stay too long. She usually only showered when Larry or the girls were home in case of an SOS signal from Jason. After toweling off, she applied her makeup with an airbrush, then dialed the number for Melissa who stayed at her friend Sammy's. She'd left a voicemail for her youngest child already and it shocked her when the phone was answered on the second attempt.

"I'm surprising your father with lunch today so I need you to come home," Karen said. "I want to see his progress on Principal Smith's house."

"But I was gonna hang out here and chill by the pool. It's, like, Saturday. You do know that, right? We bought stuff to make tacos. Can't you ask Sarah?"

"I can't get a hold of her right now. She was here last time. Isn't it your turn?"

"My turn?" Melissa said. "It's always my turn to be on JD. Sarah's like never around. I'm on summer vacation, Mom. Remember?"

"Yes, I remember. And I'm sorry, but I won't be long. Your—"

"That's what you always say and then you're gone for like three hours."

"I'm never gone that long. You're being dramatic. I can't . . ." Karen caught herself getting reeled into a fight and stopped. She knew where the conversation was headed. "Listen, your brother is going away soon and you won't have to deal with it much longer."

"I won't have to deal with any of it when I go off to college and never come back."

Karen ignored the jab. Her daughter was too young to understand. She'd already explained to both girls what was unfolding, that Jason would be leaving for an indeterminate period of time. It pained her to witness their reactions because they were too much like their mother—bad liars who battled masking their emotions. Their expressions weren't only of relief, but a contained excitement.

The phone fell silent.

"So?" Karen said. "I'm waiting. When will you be here?"

"This is so unfair. This is bull . . . I'll be there in like an hour."

"Can you make that a half-hour?"

"Jesus Mom, I—"

"Hey!" Karen said, chastising her. "Watch your tone. I'm not some classmate."

"Freaking fine. A half-hour then."

"Thanks. I'll make it up to you, okay? I love you."

"Whatever," Melissa said, and mumbled in a flat tone, "Love you too," before quickly hanging up.

Slices of wheat bread were spread on the counter as Karen prepared to make sandwiches. She reminded herself to make two for Jason, encouraging him to eat. When she grabbed the cold cuts from the fridge, a photo of her and Larry caught her attention. It was stuck to the door by a magnet shaped like an avocado. The entire fridge was covered with magnets from places they'd visited and the freebies distributed by local businesses.

She stared at the black and white photo snapped at a friend's wedding. Both Karen and Larry agreed it was the best picture they'd ever taken together. She appeared so much younger, as if she were a different person. *Did I really look like that?* she thought. *Where has the last decade gone?*

It mystified her why she never appreciated her looks when she had them; not in her teens, not in her twenties, and not in her thirties or forties. Only in hindsight could she recognize her youthful beauty. Unaware, she did again in her fifties. Every flaw was magnified, every imperfection critiqued. She focused solely on the negativity as the weeks passed fast and the months passed faster until the years piled up. It took an old photo to show her how blessed she'd been.

She layered a piece of cheese on top of some ham, reminiscing about when she first got married. Their romance was alive and well back then. With a state park only minutes away from their one-bedroom apartment, they'd go for picnics all the time. The question of how many children to have would always come up while they cuddled on a large striped beach blanket. She said five. He said two.

Their lives were visualized with a confident ease. Everything was going to be effortless, or at least not difficult to the Nth degree. The Turners had big plans to be simple ordinary people. They could appreciate that. Predictably, with a romantic view overlooking the lake and the spontaneous hormones of youth on their side, the picnics always led to some kind of sex. They even once got caught. She left her bra in the woods as they scrambled to the car in excitement and their hearts beat fast the entire way home.

A smile creased her lips while she zipped up the cooler but it was short-lived. The front door slammed, rattling the windows. Melissa entered the house and cranked up the volume on the TV.

"You want a sandwich?" Karen yelled from the kitchen.

Her question went unanswered, so she made one anyway. She went to the living room and handed her daughter a plate, who refused accepting it.

"It'll be here later in case you get hungry," she said and set the plate aside. She considered staying with Melissa to try and talk, one on one as they once did. Perhaps she should take the time to pierce the bubble of teenage confusion and contempt for her. But time, like always, wouldn't permit it. Karen was too busy. Maybe she'd try again later when things settled down. More likely though, maybe not.

CHAPTER

When she entered the driveway of Principal Smith's house, Larry wasn't there. She knocked on the door after ringing the bell but nobody answered. Her calls went directly to voicemail. Karen maneuvered along the wraparound porch and peeked in the windows as the floorboards creaked beneath her. Maybe he ran out to get supplies or was estimating another job. She thought about waiting to eat with him, then decided on dining alone. The first half of her sandwich was finished when Larry pulled up and killed the ignition.

"Where've you been?" she asked as he climbed from the cab. She walked toward his truck and noticed he didn't have a splash of paint on him. "I tried calling. Thought maybe you played hooky since it was Saturday."

"Had to run to the bank before it closed, take care a few things," he said, and cleared his throat. The bed of his truck had a tarp stretched across it that wasn't usually there.

Karen motioned to the house with a tilt of her head. "Looks pretty good, what you've got done. You almost through?"

"There's a lot to do on the east side yet. It's steep over there, makes things slower. But there's also been a development. I spoke with Doug this morning and for some reason he's had second thoughts about the color. Wants to put it on hold before he makes a decision."

"That's odd. His house has been the same color since he became the principal, when we first moved here."

"Exactly," Larry said. He took the sandwich she gave him and cleared his throat again. "He's thinking about maybe trying something new."

"What about the stuff you've already painted?"

"I guess I'd have to paint it again if he changes his mind. Could be good for business. But I doubt he will. It'd cost too much money."

She shook her head, taking pity on Doug Smith who was twice divorced and turned fifty in the fall. She assumed he was going through a midlife crisis. "When does he think he'll know?"

"Not sure. So we'll have to wait a little longer before I can finish and get the last check. But the good news is that I have another job lined up. It doesn't start until August and should take me through until school begins."—he flashed a big smile—"I thought I'd use this time to head up to the cabin, like you wanted. I'll try and get everything repaired so we can sell it."

"Seriously?"

He nodded.

Karen launched herself onto him and he almost fell over. She kissed his cheek before erasing the lipstick smudge with her thumb. "You don't know how much that means. It's been wearing on me. I feel bad having to ask."—she kissed him again—"When do you plan to go?"

"Monday."

"Monday? Fantastic. Thank you, Larry. Thank you, thank you, thank you. What a huge relief."

"I thought about what you said. See, I do listen. And you're right. Why wait? Because we're gonna need the money sooner than later. I might even take your advice and ask Jason?"

The smile on her face vanished. "My advice? What advice? I never said—"

"Yeah you did. At the barbeque. You said we shouldn't stop asking him to do things because you never know when he'll say yes. I could tell it bothered you, when I said no. I should've asked. So I'm gonna ask now."

Karen did recall saying that to Larry, and while she didn't like his timing to suddenly take her advice, she knew Jason would never go. Her husband had no chance. For the first and only time she remembered, she was glad about that.

They leaned against the hood of the minivan and finished their lunch, swatting every now and then at a pesky fly. "They're coming to get him Friday," she said. "They suggested I go out separately to make it easier, that I should wait a day. My flight leaves on Saturday."

"Who's they?"

"Pine View."

"You called?"

"Yeah. I was surprised they were open. And glad. Because the arrangements are made and I can put it behind me. They're handling everything now."

"How about you?" he said. "How are you gonna handle it? Could be messy when they take him."

"It can't be any messier than finding him half-dead in the bathroom. I've got scar tissue now."

"Unfortunately, me too."

"After seeing how defiant Jason acted yesterday, I didn't see any other way to get him out there."

"Seems like the boy won't go nowhere on his own."—Larry adjusted his sunglasses—"How much are they charging for the—"

"I should get home," Karen said, turning up her wrist. She expected to see a watch that was no longer there. She passed him a neatly wrapped brownie and grabbed the cooler. "It's hard to believe he'll be gone soon."

"We might as well get it over with."

The sentence hung heavy in the afternoon air and it was a statement she never thought she would hear. Karen knew what her husband meant. Dealing with Jason had turned into a nonstop string of unpleasant tasks required to be checked off the list.

"It's weird," she said, opening the car door. "But when he's out there, I'm not sure what I'll do. I'm kind of concerned. These last few years have been, well . . . I've devoted myself to his care. Entirely. Now, in an instant, I'll have free time just for me again."

"You'll have a void to fill. We both will. Everybody knows what you've sacrificed and what you gave up. Why don't you make an appointment with Dr. Baker?"

"We had a nice lunch, so let's not go there."—she hopped in and rolled down the window—"How about I make a fancy dinner tonight to say thanks for the cabin?"

He leaned forward and rested his arms on the door frame. "After getting back from Virginia, maybe you could focus on work more. It might be helpful. Maybe start up again full-time at the museum. They love having you there and another income would be great. I was thinking . . . What about Monday? Make it a whole day and see how it feels. I'll be home to watch Jason so you don't have to worry. I'm not leaving until the afternoon and one of the girls will be there by then. I have to swing by first and get Chip anyway."

"You're taking Chip?"

"That's why I'm not going tomorrow. There's no way Pauline will let him go on a Sunday. They got church. But I don't want to get on that roof by myself to clear any branches, and he's handy with a chainsaw."

"How is Chip?" she said. "You haven't talked much about him or Pauline lately."

"They're both good. At least as good as they're ever gonna be."

"Their own child, a mass murderer. It makes our situation seem tame."

"Think how we feel, and multiply the guilt by a million. Then consider that Wesley was their only kid."

"I can't even imagine," she said, buckling her seatbelt. She started the engine. "I'll give it a thought. About Monday. It's just that . . . what's happening with us seems so sudden and big."

"We have to learn to live again. He won't be around the house forever."

Karen looked at Larry and felt nervous by what he'd said. How would she live again? Did she even know what it meant anymore? In trying to help and protect her son, she too had become part of the lost.

"I'd better get back to it," he said, and stepped away from the car. "See you tonight."

"I thought the house was on hold."

"The painting? Yes. But the scraping on this thing won't quit. And Doug wants me to review some possible new colors with him later."—he paused—"You should really go to work Monday. I mean it. It'll be healthy. You should really go. I think it'll be—"

"I heard you before."

"Just saying, it could help."

"I said I'd look into it."

Karen pulled from the driveway and watched him wave in the rearview mirror. Her foot pressed the brake pedal. The minivan idled as she drummed her thumb on the shifter. The extraction of Jason was bothersome. She envisioned a SWAT team in tactical gear descending on his room with dart guns and Chloroform. They'd remove him in a straitjacket with military precision while her little boy cried helplessly on a stretcher. Had she seen too many TV shows? Read too many stories? Would her son ever forgive them?

She reversed the car to where Larry stood and rolled back down the window.

"You think we're doing the right thing, don't you? To send him to Pine View. To bring them in using force."

"Are you having doubts? Because if so, then maybe we shouldn't. I'll do whatever you want."

She faked a grin. What she wanted was reassurance. Why couldn't he see that?

"I guess I'm getting cold feet is all. Dr. Baker said this may happen, that it's normal. No, he's definitely going. That conversation is done with. I only wish there was a different way to get him out there. Something more civilized. But it's more than that. Do you think it's right, philosophically?"

"I like things nice and neat. That's why I gravitated toward science. You can measure stuff and rely on data. Nothing is neat when it comes to Jason. It gets blurry with what we've been through, what needs to be done. Nobody can tell us what's right or wrong unless they've walked a mile in our shoes. And we've walked plenty . . . We're trying, Karen. As long as we're trying, I think it's right."

Larry touched her hand and she caressed it.

"You and me," he said, "we're in this thing to the end."

"Always."—she reached out for a kiss, this time on his lips, and it was warm and sweet—"Now, when you see Doug, tell him to go with blue."

CHAPTER

The windshield wiper fluid neared capacity but he topped off the tank anyway. The oil on the dipstick registered full. All four tires were inflated to 35 PSI and the brake fluid, antifreeze, and power steering fluid were at optimum performance levels. The transmission had recently been replaced and there was a new battery and new spark plugs. With 130,000 miles, the truck was mechanically sound. Because it had to be. Breaking down would be the end for them all.

Larry had plenty of water and ice, and more than enough food. While it would be a tight fit with the coolers, tents, and the rest of the camping supplies in addition to the materials for repairs, his son would be able to fit.

He sliced holes along the tarp at twelve-inch intervals with a utility knife, ensuring there'd be enough air to breathe. An accidental suffocation was the last thing he wanted as the trip to the cabin was a long one—three-hours of driving in the summer heat to a 5,000-foot elevation in the mountains. A ladder was fastened to the roof rack, and he cleaned the headlights when a taxi pulled up.

Out stepped Chip with a faded brown duffle bag draped over his shoulder. He wore full-on camouflage from his days as a hunter, accompanied by a cowboy hat. Larry nodded, Chip nodded back, and they met in the corner of the garage.

"Pauline wouldn't drop me off," Chip said, shaking his head. "You believe that?"

"Why not?" Larry asked. He signaled him to lower his voice.

"She said we were up to somethin'. Said if there was one single hair hurt on that boy's head, she'd call the police."

"The police? That's not what I need to hear right now. Can you speak to her, try talking some sense? I'd feel a lot better if she was on board with this."

"Don't worry. That woman is more afraid of being alone than I am. She'd never turn me in. I'm all she's got. But since we only have one vehicle, I couldn't leave her stranded for the next couple days."

Larry pulled at the skin around his eyes and his heart fluttered. He could've sworn he developed an arrhythmia. "She's not the only one who's scared. I'm not feeling so great either. Slept awful last night. Got about three hours. Been up all morning messing around the garage and the driveway. I uh . . ."—he rubbed his belly to sooth the cramps—"I don't mean to overshare, but I've had diarrhea since about four a.m."

"Good," Chip said. "Serves you right. I read somewhere that scientists consider the stomach to be the second brain of our bodies. Sounds like your second brain is tryin' to get through to you, tryin' to make up for brain number one that's on vacation."—he pointed to the road—"I can get that cab back and head on home, you know. He'll be here in a jiff. It ain't too late to stop your stupidity."

"In a perfect world I'd agree with you, but the world isn't perfect. I need you with me."

"Just testin'. Makin' sure you're committed. Because this can't be done half-assed."

Chip threw his bag in the passenger seat and they entered the truck. Their plan was rehearsed a final time.

"You have to do all the talking," Larry said. "He'll obviously recognize my voice, and you guys have never met. Be sure to keep an eye on me. I'll use my hands to guide you . . . Did you bring them?"

"Am I gonna get these back?" Chip asked. He passed over a set of noise-cancelling headphones that cost him 300 bucks.

"Yes. If not, I'll buy you a new pair."—Larry strapped on the headphones and gave a thumbs up—"These'll do for when we get him out of his room. Wait here while I make one more sweep of the house. Karen went to work, thank God for that. I prayed hard and feel bad about manipulating her. Melissa stayed at a friend's and Sarah didn't call or anything, but she never came home last night. Her bedroom door is wide open with clothes all over the place. She's doing that now, not even calling us. It makes Karen nuts. But the coast should be clear."—before exiting the truck, he retrieved a piece of paper tucked in his pocket and unfolded it—"I wrote a few things down he should hear. Try to memorize it while I'm in there."

Chip examined the paper and a questionable expression came over his face. "You think this is what a kidnapper would actually say? Sounds . . . I don't know. Sounds kinda corny."

"I have no idea what a kidnapper would say, because I'm not one. So please just read it."

Larry walked quickly across the driveway with his head down. He leaped on the deck and it felt like a thousand probing eyeballs were somehow watching him. Within minutes he'd captured, found guilty, and burned at the stake alive. He dug his fingernails into his hand and upon opening the back door, he recoiled in panic.

"Heeeeeyyyyyy," he said in the calmest voice possible, knocking into the doorjamb. Sarah stood in the kitchen buttering a slice of toast.

"Hey to you too."

"What're you doing here? I mean, where'd you come from?"

"I'm feeling a little under the weather. I ate like some bad fast food or something last night. We hit the drive-thru around midnight and they dropped me off. I snuck upstairs. Didn't want to wake you guys. I slept in Melissa's room since she wasn't home and her bed is like so much more comfy than mine. Figured I'd bum around the house today until feeling better."

His tongue was thick as his blood pressure spiked and he stared with his mouth half-open. Larry didn't know what to say.

"Are you okay, Dad?" she said. "You look upset. And worried. You want something to eat?"

"I'm uh . . . I'm fine. It's fine. Everything's fine. Surprised to see you here is all. You're practically never here. Never. We usually have to beg you to come home. Now, you're standing smack dab in the middle of the kitchen."

"Yep. And making toast."

"And making toast."—he took a step further and went to the sink, where he filled a glass of water and chugged it—"You look healthy by the way. Good color. No paleness. Maybe you should do something. Get out of this dusty old house and go for a bike ride or a jog. Enjoy some fresh air."

"Are you trying to get rid of me?"

"What? No, no. Why would I? For what?"

"Aren't you supposed to be at work?" she asked. "Where's Mom, anyway? You're acting like weird and stuff."

"Don't worry about what I'm supposed to do," he said, his tone harsh. "You need to worry about yourself."

Sarah stopped mid-chew and glared at him.

He avoided her gaze and refilled his water. "I'm about to leave for work soon and Mom's coming home. You don't need to be here. Really. Everything's taken care of."—Larry took out his wallet and removed a twenty—"The best thing to do when you're not feeling good is move around, occupy your mind. Why don't you go to the bookstore or the mall?"

She snatched the bill from his fingers. "If you throw a little more on top of this, I guess I could like go shopping. Maybe that'll make me feel better."

He added two more twenties and worried that Chip would barge in and ask what the hell was taking so long, or worse, saying he'd changed his mind.

"When can you leave? Right now? I mean, do you need a ride?"

"I can leave as soon as I call my friends to pick me up. Relax, Dad. Jeez. And how would you give me a ride?"—she looked at the ceiling—"JD, remember? Like somebody has to be here. It's your rule."

"Yeah, I knew that. I wasn't saying. I'm just saying . . . I could call you a cab or something."

She chucked the toast in the garbage, then banged her plate in the sink. "You guys are so freaking annoying. First, you want me here like all the time, to help watch *him*. You're always ragging on me to come home or lecturing about the importance of family. That's why I stayed, you know. That's why I went to college near this rinky-dink town. I stayed to help. For both of you. But I'm tired of it. I've sacrificed too, Dad. So has Melissa. It's not just you and Mom. Now I'm here like you asked, and you can't wait for me to go. Like which is it? I wish you'd make up your mind."

"Sarah, I didn't mean—"

"I'll be gone in like twenty minutes. How about that? Even though I feel sick, I'll leave the house for you. Will my father at least grant me the privilege of bathing before he kicks me out?"

Larry knew he'd handled the situation badly but what could he do? She wasn't supposed to be there. Larger and more critical issues were in play. He set another twenty on the counter.

"You have to trust your parents sometimes. I hope you feel better. For the record, we love having you here."

"Yeah right," she said, storming from the kitchen.

He sighed. His face felt flushed and when he returned to meet Chip, Larry was still exasperated. "She's never here anymore," he told him. "At least not of her own accord."

"Maybe it's a sign not to do this."

"Can you stop with the signs and the stupidity and the testing or whatever? It's stressing me more. Her being here is nothing but Murphy's Law. That's all. Murphy's Law at its finest."

"Mr. Murphy. That sonofabitch. You're right. I won't mention that it could be your second brain gurglin' around your gut, tryin' to warn that you might be makin' the biggest mistake of your life. I won't mention it again."

"Thank you."

They waited forty minutes, not twenty, and observed the house, the street, and the neighbors. Larry wondered if Sarah would actually leave or if she'd stay in defiance. He continued to rub his stomach as his legs bounced under the dash. When her friend arrived and beeped the car horn twice, he watched in shameful relief while his confused and upset daughter vacated the house. Had he known what was to come, he would've spoken to her so much differently.

Chapter 24

He backed the truck to the edge of the deck and left the tailgate open, the engine running. *Why didn't I buy a house with a connected garage?* Larry thought. The two men slipped in the kitchen, tiptoed through the living room, and creeped up the stairs. They stood side by side on the landing wearing ski masks and sunglasses. The job was to be a simple grab and go, in and out, like a jewelry heist. Three minutes was the allotted timeframe.

Breathing heavily, they exchanged glances. Larry's throat constricted like a python was wrapped around it. Everything became real. He heard the sound of ocean waves from Jason's noise machine and uncurled his fingers one by one in front of him. On the count of five the words *Go! Go! Go!* rang inside his head.

They breached the room in silence. Chip instantly got tangled in the curtain and flailed about like a frightened bird. He spun around and around, entwining himself further until he lost his balance and stumbled into a wall. Larry untangled him as Jason rolled over. He appeared groggy and dazed. For a moment, nobody spoke.

The captors stared. The captive stared back. Until Jason screamed.

Larry lunged for his son's face and covered his mouth with one hand—he restrained him with the other. Chip was supposed to have the duct tape ready but remained frozen with a circle of pee dampening his pants. When Larry reached over with his foot and kicked him, Chip ran from the bedroom to the end of the hallway.

He blasted in and out of the room several times, whipping through the curtain while he hummed loudly. Larry watched his friend have a meltdown and knew this may happen. Earlier that year he'd witnessed Chip come unglued in a parking lot when a delivery truck backfired, resembling a gunshot. Chip yelled at everyone to get on the ground, and he wouldn't stop making a scene until the police arrived. Nothing could be done until his episode passed.

Larry shoved a pillow over Jason's eyes and pressed his body weight on him. The muffled pleas for help were heard by no one. His son squirmed to get free but he was weaker than his father. Beneath the mask, Larry didn't smile or glean pleasure in the abduction, although he did feel excited. Jason had resisted being taken. He fought and was combative. His spirit indicated a desire to live, or at least not die, and he showed fear. True fear. Fear meant a person had something to lose, something they cared for. That something had to be life.

Chip, now panting, sat at the desk and slid a few pills into his hand from an orange plastic bottle. He lifted the mask above his mouth and jerked his head back to swallow.

"Sorry," he said, re-emerging into the crime scene. He ripped off a long piece of tape. "It's been a while. Thought I was done with all that. But I still can't seem to control it."

They sealed Jason's mouth and tied his arms together, then his legs. The only thing left was the hood. What was it about the hood that spooked Larry so? The finality? The coldness? The cowardice? He stared into his son's bulging eyes, at the veins that protruded from his neck. It was sheer terror unlike he'd ever seen. *I've done this*, he thought. *How have I done this?*

He felt dizzy and when his knees buckled, he latched onto Chip for support. The excitement he experienced a few minutes prior that his plan might work deflated to a new low. All the scheming and justification, it'd been performed in the science lab of his mind with the perfect variables in the perfect circumstances. Everything was always ideal, always correct. But the divide between intention and implementation was often cloudy, the reality far more gruesome. Larry was unprepared for the gritty unsightly emotions.

The sounds were guttural and the visuals raw, stabbing his mind. He'd inexplicably blocked out the ugliness in *his* version of Jason's extraction because the kidnapping was imagined to be mechanical and innocuous, like the removal of an appliance or hoisting a piece of furniture. Could he be that delusional? Was he really that naïve? He shook his head and handed over the hood as if suddenly allergic.

"It's alright," Chip said. He wrangled the hood onto Jason's face and pulled it tight. "I got you, partner. I got you."

Larry slid onto the carpet and tried to collect himself. He searched to maintain his resolve. Cold feet—that's what Karen told him the other day; she was having cold feet. It was normal. Now so was he.

He scanned Jason's self-imposed jail cell and knew they took too long. Three different women could unexpectedly come home and blow the charade apart. He ordered himself to proceed, to get Jason prepped for transport, to vacate the house immediately. But he couldn't. Like an athlete who choked in crunch time when the big game was on the line, the pressure withered him while his mental strength faded away.

That's when he saw it. How could he not? It was always there, staring, and it haunted him. The patch on the ceiling was different in texture, smooth from the sanded spackle. It was so smooth that three coats of paint still weren't enough to seamlessly blend it in. That's where he found his son dangling unconscious six months earlier, clinging to an unwanted life. That section of the ceiling where they'd mounted a chin-up bar, where Jason once pushed his body to get stronger—then pushed it to end.

When Larry dismantled the vile piece of fitness equipment he did so in an angry fashion, not pragmatic. He tore it violently from the ceiling. Two large holes in the drywall were left behind. For weeks he blamed the chin-up bar as if it were a person who betrayed him because he had to blame somebody. He had to blame something. It wasn't *his* fault.

Larry despised that chin-up bar for the pain it caused and neither him nor Karen nor his daughters fully recovered. Maybe they never would. Perhaps the entire dynamic of his family had been altered forever. That's why he was there, he reminded himself. To stop that kind of pain from ever happening again.

He sprang from the floor and approached Chip. They needed to get Jason into the truck because they were going to the cabin, they would bring him in the woods, and he would no doubt save his son. His obligation as a father spurred him.

"We are not the enemy," Chip read. He looked at Larry, hesitated, then focused back on the note. "The enemy lies inside all of us. We must battle it. Unforeseen circumstances have brought us together. People you know owe us somethin'. You owe us somethin'. We want what we used to have and you are the only one who can make that happen. You have the power to control your destiny."

They spread out a tan canvas drop cloth to wrap him in. Chip secured Jason by the feet, Larry by the arms. But as he thrashed around like a cornered animal, their attempts to move him were futile. They changed positions, then changed back, and struggled for a solid grip.

"Hold on," Chip said. "Let's try this."—he slid three pills from the orange bottle into his hand—"It'll sedate him. Unless you know someone else interested in helpin' us commit a felony."

Larry took off the ski mask and wiped his brow. His skin felt blotchy and irritated. He mouthed the words, "What are they?"

"Valium."—Chip tore off his own mask and scratched his scalp—"Are we gonna do this or not?"

Jason had been prescribed a catalog of anti-depressants since his cutting was discovered. After each new worsening incident, the cocktail of drugs got multiplied and tinkered with. Larry inspected the pills. How bad could three little Valium be? He nodded and was surprised how assertive Chip became when he raised the hood and shoved the pills into Jason's mouth, making him swallow like a dog getting meds.

"About fifteen minutes should do it. Then we get the hell out of here."

The kidnappers sat quietly on the edge of the bed and waited for the drug to take effect. Once Jason mellowed enough to where they could lift him, he was deceptively heavy. It was difficult to carry his tall, lanky body down the narrow stairs. Both men were sweating. They stopped at the halfway mark to readjust their leverage and rest. When they reached the bottom, Larry cut the corner too sharp and whacked Jason's head on the bannister, hearing a grunt through the cloth.

They lingered near the back kitchen door as Larry peered through the window for neighbors. None were spotted. Swiftly, they shimmied across the deck and navigated the three small steps that led to the truck. The rolled-up body was stuffed under the tarp and the tailgate slammed closed.

Larry returned inside to pack a bag for Jason. He knew Karen would ask about it. She'd probably rifle through his dresser to ensure they brought enough clean shirts and underwear. He made the bed, fixed the curtain, and erased any signs of a commotion. After locking the house, they exited the driveway.

With his hands at ten and two, Larry drove through the development, then the suburbs, at the exact posted speed limit. His eyes looked straight ahead. Their seatbelts were buckled. The radio was off. When they merged onto the highway leading to the mountains he popped in a stick of gum. The shaking of his hands dissipated as his heartbeat began to slow.

Desperation had besieged a desperate man, a desperate parent. He wanted to yell and cry, hide and hug somebody. But he didn't. He simply drove. A father on a mission. Phase one complete.

CHAPTER

Is that a cop? Larry thought. He checked the rearview mirror for the hundredth time and piloted his truck in the slow lane with the cruise control set. Every vehicle on the road was envisioned to be a police car or an FBI agent. While his paranoia escalated with each new billboard and exit sign, he also worried about Jason. Was his son safe back there? Could he somehow miraculously escape his confines?

His hands hurt from a white knuckle grip on the wheel so he took some aspirin. He looked over at Chip. His friend slept for the second half of the trip. The first half he spent playing games on his phone where he'd swear under his breath when he lost a turn and had to start over.

They made a total of five pit stops, doubling their estimated drive time. The first one was immediate so Chip could change his soiled pants. The others were because of Larry's stomach woes which no amount of convenience store medicine seemed to eradicate.

When the highway finally ended, they drove along a curvy road with no shoulder and sparse traffic. A few small towns presented themselves and one had a dilapidated diner. The other had a single blinking light. Driving deeper into the woods and higher up in the mountains, they veered left at a fork, then turned onto a rutted dirt road called Beaver Ridge Lane.

The Turners were one of the last people to secure a camp at the lake. Soon after their purchase, legislation was passed protecting 4,000 acres of wildlife from not only the logging industry, but from any future development as well. Because of this, Larry had no neighbors at all to the north and west. To the south was Lake Moonset itself which stretched eighteen miles through a granite basin. It was carved from pre-historic glaciers as large as a city and filled with the melt. The only neighbor the Turners had within walking distance was to the east. Their place was still six miles away.

The cabin was isolated, in the middle of nowhere. While Karen raised concerns about response times in case of an emergency, Larry reassured her they'd be fine. Privacy is why they bought the camp—that's what he told her. And that's why he and Chip were there. He'd been to Lake Moonset hundreds if not thousands of times to hike, fish, and explore. Larry knew the woods, knew the mountains and the terrain. When they let Jason go, they'd steer him to the north.

Built in the 1960s as a hunting retreat, the cabin was crafted from redwoods that once loomed as tall as skyscrapers. It measured twenty feet by twenty feet with a limestone fireplace and a walnut mantel. A lean-to was added to keep the firewood dry and provide extra storage. There was a tiny sink with running water and in the center, where everybody gathered to eat or play board games, resided a long, oval table.

Larry scampered from the truck when they reached the cabin and immediately opened the tailgate. The drop cloth wiggled and for the first time since leaving the house, his stomach untightened. Jason was safe. Stepping back, he admired the view as the sun sank closer toward the peaks in the distance and streaks of purple and orange clouds floated overhead. The trees were taller. The sky seemed grander. Like an old friend not seen in several years, he knew it had been too long.

When Chip snapped his fingers and interrupted him, Larry turned his attention to the cabin. The neglect was evident. An enormous tree branch was strewn across the roof and several of the shingles were missing. The window to the right of the front door was cracked like a spider web while the one on the left was smashed completely, both casualties of a hailstorm he presumed. The door itself needed to be re-stained and many of the planks surrounding the entrance were rotted.

Larry clicked on his flashlight. He crossed the threshold and expected to find water damage or mold. It wouldn't surprise him if a family of racoons took residence as squatters.

"All clear," he said after shining around the light. He then clasped his mouth, concerned Jason might hear him through the headphones. "All clear," he repeated in a hushed tone.

Chip came in with his own flashlight and scanned the floor like he was a detective. "Looks like somethin' was here," he said. His foot pointed to a clump of animal feces. "It stinks."

"I'll take care that in a minute. We need to get these windows boarded up to keep out the bugs, then start a fire. The debris on the roof, we'll address that in the morning. Before we leave. Let's get him in here to get fed and settled."

Jason flinched when they grabbed him but didn't try to resist. They dragged him from the truck in his now dirty sweatpants, the white socks brown on the bottom, and tied a rope around his waist. Delicately, Larry lifted the hood above his son's mouth to tear off the tape.

The guilt gnawed at him and he nearly fell apart to confess right away. How could it be explained that he was sorry, but that the kidnapping was for his own good? How could he tell Jason to give the experiment some time? Larry wanted to declare the extent to which he missed his son, to proclaim his fatherly adoration. He gave him a drink of water instead.

"There's no use yellin', because nobody can hear you," Chip said, following Larry's instructions after they removed the headphones. "Do as we say and you'll be alright. We're gonna take you to the outhouse, then you'll get some food, and that'll be all for today. Don't try anythin' dumb or we'll have to get drastic."

"What the fuck is going on?" Jason asked. Water droplets dribbled off his chin and there was a salty residue on his cheeks from crying. "I want to talk to my parents."

"Why would you wanna do that? From what I hear, you don't even like your parents."

"What?" Jason said. "What're you talking about? Who the hell are you?"

"I got instructions, kid. Now go take a whizz and if you gotta go number two let me know, I'll give you some TP. Try gettin' some sleep tonight and save your strength. Come tomorrow, we're all gonna need it."

Larry nodded in approval. While Chip went a little off script, he remained calm. That's all he could ask for when it came to his friend—for him to remain calm.

The three of them dined on roast beef subs and their captive was difficult at first. He wouldn't eat. But Jason surprised them both when he changed his attitude and finished his entire meal plus a bag of chips. They propped him up on one of the beds with his hands bound and his feet tied again. The hood was pulled down past his chin, the headphones nestled tight.

"Did you call Pauline?" Larry whispered. He sat in front of the fireplace as the flames flickered and the sound of the bugs outside kept them company. "Does she know where you are, that you're not in danger?"

Chip grinned. "One of the few things I like about modern technology. No need to call, only text. Told her what I had to without sayin' a word."—he threw his sub wrapper in the fire—"What about you? Your phone workin'?"

"Everybody's does because of the towers. I'm about to call Karen, just trying to get it straight. A text won't work in this situation."

"I'd think not."

"Don't know what I'm more nervous about—taking him in the first place, or making this call."

"You'd be best to get it over with. The meters runnin' on how much shit you're in."

"I'm afraid you're right," Larry said. He walked over to Jason and stared for a minute, then trudged towards the truck with his shoulders slumped. A hands-free flashlight attached to his head showed the way.

He hadn't checked his phone all day on purpose. The aftermath that was sure to come about when Karen got home and the house was empty would be apocalyptic. It would get even worse when she read the note he'd left on the dining room table.

GREAT NEWS! JASON CAME TO THE CABIN. COULDN'T BE MORE EXCITED. DON'T WORRY, I BROUGHT EVERYTHING WE NEED. COULD BE THE TURNING POINT WE HOPED FOR. CALL YOU LATER. LOVE LARRY.

His voicemail indicated there were seven new messages in addition to another ten calls. He listened in trepidation as they progressed from inquisitive and concerned to hostile and angry. Contributing to the phone assault were a string of lengthy texts.

Larry reached for the door handle but decided to forgo sitting in the truck. He began to walk and thought the night air may clear his head. A knife occupied his left front pocket and he had a bottle of bear spray clipped to his belt. He wasn't concerned about getting mauled by a rogue black bear or having his throat ripped out by a ravenous mountain lion. The chances were slim. But he was petrified to death of a five-foot-six woman who had the power to decimate him.

Chapter 26

He stopped and turned off his light a half-mile from the cabin. Thousands of stars twinkled in the sky while the planet Venus glowed brightly. Larry didn't ponder the size of the galaxy or the meaning of life—he was too busy fretting. Alone in the dark, his breaths were shallow and quick, as if psyching himself up to jump off a cliff or run into a burning building. He closed his eyes and waited . . . and waited . . . until his thumb hit the call button. When she answered right away, his voice sounded squeaky and timid. He seemed positive every creature within earshot ridiculed him.

"I, I'm sorry, my battery died, I—"

"What's going on? Where've you been? Where's Jason? I saw your note and I've tried to reach you and you're not picking up and . . ."

Venting, that's what she needed, so he let her. There were times in their relationship to plead his case and others to make like a statue and shut it. He chose the latter. His wife was scared and concerned, justifiably irate. Had he been in her situation, Larry would've felt the same. When Karen paused and came up for the slightest amount of oxygen, he cleared his throat. His semblance of a rambling explanation was given.

"Stop! Just stop for a minute," she said. "So that's it? All of a sudden, completely out of the blue, he decides to go with you to the cabin after he hasn't left the house in forever."

"That's the gist of it. Yeah."

"I don't like this, Larry. It makes me very uncomfortable. Sarah said she was here earlier today, that you acted weird. She said you kicked her out of the house. What is she talking about?"

The reflective eyes of an armadillo or some other critter glanced at him and he clutched the bear spray. He kicked a stone into the brush before it scuttled away.

"She's a moody teen, Karen, what else can I say? You know how they can be. She's mad because I suggested she go do something productive. She didn't look sick to me, so I told her."

"But we want them around the house. That's the point. We need their help with Jason. You always tell me how much you wish they were home more often, that we could be together as a family. Your attitude today certainly isn't going to help."

Larry could feel her intensity through the phone and he had to agree. His excuses were absurd. "I guess I screwed up. I'm sorry. I'll apologize to her when I get back. I got a lot on my mind right now."

"You've got a lot on your mind? Pine View will be here in four days. Jason better be home by then. I'm serious. I don't like that you took him without consulting me first. Don't mess up this opportunity to . . ."

She continued to pepper him with questions and concerns and he answered the best he could—with vagueness. He dodged, deflected, avoided, and lied. When it became apparent the conversation wouldn't end as they rehashed what was already said, Larry knew what had to be done: act mad and defend his character. That was the only solution.

"Our son is here with me," he said, raising his voice. "Not some stranger. I'm his father in case you forgot. So why don't you cut me some slack? Rather than being mad, you should be elated. He's finally out of the house. Isn't that what we wanted? This may be exactly what he needs instead of wasting all our money on that looney bin in Virginia."

"How can you say that? That place is our only chance."

"No, Karen, it's not."

"I want to speak with him. Right now!"

"Hold on, I'll ask."—he covered the mouthpiece and waited until the count of twenty—"Jason says he doesn't want to talk right now. He hasn't said much to me and is half asleep as usual."

"What about a video chat, so I can at least see him? You know how to do that?"

"No, I don't. I'm not gonna do it anyway. I get it, you're worried, and this is unexpected. But he'll be safe. Believe me. Chip and I have a lot of work to do. My guess is that Jason will sit on his bed and do nothing, like he does at home."

"Did you bring his meds?"

"Yes."

"What about food? Did you bring enough food? You know how picky he can be."

"I've got tons of food, enough for a small army."

"And clothes? It gets cool up there at night. He might—"

"I brought clothes, Karen. I'm not an idiot."

She fell silent for a minute before saying, "I don't know, maybe I should come up. I'll see if the girls want to go. We could leave in the morning."

Larry's spine stiffened like it would snap in half. That kind of reaction was never anticipated. How had he underestimated his wife's emotional damage, her overprotectiveness and dependent relationship with their son? How could he be so obtuse? His mind fled as he stared into the woods, watching his doom unfold.

"Are you still there?" she said. "Can you hear me?"

"I uh, yeah, I'm here. Not sure if . . ."

"What do you think? Sound good? I can even help with the repairs, maybe add a woman's touch."

"It's probably not the best—"

"Did you bring any extra sleeping bags or are they still in the shed?"

"Maybe you should wait and we'll do it some other time."

"I'll buy some steaks for dinner tomorrow. Baked potatoes too. The girls like those with sour cream. I'd better call and see if they'll come before it gets late."

"Karen, I was hoping to . . . Forget the repairs, I can—"

"I wonder where my hiking boots are. Not sure the last time I used them. I bet they're in the garage next to the lawn chairs."

This was it. The pivotal moment of not only his plan had come, perhaps his life too. She'd never take a hint, subtle or not. Without serious interference his wife would be in front of the fireplace by noon the next day with a package of sirloins and a bag of spuds. Any form of explanation would be humanly impossible. Larry hated himself for what had to be said. With no other alternative and limited time, he went for the jugular.

"You're gonna ruin it, you know. You're gonna suffocate him like you always do and push him further away. Maybe that's half the problem. You never leave him alone. You constantly reinforce his self-pitying behavior and act like his personal servant most of the time, not his mother. And you won't go to therapy, so you can't even see it. He doesn't want you here right now. Maybe he wants a break. I don't want you up here right now. Do realize what the chances are of Jason coming to the cabin with me again? Beyond slim. So let me have this special time with our son. Stay home and leave us be."

He could've continued his rant. All the bottled-up anger and frustration swelled inside him—the anger he never released because everything was always fine and he was an actor incapable to perform any other role. He could've gone on and been crueler to not only his wife, but himself too. He could've been crueler to his friends and his neighbors and his co-workers and God and the universe, and he could've directed his resentment back to the beginning of time and the creation of the Big Bang. But that's not who Larry Turner was. That's not who he wanted to be.

He put the phone on mute and screamed, "I'm sorry!" His words crushed her, he knew it. "Don't you understand? This is how we're gonna save our son. This is how we're gonna save us all."

It surprised him that he cried for the first time in months, on that dirt road, in total darkness. Because if there was anybody he didn't want to hurt, it was Karen. They were a team and had been through so much together. He loved his wife more than anything. Including his kids. He'd never confess that to another living soul and would deny ever thinking it. In the age of political correctness, it was a super incorrect thing to say. But it was true. He did. He felt bad that he thought it, worse that he felt it, and accepted he was in the minority. Some people live solely for their children and forget about the one chance they have at life, others journey to find a balance. Everything Larry ever did, is doing, or will do, was for her.

"Please guarantee me you won't leave him alone," she said in between sobs. "Not even once."

"He'll be in my sights the entire time. And I'll call you first thing in the morning."

They exchanged a few more words and limped to the finish line, two spent boxers punch drunk and weary. Finally, the long conversation ended.

Larry returned to the cabin with his eyes burning and his nose stuffed up. All day long he'd been on high-alert as the adrenaline trickled into his bloodstream like an IV drip. A fatigue he'd never experienced crashed over him.

He saw Chip stare into the flames with a pained expression and assumed his friend thought about Wes. He then looked across the room at Jason. Whether his son was asleep or awake, it seemed irrelevant. Because his son was *there*. They were *there*. If it was a dream, he didn't want to wake. If it wasn't a dream and the kidnapping had actually gone through, Larry would do the right thing for everyone. That was the reason they were in the wilderness. His boy would soon be free.

CHAPTER 27

Why couldn't she go to the cabin? It wasn't an unreasonable idea. What was the big deal?

Karen stood near the window in Jason's room after she cried herself out and called Larry every bad word her limited vocabulary of swear words permitted. How could he say those things? It was so uncharacteristic. The more his comments were considered, the more she felt obligated to rationalize and defend her actions.

She spoke aloud, as if to a panel of judges, explaining how a child needed their mother, especially in crisis. That was all. It's that simple. She loved her kids more than anyone—it only seemed natural—and she'd do anything for them. She never suffocated or smothered Jason, never reinforced any type of negative behavior. What was Larry talking about? She only tried to help. So what if she cleaned his room or served him food. What mother wouldn't? The boy has to eat.

As she continued to think about their discussion, the less she second-guessed her parenting skills as a mother. She closed the blinds and sat on the bed. How dare he speak to her like that? Who did he think he was? Suddenly he's father of the year, the best dad ever? Her annoyance with him transitioned to anger and there was plenty to be said right back.

She could've demonstrated how he worked all the time not only for the money, but to bury his feelings, to avoid being at the house. She could've shown that in spite of attending his weekly support group, his attitude and behavior hadn't changed. Everything was still *fine* with him, even when it wasn't. She hated that word! He hadn't progressed or tapped into a greater understanding of who he was. Maybe if he wasn't so hands-off with Jason anymore and made a better effort to communicate, maybe if he helped more and didn't expect her to take care of everything; maybe then things would be different.

Karen then stopped shredding her husband and questioned what was happening. It wasn't like her and Larry to be mean to each other. They'd always been kind and supportive. Why did he act so strange? Why now?

A cooling off period, that's what they needed. She would allow her husband some time at the cabin to regain his sense and realize his errant way. How much time, she couldn't say? But one thing she knew for sure was that when Pine View arrived in four days to remove Jason and transport him to the plane, he'd be ready. And so would she.

She looked around the room and tried to remember the last time her little boy wasn't in the house or that she wasn't with him. But she needn't try very long. No need to play that game. Because she knew. She knew the exact day and the precise minute. It wasn't a proud memory like when a child went off to college, but rather a disturbing one—her son in a hospital psych ward with rope burns around his neck being monitored by an orderly.

The house was silent, but a different type of silent. *Is this how it'll be when he's gone?* Karen asked. She never desired to be an empty nester and was terrified when all the kids left for good one day. Eventually the cord would have to be severed, she understood that. The Turners promoted independence and believed that was how young people matured to discover themselves. But over the last several years she'd changed her mind, becoming selfish. She used to mock parents who hid behind their children and used them as excuses not to lead their own lives. Now she had joined them. At the age of fifty-four, Karen couldn't comprehend how it'd happened.

She got up from the bed to exit the room when a small wad of tape on the carpet was noticed. It was gray and resembled duct tape, the kind that hung on the wall in the garage. *How'd that get there?* she thought, unsticking the tape and placing it in her pocket. Karen turned off the light and went downstairs to the kitchen. She put on a pot of coffee. Sleeping that night, with or without the aid of pills, was not going to happen.

The oven pre-heated and the TV was on. For no reason at all she whipped-up a batch of peanut butter cookies. She wasn't hungry and had little desire for sweets anymore but when the cookies were finished, she still felt anxious. She needed something to do.

Larry's dress shirts for school could always be ironed and while stretching a neatly pressed Oxford across a hanger, she spotted her suitcases in the back of the closet. *Why not?* she thought. *May as well start packing now for Virginia.* She unplugged the iron and folded up the board.

She grabbed her red suitcase, the bigger of the two. The duration of her stay in the Pine View area was still unclear and she wondered how long it'd be before getting asked to leave. A couple days? Maybe a week? As usual, Karen over-packed. Half of the clothes jammed inside would never be worn.

Next, she grabbed the smaller suitcase, and set that on the bed as well. She dragged her fingers across the coarse blue fabric and replayed the conversation with Larry. *Stay home,* he'd told her. *Leave us be.* He didn't want her up there.

The first item she threw in was a beach towel followed by a baseball hat and a bottle of sunscreen. Within minutes she found herself rummaging through the attic for her walking poles. When she ventured to the garage in search of her boots, she noticed the duct tape didn't hang on the hook near the door as usual. Maybe Larry needed it to fix some things at the cabin.

She thought about the wad of tape discovered on Jason's carpet. It seemed strange. Karen knew every square inch of his bedroom in detail and never saw anything like that before. Perhaps she'd mention it to Larry when they spoke in the morning. Because that's what he'd told her—he'd call her in the morning. *I won't go up tomorrow,* she said to herself. Let him have his one full day. But the day after that was no guarantee.

Her cell phone rang and she was stunned by the caller. "Melissa? Is everything alright?"

"I'm good, Mom. No worries. What's up?"

"Nothing. Why? Do you need something?"

"You haven't like called me all day. That's a first."

"I figured you'd enjoy not hearing from me for a change. You've got the day off from me bugging you. In fact, you have several days off."

"You know I don't mind. I like it sometimes. It's just that you can be . . . You know."

"Are you at Sammy's?"

"Yeah, I'm gonna spend the night. If that's okay?"

"Since when did you ask for permission?" Karen said, a tad curtly. She locked the garage and headed back in the house. Melissa began staying at Sammy's on a regular basis right after incident number one.

She tried to think of something to say and desired to have a real conversation. But as usual, she had nothing. If the schedules of her daughters weren't inquired about to coordinate JD, they didn't have much to discuss. Karen wanted to talk about art or books or learn of their interest in boys, maybe carve out a few hours to watch a movie. None of that ever happened. She didn't try to be their best friend and understood teenagers need moms to be moms. The boundary was respected. But what perplexed her most was that she and the girls used to hang out all the time. Now they only hung out when they had to.

The relationship with her daughters was a slow steady decline, like a water faucet losing pressure. Whenever she requested Sarah and Melissa do something fun with her, the answer was consistently no. They were always busy. So Karen stopped asking. And the girls didn't seem to mind.

When she got back from Virginia she'd try harder—that's how she comforted herself. A serious commitment would be made to reconnect with her daughters and truly understand the young women they'd become. But as always, she attended to her son not only first but second. Then third. Then fourth. Then fifth. Her daughters knew it. Everybody did.

Melissa smacked her lips, interrupting the long silence. "So, I guess you kind of like have stuff going on or whatever. I'm gonna go. Just wanted to check in case you were looking for me."

Karen thought for a moment and stuffed her mouth with a cookie. Her shoulders tensed. She feared the rejection and winced, but asked anyway. "What are you doing on Wednesday?"

"Nothing, I guess. Like the usual."

"You want to go to the cabin?"

"You guys are heading to Lake Moonset?"

"Dad and Jason are already there. It'd be with me."

"Jason's there? How'd that happen?"

"He went with your father."

"Seriously, like what's going on?" Melissa said. "You haven't called me all day, Dad's up at the cabin for the first time in forever, and Jason actually left the house."

"Maybe things are changing around here for the better."

The phone was silent again as Karen waited for a response. She ate another cookie out of nerves. And another. "How about it?" she finally said.

"What time you leaving?"

"Eight o'clock."

"That early?"

"It's a long ride."

"Like how long are you gonna stay? If it's only a—"

"You know what?" Karen said, already feeling an upset stomach from the sugar. "Don't worry about it. I don't have time for your antics. I'll put some money on the counter for you to eat."

"No, wait. I didn't say for sure . . . Can I bring Sammy?"

"Why not?" She listened as Melissa asked her friend to come along and try to con her into it. "Be sure and run it by her mother first."

Karen went to the living room to lay on the couch. She placed the back of a hand to her forehead. "If you're here when I leave I'd enjoy the company, if not, maybe some other time."

"Mom, chill. I'll go."

She smiled. "Great, see you then. Be sure to bring your bathing suits."

"Is Sarah coming?"

"I'll ask. And do me a favor. Don't tell Dad. I want to surprise him."

For the rest of the night she stayed on the couch, unable to get rid of the taste of peanut butter. She called Sarah only once about the trip and left an upbeat voicemail how she *and* Melissa were going to the lake. It felt nice to say *we* instead of *I* for a change. She hoped her oldest daughter would join them but a response from the invite wasn't expected. Out of her three kids, Sarah was the toughest to get along with.

In addition to her proclivity for holding grudges, the Turners' middle child had a much harder time than her younger sister dealing with Jason's depression. She was closer to Jason and took his self-inflictions personally. Because of her age, expectations for her help were also higher. Karen was certain that Sarah remained upset with Larry for kicking her out of the house and knew it would be held against both parents. Why had he done that? It was so unlike him.

Everything he did that day seemed atypical for such a passive man. Something was off. She couldn't explain his behavior, but if Jason miraculously left the house then she needed to see it with her own eyes, not hear it on the phone from hundreds of miles away. The steak dinner she offered to make occupied center stage in her mind. It was to be prepared over the open campfire at the cabin, not on the electric stove of the house. When it came to their son, nobody could tell her what to do.

CHAPTER

Larry found Chip by the fire pit playing games on his phone. The volume was turned off and he lounged in one of the Adirondack chairs they had stored in the lean-to. The chair was white, the paint chipping. All three names of the Turner kids were carved into the arm.

Chip never took his eyes off the screen and his tongue poked from the side of his mouth, when he asked, "How you feelin'? Man, you were out. Dead to the world as Pauline would say."

"I feel like garbage," Larry said. He rubbed his face with both hands and yawned.

"Suppose that's normal for what we done."

"I meant I think I overslept. I've got a headache."

"Never more than six hours. I won't do it. It only makes you feel worse."

"Good for you," Larry said, yawning again. He retrieved another chair from the lean-to and sat next to his friend. His feet rested on the sunken rocks that were covered in pine straw. "I checked on Jason. He seems good but might be sleeping. I can't tell."

"I know," Chip said. "I checked on him too. Made sure he had enough blankets and a nice fluffy pillow."

The morning air was calm, absent of noise. It was Larry's favorite part of camping. There were no cars driving by or lawnmowers buzzing, no neighbors using weed whackers or leaf blowers or pressure washing their house at 7 a.m. on a weekend. The silence nourished him and drew him into the wild. It enticed him to live there on a full-time basis.

He looked to the east and saw the sun rise among the oak trees and evergreens. The light filled the gaps with sharp golden beams. A picture like that deserved to be in a museum somewhere, signed by the artist and framed. He thought of Karen and set the alarm on his watch so he wouldn't forget to call her.

"Did you happen to bring any type of battery-operated coffee maker?" Chip asked. "Hell, I'd even settle for the instant kind."

"No, but I can offer you a diet soda if you need some caffeine."

"I'll pass."

Larry cleaned out the pit and started a fire. He convinced Chip to stop playing games long enough so they could untie Jason. Each of them stood beside the bed with a hand on the young man's elbow and when they lifted him to his feet, he was taller than both of them, especially Chip.

His bony shoulders framed his baggy shirt like an oversized tent and he scratched at his wrists that were red and irritated. A bottle of water was requested which they quickly gave him. After a trip to the outhouse, they ordered him to change. A shopping bag was thrown on the bed and they made sure he kept the hood pulled tight as he put on his hiking gear.

The clothes Larry bought were of the highest quality and he didn't skimp for a second on the material or price. The pants were a tough gray nylon, wind resistant, and could be unzipped at the knees. A Gore-Tex shirt was not only breathable but designed to wick away any moisture. Multi-layered socks that costs thirty dollars were advertised to prevent blisters and the boots were guaranteed to be the most waterproof footwear constructed.

They brought him outside for breakfast where he was fastened to a chair. Larry found the cast iron skillet hidden in the kitchen and set a grate above the fire. The aroma of crisp smoky bacon with fried eggs soon filled their noses. The trio ate quietly as the popping of grease accompanied them and he watched Jason the entire time. It amused him how Chip encouraged his son to eat, scooping more food onto his plate until there was nothing left.

Over the years, Larry studied Jason like an animal in the wild. He observed facial expressions and body language in an attempt to gauge thoughts or feelings on his subject's disposition. But the subject was usually stoic, and that morning remained no different. He couldn't conclude if Jason was rattled by the situation or merely settling in. Was it just one more environment to endure while waiting out a life sentence of misery?

After they finished breakfast, he unloaded the plywood from the truck, then the tools. He listened as Chip gave his second lecture of the morning. This one touched on dental hygiene. Chip stressed the importance of proper oral care and made Jason brush his teeth, floss, and rinse with Listerine. He explained that if a girlfriend was on the agenda then bad breath and bleeding gums were a deal-breaker. Yet, when Larry looked over, he saw him handing Jason a candy bar. He shook his head and would have to speak with his friend. Chip already acted too motherly and was turning out to be the sweetest kidnapper in the history of the world.

For the next several hours they repaired the cabin while Jason stayed tied to the chair with the headphones strapped over the hood. He didn't argue or fight or squirm in his seat, didn't ask any questions. Larry tried not to consider the implications of his son's passivity on the overall outcome of his plan.

Sheets of plastic that covered the windows were replaced with plywood and a fiberglass ladder leaned against the roof. Larry climbed atop the cabin with a chainsaw. He cut up fallen tree branches into log-size pieces and rolled them onto the ground where Chip assembled a chopping station. They swapped out sections of decayed roof decking, resealed the chimney, and unclogged the gutter. When the last new shingle was nailed down they noticed it didn't quite match in color.

"It's close enough," Chip said, perspiring through his shirt. He complained there was nothing to drink but water and diet soda. "We ain't going to no hardware store."

"Not too shabby for a couple amateurs," Larry said, approving of their work. It was already hot, even at 5,000 feet, and there was no wind at all. "I brought some stain for the door and thought we could fix some of the floorboards that buckled. What do you think about digging a drainage line off the backside? The water comes down hard there and the ground is sloped—"

"Ain't you forgettin' somethin'?" Chip said.

"I think I've got all the tools necessary. Could always run into town if we need more stuff while you stay and rest. Should only take me an hour."

"No, dummy. I mean him."

Larry peeked over to the chair and turned away. "I didn't forget. But things need to get done first."

"They seem damn well done to me. We have to . . ."

The image of his son tied to a chair like a prisoner at the hands of his own father was something from a horror movie. It didn't seem real. Larry didn't look in that direction all morning on purpose because for so many trips to the cabin he sat next to Jason in the exact same spot. They'd roast hot dogs on sticks or blacken marshmallows by the fire. Both of them would share what their favorite part of the day was.

They talked a lot back then, when Jason was younger, and not just about basketball or school. They talked about life. He missed those conversations more than watching his son score thirty-seven points in his first varsity game or come home with a straight A report card. To simply talk, about everything and nothing. It didn't get better than that. But no matter how much Larry tried, he couldn't get the talking back.

"You listenin' to me?" Chip asked. "I'm not sayin' this for my health."

He nodded yes but he wasn't. Didn't hear a word Chip said. Didn't want to hear it. What he wanted was to continue doing the repairs, to live in the fantasy that Jason had returned from a swim in the lake and warmed himself by the fire. He waited for his father to clean the fish they'd caught and prepare dinner so they could break out the telescope and view the stars. At least once a year the Turner men would visit the lake by themselves. Whenever it was time to leave, his son always asked to stay longer. He declared that someday he'd move to Lake Moonset as a permanent resident.

Larry knew he was stalling, didn't need Chip to state the obvious. But to remain frozen in the glorious past and disregard a bleak future—that's what he wanted. His procrastination was savored and allowed the extension of the moment, because there would never be another moment like that again.

Chip spoke to him further and finally reached up. He grabbed him by the cheeks and twisted his face toward Jason.

"This is why we're here! This is what you asked for! It ain't a social call. Now times a wastin'."

He tried to pull away but Chip squeezed him harder and the only thing he saw was the back of his son. They positioned him like that deliberately. The guilt spread inside Larry until he pushed Chip aside and hung his head in embarrassment. It was never imagined he'd actually have the courage or senselessness to follow through with his plan.

As a teacher and coach for more than twenty years, he'd seen and heard it all when it came to parents, however outrageous it may have been. He witnessed mothers defy logic concerning their children and watched fathers ignore basic reason. Now his name was stamped on top of that list.

The truck door dented when he walked over and kicked it. That was followed by the tossing of a wrench which spilled a coffee can full of nails. An idea that once seemed righteous from the inspiration of a TV show suddenly felt wrong. How much further would he take it? What if he stopped right away? Jason was out of the house, that was a good thing. He received some fresh air and seemed to eat better. What if the act of being kidnapped alone was enough to uncross his son's wires? What if he'd already been saved?

Larry began to backpedal. There had to be a way to escape his predicament. Couldn't he simply bring Jason home like nothing happened? Maybe. Was the kid so damaged he'd never say a word? Highly improbable. He'd heard of Julius Caesar's crossing the Rubicon from history class and never gave much thought to the event from two-thousand years ago in a faraway land. Until then.

Karen would interrogate him like a United States prosecutor the second he entered the door, then question Jason and Chip. If still unsatisfied, she'd drive up to the lake herself for a forensics exploration and canvass the area for witnesses. Larry would confess to the crime and beg for leniency. Leniency would not be granted.

What about if he too had been kidnapped and somehow escaped to safety? He could pretend to rescue Jason, then the two of them would ride off into the sunset eating ice cream perched high on top of horses. But what about Chip? And why would anybody want to kidnap either of them? And why would they go to the lake or the cabin? Didn't he already speak with Karen? It could've been the worst excuse of a story ever. Maybe Chip was right; perhaps Larry was a dummy. Perhaps he'd been conned into recklessness from the fear of losing everything.

The phrase *time and circumstance* popped into his mind—he'd said it to his students often. All aspects of science were reduced to those two elements, all aspects in life as well. Larry realized he had no alternative but to go through with the plan as a litany of clichés flashed before him. *The toothpaste is out of the tube. The baby is on the way. The horse is out of the barn.* He also knew when it was over, whether successful or not, he'd have to tell Jason about the plan and let him decide what to do. How else could he avoid any police involvement?

Chip strolled up beside him. "I know what you're thinkin', seen the puzzled look on your face all day. If you didn't question yourself I'd be worried. It's natural to be scared. Because this is crazy as hell, partner. But you dragged me up on this mountain and I don't know if it's the air or your cookin', but for the first time in a while, I feel kinda good. Good for me anyway."

Larry took comfort in the sincerity of his friend's voice. It helped a little. He cleared his throat and said, "I'm fine, Chip. Really. It's fine and you don't have to worry about—"

"Couldn't figure why you wanted me to come along at first, but I'm gettin' it. You can't do it on your own. Don't think any lovin' parent could. You stumbled at the house and you're stumblin' now. Bettin' you knew you would. But think about Pine View and think of your family. Think of what you told me and Pauline. I'm only sayin' this because we're right here, on the doorstep. And we're in kinda deep. The hard part is over and you can't stop this now. It's already in motion. You'd always be wonderin' if Jason never got better. So do what you said, and save him. Save them all. Because how much more miserable do you wanna be?"

Chip looked at the sky, then back to Larry. "I didn't try hard enough. Couldn't see it back then because the truth is, didn't wanna. But it's clear what I should've done, and it eats me. The cabin is fixed. We did enough for one day. Now let's go see about fixin' your son. You hear?"

"I hear."

"Good," Chip said, looking at the sky again. "Because I decided. I'm dedicatin' this trip for my own boy . . . This is gonna be for Wes."—his bottom lip started to quiver—"May the boy rest in peace." He then disappeared around the side of the cabin.

"May the boy rest in peace," Larry said. He gave the sign of the cross and stared at the mountains along the horizon. He asked for God's favor in what lay ahead. The hard part was over. He wanted to believe that. When he approached the fire pit and stood behind Jason, he was unaware that the hard part had yet to begin. It was time to head into the woods and lose themselves, to mimic the success of Edgar Suarez.

CHAPTER

The first three hours were easy. They trekked through the woods at a leisurely pace as Larry noted the trees and the fauna, using boulders or streams for landmarks. A deer eating leaves was spotted on a hillside. Several rabbits hopped out of and then back into the brush for safety. Squirrels raced up and down trees as if on some kind of stimulant, and birds of all colors chirped overhead. If it wasn't for the fact that Jason walked in front of them with a rope cinched around his waist, they could've been good friends exploring Mother Nature on a warm sunny day.

The hood was off so Jason could see while the kidnappers resumed wearing their masks, which they constantly scratched underneath. They gave him twelve feet of slack but kept the rope snug as a precaution. Larry decided it was too soon to let him go and grew fearful of him running away. If he'd run at all.

On their second water break, Jason spoke for the only time that afternoon. "Where we going?" he asked.

Chip looked at his partner and shrugged. "That's for us to know and you to find out." The comment had the maturity of a fourth grader arguing with a classmate, but Chip wasn't prepared for questions. What he was prepared for was talking. His mouth wouldn't quit. It relaxed him to talk, that's what he said, and it was the first time he'd been in the woods since hunting.

Chip spouted a continuous dialogue of parental guidance and suggestions. He combined spiritual inspiration with fatherly advice and Larry wanted to chime in too because there were so many things he desired to say. But he couldn't. So he listened. He listened while Chip spoke in a lighthearted tone and started referring to Jason as *buddy*.

When they halted for a reading on the compass, Larry requested his accomplice reel in the therapeutic bombardment. He was asked to cease the joviality. They were kidnappers after all, working an alleged scheme for some type of ransom. The experience was supposed to be scary.

But Chip dismissed him. He explained they were things the boy needed to hear and it might just help to come from a stranger. It's what he should've said before and he wasn't going to stop, because he couldn't. He would never miss another opportunity again. Larry didn't know if Chip talked to Jason when he spoke, or maybe the ghost of Wes. He decided it was likely a little of both.

Upon reaching Flagler's Hill, they encountered their first real challenge of the day. The terrain was steep and not really a hill at all, belying an erroneous name that somehow managed to stick. It didn't require a rope and harness or professional climbing gear, but the angle was such to demand significant effort and conditioning.

It was doable for Larry. He worked out twice weekly on an elliptical machine during the school year and constantly traversed ladders in the summer. But the story was much different for Chip, the man whose concept of a cardiovascular activity was to get the mail from the mailbox. As for Jason, Larry figured he'd struggle too from months of inactivity. It was a striking contrast to his son's days of being a stellar athlete.

They walked as far as possible, slowly, and zigzagged back and forth in a switchback pattern. Frequent stops were made to breathe. Trees were used to anchor themselves and Larry led the way with Jason in the middle. When the hill grew steeper, they grabbed onto low hanging branches and plants for support. All three of them resorted to crawling the last 500 feet to the summit. Chip grunted the entire way as if he may die and while Jason moved cautiously, he did so without making any noise.

For the countless times Larry hiked at Lake Moonset, he'd only been the way they traveled once. It was for Jason's thirteenth birthday. He took him on the arduous trek to try something different, but halfway up Flagler's Hill they retreated. With no definitive paths, the wilderness was too dangerous and rugged. He intended to return one day when his son got older.

Most of their hikes were either toward the lake itself where they wound up swimming or to the south which contained miles of well-marked trails. If a person headed toward Flagler's Hill it meant they were going north. And north was an endless acreage of open wild even most of the locals avoided.

Larry had dirt in his mouth and leaves inside his shirt when he neared the top. He kept an eye on his son, worrying if their surroundings would somehow be recognized. But then he thought better of it. Eight years passed since they last hiked there, and Jason was still only a kid. Besides, to the novice hiker everything appeared the same.

Row after row of pines were in every direction, mixed in with sycamores, cedars, and redwoods. A canopy of dense green towered above. Trees struck by lightning or rotted from disease covered the ground and there was an unlimited variety of plants.

Chip lay on his back after cresting the hill and sprawled out in the tall dry grass, sucking in air like a vacuum. Larry rested on all fours. He drew long, steady breaths and measured his pulse with a watch. Jason bent over and gripped his knees. He glanced at the captors and opened his mouth as if to speak, then turned away.

The sky was a soft baby blue and a lone puffy cloud drifted across it, changing shapes as it went. Larry stood to take in the view of the majestic valley below. The lake glittered in the sunlight and the water was gilded, sparkling like a sacred jewel in the wild. An escarpment of exposed cliffs were to the east with a vertical rock face at least a thousand feet tall. To the west was Herrington's Peak, the highest elevation in the range. It was frosted on top with snow.

The wind blew for the first time all day and provided much-needed relief. Larry hoped observing a landscape so beautiful could serve as inspiration. Some people found God in nature or a higher power of their own understanding. Others found degrees of salvation. He wasn't sure what Jason would discover but believed viewing such grandeur had to convey there were forces in the world much larger than any one person.

Chip, finally able to talk again, declared that he was going to get in shape. So was Pauline. She'd quit smoking and he'd reduce his sweets. The grocery store was only a mile away from their RV. From now on he'd walk instead of drive, then do ten push-ups and twenty crunches.

He said to Jason, "You gotta stay in shape, buddy. Don't let yourself get a gut like me. Girls don't want guys with guts, like they got a basketball glued to their stomach and are lookin' all pregnant. And speakin' of basketball, you need to get back on the court again. I heard you were once pretty good."

Jason looked at him and his eyes narrowed. He stepped as if he may charge. Larry gripped the rope tight and pulled, redirecting his son's eyes toward the valley. He glared at his friend and pointed to a bush near a boulder the size of a car.

"Man, that feels good," Chip said, removing his mask. "This thing is itchin' like crazy."

Larry took off his mask too and wrung the sweat from it. The fresh air soothed his scratchy skin. "Maybe so, but it needs to stay on until we let him go."

"My head feels like it's wrapped in plastic wearin' that thing, like I'm gonna suffocate."

"Listen, Chip, you can't get so personal with him. Tone it down. You mentioned Pauline's name out loud."

"Guess I forgot where I was for a moment. That hill just about did me in."

"You're doing great but dial it back, keep it together. You're leaving too many clues."

"Got it. I'll be more careful. And put your mask back on. He sees my face it's one thing. He sees yours and it's all over."

They stayed behind the bush for a minute to catch a few more breezes and Larry wondered about Jason's reaction if he walked over to him and confessed. What if they'd gone far enough? What if it was time for a confrontation? He sipped some water, changed his mind, and considered something else. Perhaps in dealing with his son since the cutting and the pills and incident number two, there was an aspect of the situation that had been overlooked.

Perhaps if Jason lived in the woods he could be happy, or at least functional. Maybe they should've moved him to the cabin years ago. Some people can't handle the clutter of the suburbs or the overload of information and technology. The increased speed of society was too great. They needed to get away from it all and unplug to a simpler lifestyle. Why hadn't he thought of that before? A change of scenery. It seemed like common sense.

He recalled the image of an attractive dark-haired woman from his support group who spoke with a slight lisp. Her name was Julie Markham, and her daughter committed suicide at the age of fifteen. She slit her wrists in the bathtub on Thanksgiving. The disillusioned girl filmed the entire tragedy and streamed it online to say good-bye. Her departure was preserved somewhere on the internet, haunting her family forever. Cyberbullying was the reason she cited for ending her short life and wrecking those left behind. Whatever happened to Julie Markham, he didn't know. She came to the meetings for a couple months and then disappeared like so many parents, including Karen.

"If we stay here much longer I'm fixin' to cramp up or shut this puppy down," Chip said.

Larry capped his water bottle and withdrew from the notion that technology was responsible for the condition of his son. Even if it were a contributing factor, nothing could be done. It wasn't going away and would only get worse. Most of the students he taught or coached were fine. So were his daughters. To pack your belongings and move into the woods like a recluse wouldn't solve anything either. At least not long-term.

Problems were persistent. They were clingy. Neither Jason nor Karen nor Larry could outrun them because they'd simply pack a bag and take the ride too. It was a reach to think of such things, but that's what he'd been doing for the last five years. He reached for anything that would make sense.

Potassium pills and beef jerky were distributed before they set out again. When they did, albeit slower than before, the trio regained their formation. They waded through a fast-running creek where the water reached their thighs and descended a long gradual slope that led to a stagnant pond. Larry checked his compass every half-hour to stay on course and prevent them from wandering in a circle—which he knew was easy to do. More inclines, more switchbacks, more grunting from Chip. When they stopped for another water break, Jason was tied to a tree so the captors could fall back and talk.

"We're close," Larry said. "Not too much further. We let him go in the morning, but meanwhile be sure to contact Pauline so she doesn't worry. Tell her Jason's safe, that we're all doing good. Let's not make this harder on her than it has to be."

"I tried."

"What do you mean?"

"My phone's dead."

"I warned you about playing those games. They chew up your battery."

"Well I like them. And I find them distractin'."

"Use my phone then."

"How the hell am I supposed to do that, Larry? I don't know the number."

"You don't know your own wife's number?"

"I don't know anybody's number. Neither do you. I already looked through your phone at the cabin, and you ain't got it either."

Larry squeezed between his eyes as if trying to release a pressure valve. "I don't call her that much because I usually talk with you. I use the house phone a lot and I have an address book."

"There you go, we both messed up. Don't worry about Pauline. She'll be alright. Now, how much longer are we gonna hike? My feet are killin' me."

"A few more miles," Larry said. He rummaged through his backpack and brought out a map. After unfolding it, he pointed. "There's an abandoned fire tower along that ridge. It'll give us a focal point. We'll nudge him toward it when he gets released and beyond that, maybe fifteen miles or so, is the highway. When Jason reaches the tower, it'll be our cue to sweep in. I'd say that gives him at least two days alone in the woods. We'll tell him we settled with the kidnappers then hike to the road and hitch a ride back to the cabin . . . I only hope it's enough time for him to discover something, or at least give me what I need."

Chip wagged a finger. "They got the wrong guy, didn't they? The doctors and Pine View and everyone else. Got it stone-cold wrong."

"Huh?" Larry said, squinting.

"They want to send *him* to Virginia? The kid over there tied to a tree. Maybe it should be you instead. Me too for going along. How the hell did I let you talk me into this thing? It ain't never gonna work."

"You said you were onboard. What about that speech this morning?"

"I lied, and my feet didn't hurt then. I didn't feel like I was gonna die either. And I haven't taken my pills in a while because they can make me lazy and I knew we'd be walkin' to Timbuktu."

"I need you to take your pills," Larry said. "Right now. If you get too tired we'll stop, but remember, you're dedicating this for Wes. It's for your boy now as well."

He felt bad playing the Wes card, but another meltdown couldn't be risked.

Chip meandered over to a bubbling stream and kneeled. He pumped everyone's water bottles full using the filter, then popped a few pills. His socks were off and he picked at a raw spot on his heel when Larry sat beside him.

"Here, these'll make your feet feel better," he said, and handed over a fresh pair of socks.

"Thanks."—Chip sighed and the tension fell from his voice—"I almost forgot to ask. How's Karen dealin' with him bein' away? Did she lose it last night?"

"I think we both did," Larry said. "It got kind of ugly. I should be able to keep her at bay long enough to get this done, although part of me expects her to rappel down from that tree over there any second and start an inquisition. I guess it'll be a day to day thing."—he glanced over at Jason, ensuring he was still there—"Did you see the way he looked at the lake today, when we had that spectacular view atop Flagler's Hill? That kind of stuff can change people's perspective. The power of nature. You ever read anything by John Muir or Henry David Thoreau?"

Chip laughed. "Yeah, I saw how he looked at the lake. With a rope around his waist in a backwoods wilderness and a couple crazy bastards standin' behind him wearin' ski masks. I'm sure he was writin' poetry."

"That's not very funny."

"C'mon, it's a little funny. You gotta laugh at what we're doin' when you think about it. Could it be more absurd?"

"Not now I don't. There's too much at stake."

"People like us, Larry, we're either laughin' or cryin'. And it's mostly cryin'. Take the laughs when you can get them."

Larry zipped up his pack and stood. "Tie your boots tight and let's get a move on." The smile faded from Chip's face and he knew his friend was correct. It was absurd. But what was the alternative? To lose his family? To send Jason to Pine View? Was it absurd that Jason unraveled to begin with?

A spot circled in red on the map and labeled as *Night 1* was their destination. They arrived as dusk settled in and the bugs became predatory. Larry lit a fire for Jason and another thirty feet away for him and Chip. It would be the last time they bound his son like a hostage, and he was thankful about that.

He set up the tents while Chip cooked dinner and gave his final lecture of the evening. This one covered the importance of respecting your family. He heard his friend ask, "You understand what I mean, buddy?" and then not much else. Chip started to snore before finishing his meal.

Although physically exhausted, Larry felt mentally energized. He tried not to close his eyes because as surreal as the circumstances were, he camped with Jason again. His boy was not in a bed like some zombie waiting to be hauled off to Pine View. He was among the living. The possibility of incident number three seemed further and further away. Right or wrong, they'd done more in one day together than the last several years combined, and if that's how it all ended, Larry made peace with that.

He felt good as the fire dwindled and the chill set in. They had a positive first day, achieved a great deal of progress, and his conversation with Karen went smoother than expected. He hesitated to believe her reserved demeanor but perhaps she'd conceded. Perhaps she saw the importance of letting him have some time with their son. Everything he planned seemed to be falling into place.

Larry slipped into the dream world with his confidence high and he envisioned the next day being even better. The man couldn't have been further mistaken.

CHAPTER

Four quick knocks reverberated off the front door and it surprised her. Visitors didn't come around much anymore, especially that early in the morning. She'd finished loading the minivan and puttered around the house waiting for Melissa to arrive. Her phone was checked every five minutes. After each new updated text from her daughter that she'd be late, Karen regretted asking her to come along.

She sprang to the door and looked through the peephole before opening it. The person standing on the stoop was easily recognized. How could they not be? How many people had a white streak parting the center of their hair?

"Pauline?" she said, half as a statement, half as a question.

"Hi, Karen."

"What brings you by? How long has it been?"

"At least a few years. I think at a meeting or maybe you stopped over the RV with Larry. I can't quite remember."

They stared at each other and grinned. Karen folded her arms like a bouncer guarding the entrance at a nightclub and wasn't sure what to say. *Why was this woman here?* she thought. She caught herself being rude and stepped aside. "I'm sorry, Pauline. Where are my manners? Please, come in. Would you like some coffee?"

"That'd be nice."

They bypassed sitting at the dining room table and opted to stand in the kitchen instead. Karen didn't serve any cookies or pastries or cake. She forgot to offer cream or sugar, milk or Splenda, and both of their coffees were taken black. They engaged in small talk about the recent hot weather and the new construction project widening the Augustine Bridge.

She didn't want to leave Melissa behind but after seeing the clock on the microwave, she no doubt would. Karen refused to wait around all day, refused to play the game. There were too many times she'd been burned when one of the girls bailed on their plans at the last moment.

"I haven't heard from Chip," Pauline said. "He's not answering his phone. That's kind of why I'm here. I don't know exactly where they went. Have you talked to him?"

"He didn't tell you?"

"Sometimes he does that. But usually he'll drive around town for a few hours until he returns."

"They're up at our cabin, at Lake Moonset. Larry went to repair it from the storms. We're putting it on the market if you know anybody who's interested. Your husband went with him to help."

Pauline picked at her French tip fingernails. "Did they, uh . . . bring Jason?"

"How'd you know that?" Karen said. She paused. "Why would you know that?"

"Larry discussed it the other night, after the meeting. Said he was going to ask Jason to do something."

"He did? He told me it was a spur of the moment thing."

"Well, he wasn't sure if he was going to ask, only thinking about it . . . This is really good coffee. What kind is it?"

A pang of jealousy swirled inside Karen as her lips stiffened. How could this woman know what was going on with her son, and *she* didn't? What had Larry said to her? What had he shared? She looked at the clock again and decided not to wait much longer.

"Jason did go with him. I still can't believe it. He never goes anywhere and then wham, he's off to the lake like it's an everyday thing. I'm driving up there myself to see what's going on. As soon as my daughter gets here. If she ever does."

"It's unlike Chip to not call. I'm sure he's fine, he's a grown man and all. I didn't want to bother Larry."

"You drove all the way over here instead of calling my husband? Aren't you guys friends?"

"Seems a bit much, doesn't it? The truth is . . . I wanted to see you. To see how you're doing?"

Karen exhaled and dumped her coffee in the sink. "Did Larry put you up to this? Is this some kind of a meeting, like an intervention? Because I'm totally not interested."

"No. It's not about that, but there's something you need—"

"Sorry I'm late," Melissa yelled as she barged into the house and entered the kitchen. Her friend Sammy was behind her. "I haven't been up this early since like school got out."

"It's almost nine o'clock," Karen said. "Are you serious?"

"Exactly. It's almost nine o'clock. Anyway, we're here. When do we leave?"

"We leave now. Throw everything in the car and I'll meet you outside."

"Did you hear from Sarah?" Melissa asked.

Karen shook her head no and left it at that. Her oldest daughter never responded to the invite.

"I've got to go," she said to Pauline. "It was nice of you to stop by, but as you can see I'm busy. I'll tell Chip to call you when I see him." She stepped toward the front door and expected her guest to follow, but they didn't budge.

"I want to come along. Larry has mentioned the cabin so many times over the years, I'd love to see it. I don't mean to be forward but, would you mind? I think I can help."

"What do you mean by help?"

"Maybe I can fix something. Believe it or not, I'm fairly handy."

Believe it not, Karen thought.

Her first instinct was to hop in the car and peel from the driveway as fast as possible. She didn't want this woman she hardly knew to tag along, fearing Pauline may want to talk. And not about food or fashion or something light. But she'd want to talk about the other stuff—the serious stuff that was to be avoided. Karen would've preferred a visit to the dentist or to wait in line at an amusement park rather than discuss her feelings.

She then considered the length of the trip, the hours behind the wheel. Melissa would be asleep by the time they pulled onto the highway and neither of her daughters were good travel companions anymore. If they weren't snoozing or texting, they listened to their own private music with earbuds in. The days of singing to the car radio together were long gone—so was the concept of a conversation. Karen didn't want to admit it, but part of her was lonely.

If she could only have friends on her own terms. If people only knew how to stay out of her business. But she understood it would never happen, and that's why she'd pushed so many of them away. To protect herself. To protect her family. Maybe they should relocate to a different part of the state and start all over, a place where nobody knew them. They could begin . . .

"Or if you feel more comfortable, tell me the address and I'll drive up myself," Pauline said after no response was given. "I think it's important that I go. For me to be there."

Karen washed both coffee mugs and proceeded to dry them before putting them away. She was annoyed that Chip's wife stopped over unannounced. But why did she mention Jason? "No use taking more than one vehicle all the way there. I guess we should try to save the environment. If you really want to, you can hitch a ride with us."

"Much appreciated, sweetie."

A quick jaunt to the store to load up on snacks was followed by a detour at McDonald's. Soon the minivan smelled of pancakes and maple syrup. Karen navigated the dense morning traffic of the suburbs eating a hash brown. She glanced at Pauline from the corner her eye and noticed her stare out the window, spinning the wedding band on her ring finger. *Where to begin?* she thought. *How to initiate a generic but interesting discussion?*

At the museum, Karen spoke with patrons and guests all the time as part of her job. She never found it difficult. But this was different. It felt like anything she said could potentially be a landmine leading to a therapy session. That's probably why Pauline was there. Larry must have instigated it. For some reason, the only thing she could think of was the tragic shooting of Wes.

The story she read online about the Waltzer boy was heartbreaking and the tidbits provided by Larry only made it worse. Without realizing it, Karen had prejudged the woman who sat next to her. Opinions were formed and assumptions made. Pauline Waltzer was nothing but a poor, broken mother who'd been an ancillary victim of her son's psychotic murderous rampage. She would never be able to function properly again. Or was she part of the cause? What could she have done to that child? What kind of a home life fosters that evil behavior?

When Karen caught herself thinking this, it confounded her. The thoughts were instinctual, devoid of facts or reasoning. The frustration ballooned inside, filling her chest, because that's how she believed people viewed her—as a bad mother who did something wrong. And it wasn't right.

So why did she judge the woman so quickly, so harshly? Why did she constantly judge herself too? It was a mistake to bring Pauline along. The proximity to her was a trigger and stirred too many emotions, messing with Karen's mind. But now she was stuck. She pressed the gas harder and tailgated the car ahead of her. Why did she answer the front door?

They turned left off Route 71 and got rerouted because of an accident. When they reached the highway the traffic had thinned, and the girls were asleep in the back. The sun was bright, piercing the windows. She lowered the visor as the tires cut loudly through the air.

A Beatles song played lightly on the radio, and after adjusting the volume of the classic rock station, she slouched in her seat. The puzzlement of why this person arrived at her home persisted. There was no way Pauline came along to help—Karen was sure of it. Her mascara was flawless, she wore an expensive perfume, and her clothes were better suited for lunch at a high-end restaurant; not swinging a hammer in the woods. Besides, the woman couldn't have weighed more than a hundred pounds if she had stones in her pockets.

"The problem was I only had one," Pauline said.

"I beg your pardon."

"I only had one child."

Here we go, Karen thought, suppressing the desire to sigh. "Why is that a problem?"

"That's what Roy LaGrange from the meetings told me. He's got six. But I only had the one. There was a miscarriage before Wes and even his birth was complicated. Roy said when you only have one it's like putting all your eggs in a single basket."

"You know he's an idiot, right? For saying something so ignorant. Some people don't have any kids. You're lucky to have at least one."

"Had," Pauline said. "Past tense. Had."—she started to light a cigarette without asking for permission, but stopped—"I don't know why I let his comment get to me after all these years. But it seems if you have more than one, it might be easier."

"It isn't . . . Not that Jason is gone. In some respects it's even harder because you worry how it affects your other children."

"I know you haven't lost him, but you got three. I can't help thinking if I had that many and one of them suffered an issue, I could fall back on the rest. Maybe it's the law of numbers."

"Are you saying it doesn't hurt as much when you lose one, physically or mentally, maybe both, because you have more kids? I don't see the logic in that."

Pauline sparked the lighter and the tobacco snapped. She puffed a greedy drag, cracking the window to exhale. "You're probably right, but I'll never know."

"It's not too late, if you really want to."

"This ain't the Bible, sweetie. I'm not the wife of Abraham. Women in the real world don't have babies at my age."

"You could always adopt or maybe get a foster child. There are plenty of good kids out there who need homes."

"We're past that stage," Pauline said. She flicked her ash out the window and cracked it further. "Wes was our *one* and I'm not sure Chip could handle a number two."

The conversation ended as abruptly as it began. Karen was relieved about that. They drove quietly past giant farms of almonds, figs, and olives. Windmills and cell towers were dispersed on the landscape and when they reached the base of the mountains, she observed road signs that warned in winter conditions, four-wheel drive vehicles were required. Otherwise, it was mandatory to stop and have chains wrapped on the tires. The air conditioner blasted away as the minivan climbed higher and higher, the engine strained. The girls were now awake and watched videos on their phones. Pauline, once more out of nowhere, spoke.

"I hope I didn't make you too uncomfortable, with what I said. But it bothered me. You see, this is what we do, honey, at the meetings. We come together for a greater understanding. I don't know how or why, but it works. It's a good way to connect with others and keep it together. You ought to swing by."

"Maybe," Karen said. She leaned against the door and moved her face closer to the window. The drive couldn't end fast enough. "I'll think about it."

Larry's truck was parked out front when they arrived, but there was no sign of anyone. A pile of empty soda cans were found near the fire pit. Karen looked at the cabin. The new shingles they put up didn't quite match in color. She hated to be difficult, but the roof would have to be redone.

She tapped the plywood that covered the windows and wondered why they weren't replaced. A trip to the hardware store was atop the agenda when her husband returned. Once inside the cabin, she swept the floor, then made the beds. Every available surface was wiped down and sanitized.

Upon further inspection she discovered a small wad of tape wedged near the fireplace. It was gray and sticky, similar to the one found in Jason's room. She stared at it. What could it have been used for? Why was there tape both at home and at the cabin? She put the wad in her pocket and continued to spray a bottle of air freshener.

"Like, where is everyone?" Melissa asked as she and Sammy entered. They covered their noses. "I think you've got it, Mom. Smells like a lemon bomb went off in here."

"They must be out fishing. Why don't you girls get changed and we'll hike to the lake?"

Karen went outside and saw Pauline in one of the chairs by the fire pit. "We're going for a swim," she said. "You coming?"

"I'm gonna wait here and work on this scarf. Just need to get the yarn from my bag. You three go on."

The trail was still visible between the encroachment of flowers and weeds. It dipped thirty feet in the beginning before leveling off. Karen and the girls carried towels and bottles of water as they walked across it, their bodies shining from the SPF 50. They saw blackberries and blueberries and a gigantic tree trunk that was hollowed at the base from weathering. The winding path curled around one final segment of ferns then segued onto a pebble laden beach.

Lake Moonset contained no sand, only rocks, but the lake itself was magnificent. The water was blue and refreshingly cool all summer long. It stretched to the left like an ocean, as far as one could see. To the right, the shoreline was bordered by thick, healthy evergreens. Straight ahead were the high peaks renowned for their mountain climbing.

The girls waded in the water up to their waist. They complained how cold it was and splashed each other, telling one another to stop. Karen broke out her cell phone and dialed Larry. It went directly to voicemail. "I'm here," she said with a scowl. "Where are you?"

She removed her shoes and joined the girls in the lake. Where could he have taken their son? Why now? Why was Pauline at the cabin? A strange sensation came over her, like frigid air blowing down her neck. Something felt wrong. Perhaps it was her lack of sleep or the increased anxiety about Jason leaving. But Karen didn't want to overreact. Not yet. Her husband would've called if there was a problem, wouldn't he? She decided to wait ten minutes then dial the number again.

CHAPTER 31

An ant crawled across Larry's cheek and woke him. He instinctively slapped it, smushing the insect on his face. He wiped his hand on the sleeping bag and sat up. The tent was bright, the air stale. His surroundings were unfamiliar. He licked his lips as his mouth was dry and searched for the bottle of water. The intensity of thirst reminded him about the ease of dehydration in the mountains.

Big quenching gulps washed down his throat and with the first few movements of the day he felt much sorer than expected. He took some aspirin and ventured outside into the coolness where Chip stood with a pair of binoculars, peering into the woods.

Larry dragged himself up slowly and favored his left knee. He touched his cheek. The area began to tingle and burn. When he touched it again, he assumed the ant had its final say before getting squashed.

"What're you looking at?" he asked in a hushed tone.

"Jason."

Larry rubbed his eyes, then stared ahead. "Where?"

"He went that way," Chip said, pointing.

"What do you mean by *that way*? Why are you standing over here?"

The binoculars dangled from Chip's neck as he scratched his chin. "I've been awake for hours. Slept hard for a while, then wide-eyed as a buzzard. Came out to sit by the fire even though it was embers when I heard Jason. He called me and we got to talkin'."

"Jason spoke to you?" Larry said. He tried to make sense of the details as his morning fog lifted. "Where's the rope? Why isn't Jason tied to the rope?"

"It was mostly me talkin'. I told him how I worked in the construction business and all the places I been, includin' that six-month stint in Dubai."

"Is he tied to a tree? Is that what you're saying? And where's your mask?"

"Over there on the ground. I'm done wearin' that thing. Like I said, we were talkin' and I mentioned how you gotta do right from wrong. I told him what Wes did was wrong, it was selfish."

"You talked about Wes?"

"Sure as shit did. It felt good too. He's here in these woods with me, I can feel him."

"Where's Jason?" Larry asked, his voice getting loud. There was an uptick in his pulse. "Where'd he go, Chip?"

"As we're talkin' he tells me he's gotta take a piss. So I cut him free because you gotta go, you gotta go. I was standin' right there. Right there. I figured it was no big deal seein' as he'd been so good yesterday. The next thing I know, he turned into somebody else, like an Olympic sprinter. He was fast, man. Took his backpack and ran that away about ten minutes ago."

Larry dove into the tent and grabbed his compass. "It's still north," he said as he rotated the needle of the instrument and came back out. He pulled on a shirt hurriedly and buckled his pants. "At least he's still heading north."

"I was about to—"

"Goddammit Chip! How could you let this happen? Why didn't you wake me?"

"I was gonna tell, I swear. Hoped he'd come back before you got up."

"Why would you untie him on your own? You know better." Larry turned away and continued to speak, but more to himself. "Maybe he heard us talking about the fire tower and the freeway. That's our only chance. There's a compass in his bag and he knows how to use it. Otherwise he could be anywhere."—he let that sink in—"Oh my God! He could be anywhere!"

His hands shook while he put on his socks and he struggled tying his boots. He wanted to tear into Chip further for being so careless, for being an idiot; to get right in his face and scold him. Had it been anybody else, he would have. But he couldn't.

Chip wore a bewildered expression as if somebody stole his lunch money and he was clueless how it happened. The only person for Larry to be mad at was himself. He knew the risk in bringing his unbalanced friend. What kind of selfish person thrusts somebody like that into a high-pressure situation? Had it not been for his urging, Chip would be at the RV doing whatever he does all day.

This can't be happening, he told himself. His heart pumped like it might explode as he zipped up his pack. *This can't be freaking happening.*

"Jason!" Chip yelled into the tranquil air. "Jason! C'mon back, buddy. You don't wanna do this! Please! I promise to bring you home!"—he swung his foot and kicked a cloud of dirt as the tears dripped from his eyes—"I'm sorry, Larry. I'm so, so sorry. I . . . I didn't think he'd run like that. Thought I was gettin' through to him, that we were bondin' . . . He was standin' right there."

"I have to go," Larry said.

"Please. I can't lose another one."

"I know you didn't mean it."

"Not on my watch. I—" Chip started to gag and his face turned red. He struggled to breathe. For a second Larry thought he may faint.

"Let's sit you down," he said, clutching Chip's shoulder. "Big breaths. Count to ten. In and out. That's it. Keep breathing."—he gave him some water—"It's not your fault. But I have to go now, and it'll be by myself."

"I . . . I can't come?"

"You won't be able to keep up. It'll be faster this way. Once I get him I'll come back for you, so don't go anywhere."

"You'll find him, Larry, won't you? You're gonna find my buddy?"

"Yes. And when I do, I'll walk straight up and confront him. It's time to put this experiment to an end."

"He just took off," Chip said, staring vacantly into the woods. "He was standin' right there. We were talkin' . . . We were talkin'."

Larry slung the backpack over his shoulders and added the binoculars. He too left his mask on the ground. "It's not your fault," was the last thing he said before disappearing into the underbrush.

For the first half-mile he jumped over logs, plowed through bushes, and sprinted as fast as he could. He screamed Jason's name frantically. But like an inexperienced racer who marched from the gate too strong, he couldn't sustain the pace. The sprinting devolved to a run, which led to a jog, and after sixty minutes of the most intense workout of his life, Larry had to walk.

The terrain was steep, undulating. A person was unable to look blindly ahead for fear they may trip on a rock or step in a hole. Even a minor accident like an ankle sprain equaled a death sentence when hiking alone and nobody knew your location.

With every frenetic step he took, a sense of foreboding overcame him. Larry wished he'd put some kind of beacon or tracking device inside Jason's bag and he'd briefly considered bringing a flare gun. A set of walkie talkies seemed a prudent move in hindsight.

He tried not to think of hindsight—that vicious cruel element of the mind where everything was so obvious—but he couldn't help speculating on the ruination of their lives if he never found Jason. To lose a child from suicide was a horrific ordeal no parent should suffer through. But to lose a child because they disappeared multiplied the agony.

There was no closure in a disappearance, no body to view or funeral to attend. The parents would always be taunted by the brutality of hope. Maybe if they uncovered one more stone, searched one more clue or followed up on another lead; their child might still be alive. It was especially harsh—hope— and Larry knew Karen wouldn't be able to handle it. Nor would he. To lose physical sight of Jason was never part of the plan.

He climbed a hill near a waterfall and stopped to catch his breath. The landscape had been scoured for footprints or a torn piece of clothing, and it surprised him he hadn't found Jason already. How did his son not surrender to the elements? Why didn't he sit next to a tree or rest alongside a stream waiting to get rescued? The pain in Larry's knee now throbbed and a slight limp formed. As he continued to walk down his own road to hell regardless of any good intentions, he realized he'd succeeded.

How many times did he tell his kids, as his parents told him, "Be careful what you wish for."? The irony dawned on him that he wanted Jason to fight, to show he had a flicker of light left inside. That's all he asked. By taking off into the woods, his son confirmed what he needed to know. His plan, as ill-conceived and ill-advised as it had been, proved to be effective. And it may have cost him everything.

A twig cracked behind him and he instantly spun around. But rather than lock eyes with Jason, he stared at a red fox. The animal sized him up to be too large a prey for a meal and scurried away. Dejected, Larry stared in the fox's direction and thought about his son, about the good times they'd once had. He then considered Chip. Would he ever see the man again? Would Chip stay put as instructed or wander into the unknown? His friend could die out there and so could Jason. If Larry didn't find his boy soon, he'd be as good as dead too.

The search resumed. His body and face were covered in scratches and cuts, stinging with sweat. Three times he bent over and dry-heaved. Once he kneeled to vomit. He wasn't sure if the nausea was anxiety related or purely fatigue, but that was before his phone rang. That was before the concept of worry became redefined to a level never imagined.

CHAPTER

The caller ID flashed the name KAREN. There's no way he'd take that call less somebody shoved a gun to his temple and threatened to pull the trigger. It was early afternoon. A phone call from his wife should be expected and he'd deal with her later. First, a story of some sort needed to be concocted. Maybe he'd have Jason in his grasp by then. But later came sooner than expected when he checked the message and his wife said, "I'm here. Where are you?"

Larry listened to it again and again, trying to convince himself he'd heard it wrong. Karen's tone sounded tense and smoldering. Her words twisted a screw inside him.

"Why, why, why couldn't you leave it alone?" he screamed into the woods, punching the air repeatedly. "Ahhhhhhhhh! Ahhhhhhhhh!" He cupped his mouth as his brain melted. "Jason, are you out there? You have to come back! For the sake of your mother, you have to!" The plea to his son ricocheted off the mountain and bounced off the trees.

He tightened his backpack and ran again. His legs were re-energized, his breath felt strong. He dashed to the left, hopped to the right, crisscrossed and zigzagged his way through a mile burst of frenzy sprinkled with mania. Everything was a blur. He ignored the pain. He ran faster and faster, screaming Jason's name. But adrenaline could only take a person so far and was meant for short bursts of intensity, not a marathon in the woods.

His legs burned while his lungs gobbled up the air. Larry tried to will himself to push harder, that he wasn't tired. But still exhausted from the previous day's hike, his middle-aged body took longer to recover than expected.

Another hour of walking and screaming and pleading—no hint of Jason. He stopped and wrapped his arms around the sticky bark of a pine tree. His body was rubbery, his voice was hoarse. Larry closed his eyes and rested. It felt nice not to move. If he wasn't careful, he could've stayed there all day.

Three more calls, three more angry messages were left on his phone. He turned off the ringer. It was imperative to speak to Karen immediately. She would never leave the cabin without their son, but he hadn't a clue what to say. Honesty was not always the best policy for if it was, Larry could've come out and said, "I lost Jason after kidnapping him and don't know if I can find him. Because I think I'm lost myself. And I think I'm having an allergic reaction to an ant bite because my face feels hot and I've got welts on my arms." No, now was not the moment to sacrifice himself out of fear.

Time and circumstance, he reminded himself. *Time and circumstance*. How could he spin what transpired? How much more time did he think he could buy? He needed to find Jason before the situation worsened, before Karen summoned the National Guard or brought in the Green Berets. The call had to be made right there, right then. That was the only remedy. He pushed a hand through his hair and exhaled, pressing number two on speed dial.

She answered on the first millisecond of the first ring and blustered at him like a speed talker. Larry wasted but only a minute. He interrupted her and breathed extra hard for effect. "We're in the midst of a major league hike. Jason's ahead of me and Chip's in the rear. No, no. Everything's fine. What? I think we're breaking up."

It was a lame trick and a pathetic excuse and he was certain Karen saw right through it. But what could he do? "I can't hear you," he said. "If you can hear me, we'll be back at the cabin tomorrow. Maybe the next day. We're finally hiking Herrington's Peak and we check off number seven on the list now. Don't worry, Jason's doing great. He's in much better shape than we thought. It's tough to keep up with him. Huh? What? I think we're breaking up." And with that, he hung up.

He continued to lean against the tree as the lactic acid settled in his calves and made his legs feel twice as heavy. It was imperative to walk again before he grew stiff. The knee pain intensified and he guessed it was tendonitis or bursitis, maybe arthritis. Larry swallowed more aspirin, disheartened at his aches and fatigue. He considered himself in good shape, which he was, when using the elliptical machine in an air-conditioned gym. Even traversing a ladder numerous times a day was no match for a vigorous slog through the mountains.

His strides got smaller, leaner. He screamed Jason's name until his throat was scraped raw and a blood vessel popped in his eye. Every step he took was akin to moving through a puddle of sludge. But Larry soldiered on. Eventually he made his way from the shade of the forest into a sun-soaked field.

Bees buzzed and butterflies danced about as they pollinated flowers. The rich sweet nectar of buttercups and purple lilacs were fed upon. He found a spot to sit down and assess his wounds, to give himself time to think. The rescue of Jason required a systematic approach—something scientific. So far he'd behaved like a panic-stricken parent who lost a child at the zoo and chased themselves by the tail. His rational brain ignited again. He focused on his breathing and told himself to relax. To traipse all over Lake Moonset haphazardly without a solid plan was no plan at all, except for defeat.

A pond butted up next to the field where the ground sloped away and the rainwater collected, combining with the snowmelt runoff from the spring. He refilled his water bottle and munched on a granola bar. The calories reinvigorated him. His head cleared. Larry unfolded the map and took out his phone.

Using the calculator, he approximated how far Jason could've gone based on speed, temperature, and terrain. The square mile radius was sketched on the map in pen. While his son may have fled from their campsite like a thoroughbred, his stamina wouldn't last. It couldn't. The boy was weak, he had to be—the laws of physiology demanded it. But he wasn't as weak as he'd let on. Did he do jumping jacks or calisthenics they weren't aware of? Did he do Pilates or yoga in secret? Larry knew the strength of his son was irrelevant because *he* was the one who needed to be stronger. He had to dig the deepest.

For six straight hours he searched the woods with his head on a swivel, his observations keener and sharper than before. An organized routine was developed. Every half-hour he hydrated, every hour he halted to stretch. He traveled methodically along diagonal patterns and took notes of the sections he'd swept. The compass was checked to stay headed north and although losing his voice, he still tried to yell Jason's name.

The prayer of St. Anthony, he whispered it often. He begged the saint of lost causes for help. He begged God, Jesus, and the Holy Spirit. He begged his dad too, who he believed was in Heaven. It couldn't end like this for him and his son. There had to be more.

The sun faded and slipped behind the mountains as dusk settled in. It grew dark for the last several hours and now it was hard to see. In his haste leaving Chip he'd forgotten to bring a flashlight, but it wasn't a deterrent. The search would resume through the night or the next day or the next week if need be. His search wouldn't stop for anything.

He maneuvered down an embankment, limping badly, when he smelled something. His nose wiggled like a rabbit and the scent was registered. Smoke. For a second his mind envisioned a doomsday scenario where a forest fire engulfed him. If that were the case, then Larry assumed he had the worst luck on the planet and the God he prayed to hated him.

The smoke became stronger as he creeped forward, proceeding with caution. He had no intention to spook Jason and repeat the chase again. The meeting with his son would be eased into. First he would seek forgiveness, then mercy. He was also aware the wilderness attracted people other than those who loved nature. There were poachers and drifters, drug dealers who cooked meth, and renegades evading the law. Serious crimes like murder have been committed at some of the most venerable parks in the nation.

Darkness became fully entrenched as he shuffled from tree to tree and latched onto anything he could for support. His knee pain stabbed him with every movement. He tried to massage it but it hurt to touch and the limp degenerated into a hobble.

Larry dragged his leg like an ornery companion, sniffing again. He was close. Hope stirred. After rounding a slippery bend where he cut his hand on a thorn bush, he saw it. It was the unmistakable glow every hiker yearned for at night, and the soft orange light illuminated a speck of the pitch-black forest.

He fumbled with the binoculars and zeroed in on a figure sitting next to the flames. It was a young male with a thin neck and lanky arms. Larry fell to the ground as his legs gave way. That's all he needed to see. He could've picked that beautiful scrawny frame out of a lineup.

His body cramped, his muscles locked. He'd gotten this far on fear and determination but there was nothing left in the tank. Silently, he cried. Larry slithered along his belly to get a better view and when he did, he saw Jason stoke the flames while chewing on a stick. The fire was small and although it disclosed his position, the allure was too great. Fire represented comfort at night. Fire represented safety.

He lay on the cold dirt and sobbed. The roller coaster ride of the day's emotions were unable to be processed. The stress shaved years from his life and added wrinkles to his face. But Larry didn't care. When the bugs began feasting on him he hardly noticed. He'd found his boy! A miracle had been bestowed. And he had no idea how it happened. For the first time in longer than he remembered, God answered his prayer. St. Anthony *did* come around.

Memories of his son flooded him as he tried to move but couldn't. They were simple things, everyday things, moments so easy to take for granted. Jason doing math homework at the kitchen table, mowing the lawn, eating all the food in the house, arguing about cleaning his room, and dressing like Batman for Halloween.

For the rest of Larry Turner's life, nothing would be taken for granted again.

The kidnapping of Jason was meant to uncross his wires and realign his brain, to harness him back to reality. But it wound up doing just that for Larry instead. He didn't want to lose his son at any cost, and he'd never give up. Because Chip was right, you couldn't go back; you could never ever go back. He could see it now—so obvious, so direct. He felt mortified by the things he said, for what he thought, for what he'd done. The kidnapping plan was unconscionable at every level. How could he? Larry didn't mean any of it. He'd simply been beaten down for too long, snared in the cycle of pessimism, stuck in the cycle of pain.

If Pine View was the requirement to get Jason better, then Pine View it was. If that didn't work, they'd try something else. He'd get another job, and another, and they'd sell everything they owned. He'd borrow money from anyone, at any rate, and he'd beg and scrape and scrimp and scrounge and rob a bank if he had to. Because you could never go back. You could never, ever go back.

Larry reveled in the euphoria with his son in front of him—breathing, healthy, alive. The past was immaterial as their future lie ahead. An improbable second chance had been given. His mind turned off and his battered body shut down. He was proud that Jason ran, as proud as any parent could be.

CHAPTER

"Mom, hello, are you there?" Melissa said. She gathered the dice off the Yahtzee board and placed them in the cup. "Are you even keeping score? That's like the third time you spaced."

"Huh?" Karen said, lifting her eyes from the floor. "Yeah. Absolutely. You got two sixes and three fours. Good roll."

"That was my last turn."—Melissa stood and walked outside, followed by Sammy—"Ridiculous," she said before slamming the door.

Karen shook the cup, rattled the dice, and spilled them on the table. She counted the numbers and put them back in, then shook the cup again. The sound of dice ricocheting around the plastic was loud and abrasive. It filled the otherwise quiet cabin. When she started to shake the cup a final time, Pauline gently covered her hand.

"It's alright," she said. "I know you're anxious."

"We should play another game. Let's see what we got here."—Karen read the board games stacked on the floor—"There's Parcheesi, Trivial Pursuit, and Monopoly. We have a checker board that can be used for chess, and I'm not sure if we have all the pieces in the Jenga box."

"Maybe we should give it a break. You don't really seem up for a game right now."

Karen ignored the comment and looked around the cabin for something to do, perhaps something to clean. It was bright inside with lanterns on the table and candles on the shelves. She opened a book, read a few pages, then snapped it shut. The room still smelled moldy after sanitizing it. She sprayed more air freshener and paced the floor, stopping to inspect a pair of snowshoes hanging on the wall as decorations. *Why do we have these?* Karen thought. She never went snowshoeing once in her life. Neither had Larry.

"You want some more to eat?" she asked Pauline while starting to put the Yahtzee board away. "I can make you another steak."

"They might still want to play. Melissa was in the lead."

"Probably not. She's off pouting because I lost track of the score, like it's some great atrocity."

Pauline moved from the hard wooden chair of the table onto one of the beds. She leaned on a pillow. "Is that why you think she left, over a game of Yahtzee?"

"Who can tell with her these days? She's hot and cold with me. Mostly cold."

"Sweetie, you've been off on your own little planet all day. Isn't it obvious?"

"Isn't what obvious?"

"Your daughter. She craves your attention."

Karen's nostrils flared. "Thank you for the insight into my family life, Pauline. But I didn't ask. I let you come along, so leave it at that and save the psychoanalysis for another time." The door wasn't slammed shut when leaving the cabin—that was a pet peeve. She closed it firmly with a clenched jaw.

The night air was warm and buggy, mosquitos the size of jetliners hunting for blood. The flames in the fire pit had faded and the girls hovered near the edge of the woods. They took pictures of the lightning bugs that flashed in the darkness. Karen suggested to capture them in a glass jar, like she did as a kid, but they didn't listen. She craned her neck upward and was awestruck by the sky.

"You won't see anything like this back home. It's perfect."

"Awesome," Melissa said.

"They say there are more stars in the universe than there are grains of sand on all of Earth's beaches combined. Can you believe that? At least that's what your father told me."

"Thanks for the astronomy lesson."

Karen walked a bit closer. "Sammy, could you give us a minute? Pauline is inside. Why don't you go join her?"

She directed the flashlight to show Sammy the way and watched her enter the cabin. Unless a person was really into nature and isolation, it was kind of boring up there. She assumed Melissa's friend regretted coming along.

"What's wrong?" she asked her daughter.

"Like nothing. Why?"

"I'm sorry I lost track of the turns. It happens. Now what's going on? I want to know."

"That's the thing, Mom, you really don't."

With the windows boarded up for repair, the cabin emitted no light except what escaped under the door. The fire pit was an orangish heap of molten coals, and being in the woods at night was a different kind of darkness than the suburbs.

There were no streetlights on the sidewalk or headlights from a passing car, no back-porch flood light left on by a neighbor. Your eyes wouldn't adjust because there was nothing to adjust to. A person couldn't even see a hand waved in front of their face. Karen scanned the area with the flashlight and heard a noise. She reached for her daughter's arm. "Come on, there's too many animals out here."

Melissa pulled away and tied her hair into a ponytail. "I'd rather not."

"Okey-doke, then I'll stay too. I can turn off the flashlight if you don't want to see me. It's just you and me plus whatever that creature was over there."

"Just you and me? That's hilarious. It's never just you and me. Or just you and Sarah. Or just you and Dad. It's only you and Jason."—Melissa's voice cracked—"Do you like know that I've been here all day trying to hang out? That I got up extra early to come."

"I'm the one that invited you, didn't I?"

"Then why do I seem to be getting in the way? Down at the lake you didn't talk at all, even when I asked you questions. You spent the rest of the day moping and obsessing on your phone. You've gotten bad, Mom. It's true. The sad part is, you either don't know how to hide it or don't really care. All you think of and talk about is Jason. Which I've grown used to and which is why I don't like to be around you anymore. Neither does Sarah. For all I know, neither does Dad."

"Hey, leave your father out of this."

"Why? You won't. He's with Jason, like right now, and they're hiking. What's so wrong with that? But from the way you act, you'd think he's with some guy he met on the street, not his own father. Dad is smart, you know. He's caring. But you don't trust anyone but yourself."

"That's not fair and—"

"I don't know if it's because he's a boy or your first born or like whatever, but I wonder if you'd act this mental over me."

"I love you all the same."

"Yeah right. Don't insult me, because you've made it more than clear."—Melissa hustled toward the cabin but stopped halfway and turned—"I only came because you asked and I thought I should give it a try. For us. But I should've known better. When can we leave?"

"When they get back."

"When will that be?"

"Who knows?" Karen said. She debated whether to follow Melissa who disappeared into the cabin. But what could be said?

Her daughter was probably correct on a certain level. Maybe she did obsess over Jason at times. How would she explain it was only because she was scared to lose him? Melissa might never understand until she had children of her own and there was no reason to drag out the argument further. A parent's bond couldn't be comprehended until one was a parent.

Karen cringed as she thought this. She sounded like her own mother and it made her feel old. Maybe she was old. If she was, she certainly didn't feel any wiser. She remembered hating it when her mother used to speak to her like that, to give an almighty, all-knowing lecture. To a teenager, it comes across as nothing but condescending.

She went to the fire pit and clutched her phone, hoping it would ring. Should she call Larry again before going to bed? But why bother wasting her time? They wouldn't return that night and he wasn't going to answer anyway. *Why were they hiking to Herrington's Peak?* she asked.

The location of where they were headed was well-known to Karen. Back in the day when Jason and Larry were gung-ho for hiking, her son used to ask about it constantly. They'd hiked six of the seven high peaks in the area over the course of a few summers and Herrington's Peak was the last one left. Since it was the most challenging, Larry wanted to wait until Jason got more experienced before they made the final ascent of the *Moonset Seven*, as the peaks were referred. Once completed, they would receive free T-shirts and bragging rights from a local club in town.

Conquering the *Moonset Seven* wasn't a feat compatible to the forty-six peaks of the Adirondacks or the Seven Summits of the world. But it was still an impressive accomplishment, especially for a young person. Herrington's Peak was the only one that resided in the western part of the mountain range. Karen didn't know why they decided to hike that particular peak at that particular time. It didn't add up. Maybe it was Larry's way of saying good-bye before they surrendered Jason to Pine View.

She stayed outside and stared at the dying coals. A mosquito bite on her wrist was already swollen. The absolute silence of the wilderness felt eerie as it was only Karen with her thoughts and her concerns—nothing but worry. More bugs. Another bite on the arm. More scratching. When an owl hooted she flinched. What else lurked in the woods? She dashed to the cabin for safety and when she reached the door, laughter erupted, accompanied by the clatter of rolling dice.

The notion of laughter was considered and Karen wondered if she'd forgotten how. The last time she had a gut-busting laugh escaped her memory. It seemed such a trivial thing to contemplate given all that was going on. But when she went inside the laughter would diminish or perhaps even stop, her presence alone a buzzkill. Though she tried to hide it, the bitterness emanated from her body.

She looked at the stars a final time. What was out there? Why did everything have to be such a giant mystery? Reluctantly, she turned the knob and pushed on the door because she had nowhere else to go.

Chapter 34

The book in her lap was upside down. When Karen realized it, she hoped nobody else had. Pauline and the girls played cards at the table and while it was only ten o'clock, it felt much later, like they'd been at Lake Moonset for a week already. She crossed her legs and leaned up in the chair, then crossed them in a different direction, unable to get comfortable.

The cabin once had a peacefulness Karen yearned for. She looked forward to it. But now if she wasn't doing something productive she didn't feel at ease, as if losing valuable time. Her mind wouldn't stop and her body seemed to follow. With the prospect of sleep evading her for the second night in a row, she thought about taking a pill. But what if Larry did call? What if somebody needed her?

Both girls eventually tired of the card game and pushed two of the small beds together. They watched a movie on Melissa's phone, sharing a set of earbuds. Karen looked at her guest, who went back to knitting like she ran a small business with orders to fill. She stared at Pauline. How did the woman remain so poised? Most people would have crumbled after Wesley's death or turned into an alcoholic. Karen may have been one of them. She felt bad about being rude earlier and considered apologizing, but instead blurted out, "You almost finished with that?"

"I'm close. And thankfully I got a bunch more projects after this to keep me busy."

"I guess that's the key. Keeping busy."

"Either you keep your mind busy, honey, or it'll keep you."—Pauline patted a spot next to her on one of the larger beds—"Come give it a try. I'll show you how."

"I don't think I'd be very good at it."

"You should've seen my first scarf. Ugly doesn't begin to describe it. It was so bad I had to throw it away and I'm not sure a homeless person would've worn it. But I watched some videos and practiced. Got better. Come on, let's try."

With needles in hand, Pauline slowed down her pace. She displayed the process, and said, "To me, it's nothing more than a simple repetitive task. Something I can zone out to. It has a steady beat, like a musical rhythm. Are you into music?"

Karen nodded. "Stuff from the seventies and eighties mostly. Anything vintage."

"Just pick a song and go with it."

For the next half-hour they passed the scarf back and forth. Pauline encouraged Karen and fixed her mistakes. She began to speak a few times, as if she had something important to say, but each time said, "Sorry, it's nothing," and took another sip of her tea. Karen didn't think much of her guest's awkward gestures anymore. She kind of got used to it. She was also surprised how much she enjoyed the knitting. Maybe an alternative to cleaning had been found.

After a trip to the outhouse that was both scary and gross, she finally worked up the courage to ask what she'd thought for most of the day.

"How do you do it? With everything that happened, you seem, I don't know . . . okay."

Pauline raised her brown eyes, the lashes thick. "The word *okay* is a bit of a stretch. You're in the confusion of the storm right now. Makes it harder to see. My storm is done so there's a finality. Sure, I'll have to pick up the debris for the rest of my life, but it's over. There's nothing I can do but move on. That's what he would've wanted and it's all I got left."

"But don't you ask why? Why you? Why then? Why him? Why the whole thing happened in the first place?"

"Those are the three most dangerous letters in the English language. The why of it's not important. It's done and can't be changed. Think of it as an unsolved riddle, then don't think of it no more. Everybody asks why in the beginning and I'm no exception. The self-pity, well, it was overwhelming. But then I stopped because it won't do you no good. Acceptance. That's what I learned. Turn it over to God and let His will be done."

"His will be done?" Karen said, a tone of mockery in her voice. "I can't believe those fairytale stories any longer. I grew up in the church. It didn't help my mother any. Didn't help my son."

"You know what I say every day when I wake up and before I go to bed? I say, 'God's in control Pauline, you're not. God's in control, you're not.' I give it up. It's taken me a long, long time to get there. But that's the only way."

"Sounds like an excuse to be alright with everything bad that ever happened to you."

"You asked, sweetie, and I'm telling."

"That's it?"

"What's the alternative? To stomp my feet and try to find reason in something I can't begin to understand? To question everything I've done as a parent or look to lay blame? You'll go off the deep end doing that. And for a while, I did. Life is precious and you still have it, you still have Jason. Take something from this and help others. It'll heal you. Letting people help you helps them in return."

"I'm not sure I get it. Probably never will." Karen tried to slide off the end of the bed, but Pauline grabbed and stopped her.

"This is good, you talking. You're not alone. There are thousands of parents like us, maybe millions. We can help."

"I shouldn't have brought it up. It's . . . It's hard for me to connect. I can't imagine anyone could feel more pain than me right now, or shame, and . . . I'm sorry. I know what you must be thinking after all you've been through."

"I'm not here to judge."

"I ask myself how somebody can be more frustrated or despondent than I am. He was such a good kid, and we did everything right. There were so many expectations for Jason. Now I can only hope he stays alive."

"You think your situation is unique, don't you? That it's never happened to another parent before. But there's a long line ahead of you and a long line behind. The disease of the mind don't care what you wanted. It'll take it regardless."—the two ladies locked eyes, and before Karen knew it, Pauline hugged her—"How about we work on the scarf some more? Remember, when you're ready, come find me."

Karen squeezed back. For a minute, she didn't want to let go.

They completed a foot-long section of the pink and white scarf as the girls drifted off to sleep. Pauline told the story of how she met Chip and discussed their long journey to California. They exchanged recipe ideas for split pea soup, chatted about rising gas prices, and shared memories from when each of them got married. Somewhere along the way Karen's force field weakened. She became disarmed.

Maybe it was the thin air of the mountains or maybe it was fatigue, but she found herself rambling, unable to keep quiet. The normally super private person talked about Pine View and the cost and how far away it was. She mentioned Dr. Baker and Jason's last therapy session, how the meds seemed to no longer work.

177

The horror of incidents number one and two were described in detail. She yelled at herself the whole time to stop. Stick a sock in it. Go to bed immediately. But her lips kept flapping anyway.

"So hopefully they'll be back tomorrow," she said as it neared one o'clock. "That's what Larry told me on the phone. It should give us enough time to get Jason home for the pick-up."

"If not?"

She shook her head. "If not, then I don't know . . . I really don't know."

Pauline took a sip of tea. "Maybe we should call the police."

"The police?"—Karen thought she was kidding—"You like to do that, don't you? To just say things out of the blue. Why should we call the police?"

"I think it would be smart."

"And tell them what?"

"Chip's not in the greatest shape. I'm worried."

"I'm worried about all of them but we can't call the police because your husband needs to hit the gym. Let's hope they're back tomorrow. I'd rather not think about it if they aren't."

"They won't be."

Karen froze. "What do you mean? Did you talk to Larry? Did you somehow talk to Chip?"

"No. But maybe they're lost or ran out of supplies or something. Who knows? When they took Jason they—"

"What do you mean *took* Jason?" Karen asked. She sat straight up like somebody pinched her.

Pauline stared at her cup.

"I said what did you mean by *took* Jason? Took how?"

"I'm . . . I'm not allowed to say."

"So help me, answer the question."

"It was a poor choice of words. I misspoke. What I meant to say is when they brought him along."

"What are you saying? They took him from the house like it was planned. And you knew about it?"

"Sort of. In a roundabout way. Not the entire thing, not all the details. Larry wanted to try something. He's scared. I didn't know if he was serious. He and I are close."—she hesitated—"Let me start over. What I should have said is that when they brought him, they didn't give a timetable for their return. Larry said they'd be back when Jason was ready. I didn't like the sound of it and the more I thought about it, the more it bugged me. So I came to get you. I tried telling you earlier, a couple times, but—"

178

"So they took him?" Karen said, stepping away from the bed in a daze. "That's it. What other way could you get him out of the house? He wouldn't leave on his own. Never. You'd need force, like Pine View." She considered Larry's kidnapping comment to Dr. Baker and she thought of his odd behavior with Sarah. Her daze ignited into a boil. "What else do you know about my son? Tell me!"

Pauline slid back toward the metal headboard. "They didn't say anymore. Nothing specific. But if you don't hear from Larry by noon tomorrow I think you should call the police."

"Mom, what's going on?" Melissa said, lifting her head from the pillow. "Why are you yelling?"

"Go back to sleep. Now!" Karen dug through her suitcase with wild eyes and threw clothes on the floor. When the wads of tape were found she shot over to Pauline. She held them in front of her. "This one was in Jason's room right after they left the house, and this one I noticed as soon as we got here. What are they for?"

Pauline had no expression and grabbed the scarf. She started to knit again.

Karen repeated the question, then dashed from the cabin and slammed the door. Larry's name was screamed into the night. Her barrage of calls went to voicemail and the messages she left were the harshest of her life. The mosquitos no longer bothered her and she wasn't scared of any creatures that lurked about. If the creatures were wise, they'd be scared of her.

Hiking? she thought, ripping the car keys from her pocket. *I knew they didn't go hiking.* She turned the engine over and put the minivan in drive, unsure if the police station would be open or closed. But she didn't care. The line had been crossed. Reinforcements were needed. She floored the gas pedal, kicking up gravel and sticks, and bounced around the ruts on Beaver Ridge Lane. When Karen reached the main road, she drove even faster.

Chapter

Larry jolted awake from a nightmare slumber like there'd been a volcanic eruption. He scrambled to see if Jason remained ahead of him and when his breath returned, he dropped his head in relief. The morning light was soft, erasing the darkness. His clothes were damp from the dew.

He tipped the water bottle to rinse his mouth, then drank the rest of it. The sun was below the horizon which created a muted pastel sky, and when he tried to stand, it felt like he'd been in a bar fight or suffered a minor car accident. His throat still hurt from screaming but seemed a bit better. He tested it by saying, "Good morning," to a curious little chipmunk who clung to the base of a tree.

Larry yawned. His breath tasted sour, his stomach growled from emptiness. But more than pancakes or eggs or a bowl of cereal, he craved a tall glass of diet soda filled with shaved ice and if he was lucky, a lime wedge stuck on the rim. He took a baby step, then another. While his legs were stiff and his knee already ached, the deep sleep nourished and partially healed his body. The more he moved the looser he felt, and as he walked across the floor of the forest, a smile engulfed his face. Today would be a good day. A new day.

He blew on his hands to warm them, and sat down when he reached Jason's camp. The last four tablets of aspirin were ingested. Let the boy sleep, that's what he told himself. It was strange encouraging his son to sleep because at home it was always the opposite.

The chatter of birds intensified as the woods grew brighter and the forest came to life. In a different era, which at times seemed not long ago, they would've been camping on a summer adventure for their next big hike. To go for a swim before breakfast or to have lunch at the summit—those were the only tough decisions to make.

Somewhere between careening through the woods like a madman and when he passed out like a corpse, Larry decided he'd tell Jason everything. No details were to be omitted. He didn't know why he thought his son would understand. Perhaps he trusted that their once close relationship could surpass any obstacle, or perhaps his ecstasy in finding Jason made him delirious and naïve. But the trip was salvageable, he believed that, as soon as they patched up their differences and became reacquainted. They still had the potential to enjoy an amazing bonding experience. And fishing would hold the key.

It was their favorite activity when they camped, and as Larry's father taught him, he taught Jason. Fishing at Lake Moonset was ideal with its abundance of streams and variety of trout and striped bass. Surely they could find enough material to make an impromptu net or devise a pole.

When their bellies were full and with the Turner men reconnected, he'd call Karen to boast that Pine View wouldn't be necessary. Cancel the trip. Forget the entire thing. Inform Dr. Baker they appreciated the effort but her services were no longer required. Because *he'd* done it. Just as planned. He'd saved their son. Karen could come pick them up whenever she wanted, but there was no rush. Take your time. No worries at all.

He guessed they were about twenty miles from the highway, twenty-five at the most, but couldn't be certain. From the unconventional way he stumbled onto Jason he was unclear of their exact location. But how far or how long the journey remained no longer concerned him. Bum knee or not he'd make it, assisted by the help of his son.

As an extra treat, while they weren't technically going to climb Herrington's Peak and were probably quite far from it, they'd go ahead and check it off the list anyway. No need to get bogged down in specifics. Completing all seven peaks wasn't a school test. Maybe they'd stop in town on the way home to finally claim their free T-shirts.

Larry leaned on his side near a sequoia tree and examined it wearing a grin. The height and girth of the trees astonished him. Some species can live hundreds of years, even thousands, and to be with his son in such an inspirational setting—

Everything stopped. The sound of nails on a chalkboard stunned him.

A pudgy, bald man with a fragile mentality entered his psyche, thrusting him back into reality. The emotional ups and downs he'd endured combined with exhaustion and not enough food caused him to forget about his friend. How could he not remember that a whole other predicament awaited him?

His forehead tightened as the balloon of his fantasy popped. There'd be no fishing or swimming or strolling from the woods at a moderate, comfortable pace. Once again, he was propelled into high alert.

They had to move now and they had to move fast before anything happened to Chip. He didn't know how they would find him, but he had to try. Larry truly loved the man who steered him through so many perilous times. He imagined his friend wandering aimlessly in the wilderness, crying, verbally flogging himself that he untied Jason.

If Chip did leave, where would he go? The woods were endless. Maybe he followed directions and hunkered down like a mole, waiting for help to arrive. Larry then considered Pauline. If Karen didn't kill him, she might.

He analyzed the map as a rush of anxiety cast a giant stone upon his shoulders. The coordinates seemed vague and the route he'd taken was a mystery. Larry rationalized that Chip was an experienced woodsman who could handle any situation. But that was before Wes's death, when the man was . . . different. The hour-long delusion he enjoyed so thoroughly vanished. If they didn't come across Chip by the time it got dusk he'd contact Karen. They may have a missing person to report.

"Hey there," Larry said, his hands in his pockets. He watched Jason roll over and glare at him. "How you doing? You're not hurt are you?"

No answer.

"I guess you're wondering why I'm here, about what's going on. I bet you're confused and I get it. You see, it's kind of a long story. I want to tell you. And I will. This may sound a little crazy, but we have to go. Chip's waiting for us. You think you can pack your gear and I'll explain everything on the way?"

Jason remained on the ground.

"You probably want a little something first. Well, to begin with, I'm sorry. It's been tough lately, there's a lot going on. I was figuring a way to . . . You see, I watched this show. It started when Uncle Nathan came over on the fourth. Remember? When your mother asked you to go to the store? But his friend, this guy Edgar, he got lost. He reminded me of you. He was in Yellowstone and—"

"Don't," Jason said, sitting up. He pulled on his boots and pointed. "You can stop with the bullshit because I know."

"Know what?"

Jason got to his feet and inched forward like a gunslinger engaged in a duel.

"This can be a good thing," Larry said, "if you allow it. I want to apologize. I think it'll make more sense once I explain."

"You don't have to. I knew from the beginning."

"I'm not sure you do, Son. I'm not sure what you think you know or why."

This was the moment Larry hoped for, where they hugged it out and came to an understanding, where a father and son began anew. There was nowhere else to go in the sprawling forest. If not here and now, then when?

The person that charged at him didn't seem weak or scared or resemble the young man who hadn't left his bedroom in months. Jason grunted when he shoved Larry in the chest with the palms of his hands extended. Larry stumbled backward like a wobbly drunk until he lost his balance and fell on his ass. He lay there in awe, excited. He then stood and reset his feet.

Jason charged again and pushed harder the second go around. Larry was forced directly onto the ground with no awkward backpedal.

"I'm willing to do this all day if you need to, because I love you. Let it out. I want you—"

Larry wasn't quite to his feet when the third shove launched him with such ferocity he did a reverse somersault, flipping over. Leaves got jammed inside his mouth and an acorn stuck to his hair. He relished the taste of dirt and enjoyed the pain. If only the outburst could have been caught on video to show Karen.

It was all worth it, he thought, to witness his son get resurrected and rejoin the ranks of humanity. But the elation was short-lived. As abrupt and unexpected as the assault had been, Jason took off running. Larry watched him with his mouth agape, dumbfounded. Chip had been right. The boy was fast.

"Hey!" he yelled as he sprung to his feet. "Jason! Where you going? Wait!"

Already fifty feet behind him, Larry began to run too. Every creak, ache, and affliction in his body evaporated. There was no way he'd lose sight of him again.

Jason ran up a small hill that plateaued across a field and then up again across a rocky escarpment. A steep valley soon approached with a wall of granite on one side. They both slipped and lost their footing, using trees as guideposts until reaching the bottom.

"Jason!" Larry yelled. "Stop! Let me explain!"

They ran through a long flat stretch and swerved to avoid impassible boulders. Pine trees and bushes were weaved around and they jumped over rocks, hurdled over logs. He matched his son stride for stride, gaining a step here and there by taking smarter, shorter angles. When proximity allowed, he'd tackle Jason. That was the only option he had.

They both slowed down as they came to an embankment that led to a creek. Short, choppy steps were taken. When they hit the water, Jason attempted to run through it but his momentum was stymied. Larry dove in head-first and swam. He made up more ground. By the time they reached the other side, he was within ten feet.

He clawed his way up the opposite embankment directly behind his son. They began to run again, slower, waterlogged. He was now six feet away. Then three. With another step he reached out and swiped Jason's shirt with a finger. They ran parallel to the creek as the earth rose. The bank grew higher until a narrow spot emerged along a sharp bend.

Jason leaped into the air. His arms flailed, legs kicked. His heel hit the water on the other side, which caused him to tumble forward in one smooth motion. He quickly recovered and kept moving. Larry was in midair right behind him. Fueled by a desperate adrenaline, he jumped farther than his son. He easily cleared the water and landed on a pile of wet leaves off to the side that concealed a large, elevated tree root.

His right foot buckled. It cracked at a ninety-degree angle, the noise of the snapped bone loud and savage. He bounced forward like a pogo stick and crashed into the ground, smashing the cell phone in his pocket. His head slammed hard into a large gray river rock.

Blood poured down his face in a torrent and burned his eyes. The salty fluid on his tongue startled his awareness. He grabbed the air and tried to grab onto Jason. But his son was gone. He grabbed the air again and again until his face hit the mud and the words "Don't leave me," trickled from his mouth. His vision went cloudy. His mind turned blank. "Don't leave me," he said as the tunnel of light shrank and his consciousness faded. "Don't . . ."

CHAPTER

"I understand," Officer Odom said as he walked to his desk. He set down a mug of steaming coffee and slid into a worn leather chair. The police station, which doubled as the courthouse once a month and a part-time DMV every other Thursday, had only been open for a minute. "Ma'am, I understand," he repeated. "But I'm gonna need you to slow down."

Karen slept little that night. She nodded off in the car for no more than an hour after practicing what to say in the mirror. The twenty-four hour waiting period for a person to officially be designated as missing concerned her. She knew some states or jurisdictions had longer waiting periods, up to forty-eight hours. With Pine View looming, neither of those time frames worked. If she could get Jason back home by the following evening at the latest, they still had a chance.

She hovered in front of his desk, then leaned over it. Her hands gripped the corner of the wood. There was so much she wanted to say yet so much she didn't. Officer Odom sipped his coffee and looked up at her. He pushed his chair farther away as she gave her statement without taking a full breath.

"They should've been back already. I've called my husband repeatedly but he doesn't answer, and all their stuff is at our cabin. That's not like him, sir. I'm worried. I think something's happened to my son. He's twenty-one but still really just a boy. I need you to find him. I mean all of them. When can you leave? Right away?"

"Do you know where they were going?" the officer said, shuffling through a messy desk drawer for a report form. His black hair was combed to the side and his jaw contained neatly manicured stubble. He clicked a pen, jotted down the date, and asked, "What are their names?" With his large hands, the pen looked tiny as he wrote.

Twice he asked her to speak slower—he couldn't write that fast. Once he told her to keep calm or she'd have to come back. Karen sighed every time he interrupted her to ask another repetitive question. She wondered why they were still in the office. How come they weren't out searching for her son already?

She provided their birth dates, social security numbers, home address, and the address to the cabin. The only time she paused to think and stumbled with her composure is when he asked, "Do any of them suffer from a mental condition or have any issues along those lines? Could they be a threat to themselves or jeopardize the safety of a rescue?"

Karen bit her nails and avoided his eyes for the first time since being there. She asked, "Why is that relevant?" Her question sounded defensive and when she realized it, she let go of her grip on the desk and sat in one of the chairs. Her voice was lighter when answering the next round of questions.

Officer Odom continued to write in his meticulous penmanship as Karen scanned the room. A deer head was mounted on the rear wall with a wide rack of antlers. In the front was a double-hung window streaked with dirt stains that overlooked a town strip. Most of the buildings were painted white. A few of them appeared to be taverns. Absent was a secretary or a receptionist and every available surface was cloaked with an unsettling amount of dust.

"As you can see, ma'am, I'm here alone. I do a little bit of it all."—he set the form aside and turned on the computer—"I'll put their names in the system now to run a few checks. I prefer to log everything on paper first so I have a hard copy. In case we lose power, I know I got it."

Karen squirmed in the chair. "What kind of checks?"

"Criminal history. Outstanding warrants. Stuff like that. We don't get much crime up here. Not the kind of place you get a bunch of missing persons either."

"Don't people come here to hike? They must get lost or injured sometimes."

"It's pretty rare," he said, pecking the keyboard one finger at a time. "This place is off the beaten path so to speak. Most folks who travel up here tend to be a little more seasoned and experienced. People like yourselves who own a place. Not too many tourists visit."

"How long will this take? We're wasting time. I've told you already that they're lost and I haven't heard from them. What else do you need? I want my son back."

Officer Odom looked up from the screen. "And your husband too, right?"

She swallowed. "Right."

"And that family friend of yours as well. Chip. Let's see. You gave his last name as Walton. Chip Walton."

"Yes."

"But your son first."

"Jason shouldn't be up here. He has an appointment tomorrow that cannot be missed. It's imperative. Larry should never have taken him and I can't—" Karen stopped. The lack of sleep was finally getting to her. She rubbed her dark eyes. "It's been a stressful night, sir. I just want them back safe and sound."

"Me too," Officer Odom said, starting to type again.

He'd been the sheriff at Lake Moonset for almost four years after several decades of service in the state capital as a policeman. He planned to retire there, but it didn't seem to be happening any time soon. With an appreciation and enjoyment for his job that belied his slow manner of speech, he asked, "Are you sure there isn't anything else you want to tell me, something I should know?"

"I'm sure."

"Then that's how we're gonna write it up. Now, if you'll give me a chance, ma'am, I'd be happy to help. But we need more details first. I don't have an army to send into the field and I can't go stomping through these woods without some kind of plan. We need to work together."

She nodded sullenly like a child who'd been chastised then motioned to the coffee mug on his desk. "Would you happen to have an extra one of those?"

"Yes, but I'm out of cream. The pot's next to the microwave."

"Thanks," she said and walked over to pour a cup.

"Where did your husband say he was going the last you spoke? When was that?"

"They were headed to Herrington's Peak. That's what Larry said anyway. Must've been about three or four days ago. It's the only peak they haven't climbed yet."

"Which is it? Three or four?"

She stared upward as if visualizing a calendar and put a finger to her lip. "I'd say four. Yeah, definitely four."

"Four days at Herrington's Peak, huh? It's beautiful but tough sledding out there. At least the weather's been good." He grabbed a rolled-up map atop a slim metal cabinet and opened it on a side table. "The next town over is Portersville. About sixty miles away."

Karen joined him at the table and peered over his shoulder, holding the warm mug with both hands. "Seems kind of far."

"It's on the other side of the mountain, which isn't that bad, but there's no direct way to get there. They have a unique cave system in Portersville. Brings in a lot of people. It's not huge but it's deep. Legend has it you can't get to the bottom. A bunch of people still try and every few years someone dies or goes missing. The body eventually turns up. They have more officers than us to handle stuff like that, even have some mounted horses."

"Horses? What about helicopters or dogs?"

"Afraid not. Let me make a few calls to see if they can help."—he dialed the number, spoke to someone briefly, and was put on hold—"Would you say your husband is an experienced hiker, ma'am?"

"He used to be. But it's been a while."

"And he's been coming to these parts for a number of years?"

"Yes."

"Then I wouldn't be too worried."

"How can I not? I know for a fact something is wrong."

He stroked the scruff on his chin. "Is there anything else you want to tell me?"

"I . . . I can't explain. I believe it to be women's intuition."

"We can leave it at that, for now. But if he's familiar with these mountains, then he's probably staying up there from pure enjoyment. Especially if he hasn't hiked in a while. Maybe his phone ran out of battery."—he looked out the window with a hand on his hip as the buildings gave rise to the mountains—"If there's one thing you can say about this little town, you'll definitely get a signal. They were gonna lay a pipeline through here a few years back and marked some towns expected to prosper. Ours was one of them. They began to build a line of cell towers along the main ridge."

"When do you think you can start to—"

He held up a finger and cut her off. Officer Odom conversed on the phone for the next five minutes. Karen topped off her coffee and reminded herself not to say too much. She was concerned if Jason's mental history would somehow come up. She was even more concerned if the story of Chip's son surfaced. It wasn't pertinent to the rescue or anybody's business, and she feared it may cloud the investigation.

There was no way she'd mention what Pauline insinuated, that Larry and Chip had *taken* Jason. She considered the wads of tape she'd found and became irate. *Did they tie him up? Did they cover his mouth?* Karen would deal with that situation later. First she needed her son back. He had a plane to Virginia to catch.

She roamed about the sparsely decorated room with drab brown paneling. The only item of interest was a framed photo of Officer Odom and Ronald Reagan. She picked it up thinking how young they both looked, but almost dropped it when the officer hung up the phone.

"That's when he ran for governor the second time. I worked security down in Sacramento, at a fundraiser."

"What did they say?" she asked and set the photo down.

"The area between your cabin and Herrington's Peak is big and we'll do our best. I haven't spoken to those folks in a while. It seems they're short staffed. Budget cuts or something."

"What does that mean?"

"It means they can only lend one officer for the cause."

"One officer? So including you, that makes two people covering all that space."—she paused and counted on her fingers—"That will give us six once I come along. Chip's wife is here too, and so is my daughter and her friend."

"Ma'am, let's wait a minute. Your idea is honorable, but it'd be better if you all stayed put. You'll only slow us down and you may get lost yourselves. These aren't well groomed ski trails we're gonna explore."

"Then how are just the two of you going to find them?"

"We'll find them, trust me. But if you're really that worried I can contact the State Police. Maybe they'll get the FBI involved or some other agency."

She sipped some more coffee and squeezed the mug a little harder. The cheap grinds left a bitter aftertaste. "Does that mean the media?"

"Depends on what's going on in the news cycle. If it's slow or if they find something of interest, you might end up doing an interview for the local stations. If it blows up, who knows, maybe Fox or CNN. I doubt it would get that far, but the news can be tricky."

Karen walked to the window and folded her arms. She knew Jason was with Larry and they were probably safe. But when would they come back? How far would her husband take it? After what he'd already done, it was hard to tell. She'd hoped to avoid any unwanted attention and didn't want to get in trouble either. Her only agenda was get Jason back to the cabin as soon as possible, drive him home, and send him to Pine View. All she wanted was to save their son's life. Why couldn't Larry understand that?

"How long will it take for you and the officer from Portersville to reach them?"

"Hard to tell."

"Ballpark it."

"I'd say anywhere from three to five days. Could be a week. Maybe it's best I make some more calls and get a higher authority involved."

She shook her head. "No. Please don't. There are details I may or may not have given you."

"I know. Been doing this kind of work for a long time, ma'am. Can always tell. How about you fill me in so we do this right?"

"The kid's been through enough, sir."—Karen exhaled and glanced at the deer head—"And so have we."

"I respect your privacy, but I'm gonna need more."

She sat in one of the chairs and her left leg started to bounce. Pine View was discussed along with incident number one and two. Karen surprised herself by talking about her feelings again. It felt good to unload the burden. Why did she always act so guarded? Why was everything kept inside? Sending her son to Virginia was their last chance, and Larry may have brought him to Lake Moonset as a way to say goodbye. Now they were lost. And she was scared. That's what she stated.

But she knew the truth, or at least her version of it. Larry didn't want to bring Jason home because nobody knew exactly when their son would return from Pine View. It was impossible to tell. Would it be when he was cured enough to function in society and take care of himself? Would it be when the Turners simply ran out of money? Or would it be in a box when . . .

"I understand," Officer Odom said. "My heart goes out to you. The situation, as usual, is more complicated than it appears."—he offered a napkin to dab her watery eyes and apologized for not having any tissues—"I have another idea that may help, but it's kind of unorthodox."

"I'm listening."

"I know some guys in town who can work as volunteers."

"What's so unorthodox about that?"

"You have to pay them."

"They're like what . . . Mercenaries?"

"In a way."—he held up his hands as if to defend himself—"I know, it sounds a little weird. I normally wouldn't bring it up, but after what you told me . . .

Ma'am, these are good men who know this area better than anybody. Some of them have been out of work for a spell and could use the money. They work cheap, but it's risky out in the woods. It's physical. Within the next several hours the search could begin if you're interested. I think we'd find them in a few days."

A calculator processed inside Karen's brain as she crunched the numbers. If she took a little here, nipped a little there, and used the small amount left on their credit cards for a cash advance, the idea was doable. She'd have to find some other way to secure enough money and hang around Virginia when Jason went to Pine View.

"How much?" she said.

"One-fifty a day per person seems reasonable. I'll make sure it goes no higher."

"How many people are needed?"

"At least six. I'll take four with me and send the others around to Portersville."

"They can start in the next couple hours?"

"We'll be fully engaged by noon."

"What about you?" she asked. "How much is your fee for this arrangement?"

"My salary is taken care of by the taxpayers of this community. I didn't move to the middle of nowhere for any type of financial opportunities. I want to help you, Karen. I really do."

She saw the sincerity in his droopy eyes, the honesty on his jowly face. "Where's the nearest bank?"

"About an hour south."

"Jeepers, how do you people live up here?"

"We manage."

"Alright, get your guys. I'll have the cash. But until then, I give you my word. If that doesn't suffice, my car can serve as collateral."

"No need for that," the officer said. They exchanged phone numbers and agreed the Turners' cabin would be designated as mission headquarters.

"I'll meet you there. Don't start without me."

"I thought we discussed—"

"I'm coming, sir. I'm definitely coming. But it'll only be me."

They shook hands, and against his protests, she washed her coffee mug and set in on the counter to dry.

CHAPTER 37

Smoke billowed in a heavy cloud as the scattered wet leaves spread across the fire continued to smolder. At least on half of the fire they did. The other half burned hot and bright with Larry right next to it, and the skin on his arm felt warmer than normal. That's the first thing he remembered—the warmth of his skin.

He had no idea where he was or how he'd gotten there. His head pounded like a church bell rang deep within his skull and it hurt to open his eyes. So he kept them shut. It reminded him of the one time in life he'd experienced a hangover, when a girl named Lynette Murray convinced him to do grape flavored Jell-O shots at a college party until he blacked out. He never drank much after that and still hadn't eaten a grape in thirty-four years.

Think of something pleasant, he told himself. For some reason the continent of Australia entered his mind. He'd gone there in high school as part of an exchange program and lived in Perth for eight months. Or was he supposed to go there? Or did he want to go there? He was confused and wondered why his head hurt. That's when he recognized the bottom half of his right leg tingled and his toes were numb. *Why is my leg tingling? Why are my toes numb?*

He sensed a figure towered above him and when he peeled open his eyes, a drizzle of water poured over his mouth. Some of the water made it past his semi-closed lips and reached his dry throat, but most of it leaked across the sides of his face. He coughed and it caused the pain in his head to be a million times worse.

"You think you can move?" Jason asked.

Larry blinked for a second, then looked around. The agony intensified as he forced his eyes to remain open and it seemed like a dream where he knew he was awake but there was no doubt he'd wake up again. While his clothes were slightly wet, he felt hot. Too hot. The fire crackled beside him. He lifted his head off the ground, moaning, and stared at the foot that perplexed him. It was bent inward at an angle it shouldn't be and triple the normal size.

He reached up to touch the hairline of his forehead. The soiled bandage felt greasy and there was a large mushy lump. When his finger came back covered in blood, he thought he may puke. Larry tried breathing through it and set his head back down, wincing as he did so.

"Sunglasses," he said. "This glare is killing me. You got a pair?"

"There weren't any in my bag."

The ground was cool as he scraped his fingers into it and collected some dirt in his hand. He spit in his other hand, then rubbed them together. Like an NFL quarterback who geared up for game day, the mud was smeared under each eye.

His brain seemed cloaked in cobwebs when the events responsible for his condition were attempted to be recalled. The last thing Larry remembered was his leap across the creek bed. Halfway through the air, he thought he would make it. But rather than focus on the landing he continued to track Jason. One more swipe to grab his son was the goal.

He heard something snap in his leg and before there was time to process it, the earth rushed around him in shades of brown, blue, and green. A white light flashed. A salty fluid entered his mouth. That was it. Until he woke up. His arm feeling warm.

"Move where?" he finally said.

"We've got to get you out of here. You need a doctor."

"A doctor?"—he started to laugh but it hurt—"We both need doctors now, don't we?"

"I'm not joking. You're already pale, probably in shock."

"What about my phone? Can we—"

"Got wrecked in the fall. It's smashed to pieces."

"Help me sit up," Larry said, raising an arm. "And get me away from this fire. I'm burning up. There's a log over there near that bush. Can you prop it up behind me?" He took the water bottle from Jason and drank as his thirst awakened, then sprinkled some droplets on his head. A maroon colored liquid flowed over his nose and off his chin. The slightest amount of pressure on the wound caused him to grimace. "How long have I been out?"

"Total? About four hours. The first three completely. The last one in and out."

The sun was behind an arrangement of white wispy clouds and a hawk circled high in the sky. Larry felt dizzy, at times having double vision. Maybe something to eat would help. "Hand me my bag."—as Jason retrieved the backpack, he noticed his son's chest was bare—"Where's your shirt?"

"On your head. At least some of it. We'll have to change the bandage later."

"Here, take mine. It'll be cold tonight."

"I don't want your stupid shirt. It's a bloody mess anyway. We'll deal with the cold when we get there."

Larry fought his emotions in addition to fighting the pain. Jason's gesture to save him felt like he'd said, "I love you Dad," a thousand times over. He hadn't heard that priceless phrase in forever.

"How'd you get me back here?" he asked.

"I carried you."

"That's incredible. How?"

"Over my shoulder."

"You carried me from the creek bed? That has to be near a mile away."

"This is where our stuff was and I have matches here. We were both wet. I had to stop and rest a lot."

Larry dug out the last granola bar from his bag and split it. He gave Jason the bigger half. His mangled foot hurt even more now that he saw it.

After a lifetime of coaching sports and attending medical clinics, the injuries he sustained were bad. How bad? Larry wasn't sure, but he knew it wasn't good. The pain chiseled away at him like a sledgehammer and the first aid kit had been left with Chip. But it probably wouldn't help anyway. The kit was designed for minor cuts and scrapes and not for what he needed—an airlift to the nearest hospital.

The suitcase of worry he carried with him on a daily basis for his son and his daughters and his wife now focused solely on him. Larry was nervous. A metallic taste permeated his mouth that wouldn't go away and fresh blood coated the inside of his nose. He pressed an index finger against his carotid artery and measured the pulse with his watch. Ninety-five—much higher for him than normal. He'd check it again every fifteen minutes if he remembered.

Jason threw more leaves on the fire to ensure a steady stream of smoke. It was survival class 101 in action. *When in distress, a hiker should attempt to generate abundant smoke by whatever means necessary. This will increase the probability of being spotted, thus increasing the odds of a rescue.* Larry pictured the words in the book he'd read about outdoor safety to all of his children. Jason was the only one who embraced it.

When he looked at his son, it was hard to believe the scene that unfolded. Jason attended to the fire, collected logs and sticks, and took control of the situation as if he were a different person. In addition, he asked his father, "Are you okay?" at least every five minutes. It was a *Twilight Zone* experience for Larry and after one more thank you for saving him, he asked, "But why?"

"Why what?" Jason said, sweating. He dropped an armful of wood.

"Why'd you bother with me?"

"What am I supposed to do, leave you to die in the wilderness? You're still my father, even after—"

"You could've. Nobody would ever have known."

Jason hesitated. "Yeah. I could've. But it never crossed my mind."

"How come?"

"Part of the old me still exists somewhere. I haven't forgotten how things used to be with us. Besides, I'm not an animal. At least not to anybody but myself."

"But you could've taken off to finally do what you want. You would've been free. It was the perfect opportunity. I mean, you ran from me earlier like you just escaped prison. I presume that was to get away."

"It's not about you and Karen. That's what you guys never understand. I know you have to try, but you take it so personally."—he stared at the ground—"I wouldn't do that to my sisters anyway. I know how much they care about you. They still have a chance."

Larry tried not to consider Melissa and Sarah, and he was glad there were no mirrors present. How terrified would they be if they saw him now?

"They care about you too. A lot. We all do."

"I'm done talking," Jason said. "Enough."

This was usually the point in conversations with their son when Larry and Karen backed down—when they used to have conversations. They were both afraid to push him too far and say the wrong thing, to be the cause for incident number three. At times it was all a big game as Jason controlled his parents like a master puppeteer. He'd intimate in a subtle way, or in many cases, not so subtle, he may harm himself to get them to leave him alone.

Even Dr. Baker admitted she saw that type of manipulative behavior in patients before but warned of caution. It was the grayest of gray areas. Like any loving parent, Larry and Karen fell for it. Because how could they not? The stakes were too high, the bluff too risky. They couldn't afford the tough love approach and make the ultimate error. Because in the end, it wasn't a game. They were afraid and confused. So they caved. Habitually.

They closed their mouths when instructed and left his bedroom when ordered to. He could've demanded they do jumping jacks or roll on the floor like a dog and they probably would've complied. Unconditional love was the greatest test they faced. When Jason said, "Enough," that was the end of it. Time to move it along. The *talk* was officially over.

Larry continued to watch Jason break sticks over his knee and add them to a pile. Another fatherly defeat in their conversation history appeared imminent. But something inside him said *No*. Perhaps it was the injuries or his predicament, perhaps it was the years of pent-up frustration. Kowtowing to his son no longer seemed prudent. He sharpened his tongue and poked Jason further.

"How come all of a sudden you decided not to leave me?"

"I said enough, Larry. Didn't you hear?"

"It'll be enough when I say it's enough. Now answer my question."

"What?"

"You heard me. Isn't this what you want? To leave me. You've been trying to leave your mother and I for quite some time. Leave the family, leave the earth, leave this life. Be honest. There's nobody here to stop you. It's just you and me. And I'm in bad shape. Tell me Jason, for the love of God, why wouldn't you leave me now and get it over with?"

With a stick in his hand, Jason stopped. "For fuck's sake, Larry, let's not do this now. Let's not do this ever. Can't you understand the circumstances? This is different."

"Is it?"

"Why does everything have to be such a big deal with you? Why can't it just be?"

"You tell me. I don't make big deals."

A sarcastic grin spread across Jason's face. "Really? Then why are we in these woods? Why were we at the cabin? Isn't that a big fucking deal?"

Unwavering, Larry pointed at him. "That's it right there. The big picture. Something you never see. *That's* why we're in these woods. The biggest damn picture ever. Don't you get it? I want to live, Jason. And I want you to live. I want to be with my family and see my grandkids one day. I want to eat good food, hear good music, and coach basketball. I want to laugh and cry."

"You want to cry? That's ridiculous."

"Crying can be good if you let it. It doesn't mean you're weak. It's healthy and normal and means you're human, that you're alive. They can be tears of joy or relief, not just sorrow."—he raised his voice further, burning his throat, and the bandage leaked more blood on his face—"No more bullshit, Son. Be honest with me for once. Why do you want to die? Why won't you come back to us?"

"You wouldn't get it."

"So teach me. You've got nothing to lose. Make me understand."

Jason threw the stick against a tree and glanced off into the distance. It was quiet for the next few minutes until a squirrel chirped on a thin branch above them. A moment later, it chirped again. He bent down and leaned on one knee, covering his eyes with a hand. When he spoke, his voice sounded weak.

"Because . . . Because I don't know. I really don't. And it makes it so much worse. I wish I did, but I can't get the idea out of my mind. I don't know how the thoughts started, or why. But they won't go away . . . When I wake up, it's there. When I go to bed, it's there. When I look in the mirror, it's there. Like a tidal wave. Like a set of handcuffs. But it's more than sadness. That's what people don't get. It's hopelessness. The lack of excitement. Whatever I do, it doesn't seem to make a difference."—his bottom lip quivered—"Things that used to bring me joy, that I could count on, they don't anymore."

"We'll get you the help you need," Larry said, beginning to cry. "Let's go to Pine View with an open mind, all of us, and see what happens. Together, I know we can turn this thing around. What led us here today is fate. A new beginning. Yeah, maybe life will be different than before and not what you thought it would be. But it can still be good. It can still be rewarding."

"You know what I miss the most? A clear head. Like when I was younger. Being able to see and think without all the clutter. Sometimes I question if I ever had it, if that was really me. This thing I have . . . I feel like I got sucker punched. Because now my mind is always cloudy. It plays tricks on me. Now I feel miserable and alone, even when people are around."—Jason brushed a tear aside, then paused to collect himself—"The pills Dr. Baker gives me make me numb. For the good and the bad. That's why I don't always take them. But when I don't, I feel fucked up in the head even worse. It makes me want to give up."

"I'll never give up on you, so don't give up on yourself either. You're young and strong and you can do this. But you have to fight every day with all you got. I'll fight with you. So will your mother and sisters. And when you return from Pine View, we'll get you back in the game. I think you'd make an excellent addition to my coaching staff. How about it?"

Jason stood. His face was dirty, his hair grimy. He rubbed the back of his neck and exhaled. "We need to get you out of here." He walked to a tree laced with vines and pulled on it.

For a while, Larry beamed inside. All the pain got shoved away, usurped by the delight of their momentous breakthrough. It was their longest conversation in recent memory and they were off to a good start, more than he could've hoped for. He only prayed to be around long enough to see the finish.

Chapter 38

The wind blew harder as more clouds rolled in and morphed the sky into a gloomy overcast sheet. Larry rested, at times feeling lightheaded or disoriented. He watched Jason organize the materials into five distinct piles around him. One was for logs about seven feet in length but less than six inches in diameter. Another was for sticks, up to three feet long. There was a pile of bark, one of moss, and vines cut into various sizes.

Jason squatted down next to him. "Time to get ready. I got everything we need to move you."

"I'm tired of wandering through the woods," Larry said. "I like it here. Just you and me."

"If you want to see Karen and the girls again we can't stay. Your ankle is definitely broken. You got lucky the bone didn't bust through the skin."

"Stop trying to cheer me up. And can you get me some water? I feel so thirsty."

Jason handed him the bottle. "I figured a splint may help when we move you. It should stabilize your foot, at least to some degree."

"Do what you think needs to be done. You're a good boy and I trust you. But you need to work dribbling left. When you get to college, the scouts will look for that. I'll show you some drills in practice today. How we getting there anyway?"

"We don't have practice today," Jason said, visibly taken aback as if somebody slapped him.

"Yes we do. And we have a game tomorrow night against Brustling Academy. You scored thirty-three against them last year. But they're probably gonna double team you, so be on the lookout for the open man."

"I uh, forgot to tell you. They called off practice today. There was a problem with the lights in the gym."

Larry sighed. "I'll see if I can fix them when we get there. If not, I'll show you those drills in the driveway."

"Yeah. Sure thing."

"Hey, remember in the ninth grade when we played Hoosick Falls. Petey Reynolds got the rebound and landed on your foot. I could hear the crunch from the bench. Then his mother ran onto the court and yelled, "My boy, my boy!" before she fainted. Poor Petey. I don't know which was worse, the ankle or the teasing he endured afterward."—Larry took a long drink and splashed some water on his face as Jason suggested. It seemed to revive him. Once again he noticed his surroundings—"What's all that for?" he asked, motioning to the piles near him.

"For the splint I mentioned. You're cool with it, right?"

"What splint?"

"The one I'm making."

"You're making a splint? Great idea. It should help my foot with the transport."

"That's what I figured."

"Did you ever think Karen Turner's mandatory first aid classes would come in handy? You remember taking those, Jason?"

"At the end of every summer starting in the sixth grade. There was always a test too."

"Your mother wants to be prepared for everything. It's part of her charm. She's been that way since I met her in college. University of Kansas. Rock chalk, Jayhawk, KU. I joined a study group to try and talk with her. Microeconomics. Still got a C."

"There's something else," Jason said. "I can't carry you all the way out of here. It's too far and I'll have to drag you. Most of this stuff is for a stretcher."

Larry sipped more water. The nausea he experienced earlier went to a heightened level as a surge of vomit gurgled halfway up his esophagus, then receded, burning his chest when it did so. "I wish we could stay for a while. Plenty of nice clean air, peace and quiet. I bet the fishing is fantastic. You think when it's all said and done, we can come back?"

"We'll definitely do that. But first I need you to help me with the stretcher."—Jason placed a hand on his father's cheek—"How about next summer?"

An odd mixture of excitement and fear cascaded over Larry, sprinkled with cheer. He felt an exuberance for life that he thought was gone. There was more hope than ever for his son as Jason helped *him* for once. There was more hope than ever for his family.

He thought about Pine View and the kidnapping. Then it dawned on him. If the only requirement to bring Jason back to life was severely crushing an ankle that may never let him walk normally again and suffer a traumatic head injury, he would've gladly jumped off the roof of the house a long time ago. Because as Karen used to say when they discussed the best way to help their oldest child, "Some parents will do anything for their kids. And we have to be those kinds of parents."

"Does anybody know where we are?" Jason asked. "Besides the weird bald guy, who since he's not here, I'm guessing is lost."

"Chip's one of the good ones, and a dear friend. Remember that when you see him. He likes you and the man's had it rough. Your mother knows we're out here. She knows because she always knows everything." Larry cleared his throat, slightly. He didn't let on that nobody knew their location. In an effort to get Karen off the phone and tell her something that sounded plausible, to buy himself some time, he made up the scenario about Herrington's Peak. In reality, he guessed they were quite far from it. But he did believe they weren't that far from the highway—that's where they needed to focus their attention on finding.

"You got anything to eat?" he asked. "Maybe some food will settle my stomach."

Jason shook his head no.

Right, Larry thought. *We weren't going to stock up his bag until letting him go.* "At least we'll have fresh water for as long as we're here. That filter is the best thing I ever bought. And once we adjust to the hunger, we can go a long time without eating." His head pulsated in a rhythmic beat with every pump of the heart. Even though elevated, his leg was not far behind.

"I'll apply that splint now," Jason said, moving closer to him.

"Before we do, let's try to straighten out my foot. I think the circulation is getting cut off." His toes were still numb and the skin surrounding his doughy, swollen ankle was dark blue and purple.

"You sure about that? Might make it worse."

"We should try something. I've never seen an injury of this magnitude before."

"And you want me to do it?"

"Well, I certainly can't."

"But what if I hurt you more? I don't want to."

"When you learn there are things in life we don't want to do but have to, it'll get a whole lot easier. Don't think, just do. Do it on three. And do it fast."—Larry jammed a stick in his mouth and clamped down—"On three," he mumbled.

Jason paused, then placed the foot between his knees for support. One hand grasped the toes, the other grasped the heel. He counted out loud. Slowly, he twisted the foot as Larry bit into the stick and screamed. But the foot didn't move far enough, so Jason twisted harder. The fibrous tissue shredded like a stale loaf of bread getting torn in half. Jason moved the foot upward and leaned forward, gripping tighter. He grunted. More pressure was applied. Then a little more. The foot twisted, loosening like a rusted bolt. Larry smacked the ground with his hand. A hard jerk. A final yank. Something gave way. The foot snapped back into the correct position, hanging limply.

"It's over," Jason said. He clutched his father's hand. "It's all over."

Larry nodded feebly, his lips coated in spittle. The stick fell to his chest and rolled on the ground before he passed out.

Curved pieces of birch bark were packed with moss and wrapped on his foot with vines when he awoke. The pain at his extremities competed for supremacy like dueling pianos. But seeing his foot in proper alignment again lifted his spirits. It also helped that when refilling the water bottles, Jason discovered a patch of blueberries. They weren't quite ripe and a bit tart, but being ravenous, anything tasted good. Larry checked his pulse and it was down to seventy. Perhaps their fortune had changed.

"If you're feeling strong," he said, "we should be able to average about eight miles a day, depending on what we come up against. How do you feel?"

"Strong enough."

"How? How do you have any strength left at all when you never used to leave your room? How did you carry me back here?"

"I told you before. Circumstances demanded it. Being in this situation, I don't have time to think. The only thing I'm concentrating on is to get you home."

"Tell me. I want to know."

"There's no quit in you today, is there Larry? Let's get it over with then. I'm only twenty-one. I have youth on my side, as you always say. And yes, I've lost a lot of weight but I still weigh almost a hundred and seventy pounds. I eat, just not as much as you like. Food has lost its flavor. My blood pressure is normal and I have very low body fat. I'm still six four. I haven't shrunk. My blood type is O negative. My sugar is normal. So is my sodium. Cholesterol—good. Liver enzymes—good. Is there anything else because Karen makes me get lab work and a physical every four months? I don't like going outside, that's why I look like a vampire, and—"

"I get it, Son."

"My vitamin D can be low—"

"You've made your point. It's easy to forget how you once were."—Larry glanced at his watch—"We should try to get the stretcher done before I start feeling horrible again."

He didn't know how far they'd travel before setting up camp for the night. Images of Karen, Chip, and Pauline floated through his mind but he ignored them. He had enough on his mind. And his mind hurt.

They continued to work on the stretcher like a well-run team. The days of their past were revisited when they did stuff together.

"Pass me that strip of vine," Jason said. "Then hold one end there while I tie it."

"How's that?"

"Not bad."

Not bad at all, Larry thought. He looked at his son. His son looked back. It was their first meaningful eye contact in years.

CHAPTER 39

The front area surrounding the Turners' cabin turned into a parking lot that could've been mistaken for a used truck dealership had someone randomly stumbled upon it. There were Ford F150s, Chevy Silverados, Toyota Tundras and the occasional Dodge RAM. While a few of the pickups glistened with a fresh shine off the showroom floor, the majority were pocked with rust from Lake Moonset's harsh winters. Most had gun racks mounted behind the cab—some had spotlights. Others were attached to trailers that carried ATVs and the supplies necessary for a deep woods search and rescue.

Officer Odom stood near the lean-to holding a clipboard. He instructed people to sign in and monitored their signatures on the liability release form. His request for paid volunteers produced a far greater turnout than expected.

Some of the people who showed up refused any payment whatsoever. They merely wanted to help. A married couple held hands and claimed they did everything together. Three teenagers had been pressed into service by their parents, and a seven-month pregnant woman dropped off sandwiches and lemonade.

The scene was loud and chaotic with dogs running around, barking and playing. A debate started about the best route to take into the mountains, followed by rumors of how the party got lost. Were they attacked by wild animals? Had they fallen off the mountain while climbing? Did they drink bad water and get sick? Were they dead? A sense of excitement spread across the camp as the citizens of Lake Moonset were cognizant that events of noteworthiness in their town were rare.

Melissa sequestered herself in the cabin and refused to go outside. She asked her mother a barrage of frantic questions, then tried to contact Sarah. She left voicemail after voicemail for her older sister and yelled at her for not answering, for not being around when the family needed her. Karen attempted to calm her daughter with no success. She called Sammy's parents to come get the girls immediately.

Pauline sat out near the fire pit in the midst of it all. She chain-smoked and worked on knitting the scarf. Once debriefed on the situation, she said very little. Her composure was akin to somebody who'd suffered such extraordinary acts of misery in life that nothing could penetrate far enough inside her to take away anything meaningful again. Like a dressed-out deer during hunting season, she'd already been gutted.

"It's in God's hands now," was the only thing she said after telling Officer Odom that she was not, is not, and has never been in control. Neither were they. That was God's job. His will was to be done. She wished the officer good luck and lit another cigarette.

Unsure what to do or where to stand, Karen was overwhelmed by the beehive of activity. She kneeled next to Pauline and thanked her again for helping to pay for the search party. While still mad at the woman for not telling her about Jason sooner, she was desperate to hear, "It's gonna be alright, sweetie," or "They'll be back before you know it, honey." She wanted to hear *something* to make herself feel better, but got nothing.

Pauline acted indifferent. The needles spun through her fingers at warp speed. Karen wasn't sure if she observed a bedrock of strength in the woman or witnessed a mother so devastated by the loss of her son and the way it transpired that part of her died as well. Maybe Pauline couldn't feel anything of significance anymore. Maybe she was desensitized.

Karen wondered if that was how it'd be should something happen to Jason. She wondered if that's how it was with all parents who lose a child. They moved on like a detached robot, unable to connect with humanity as they once did because there was no other way to cope.

"We're heading out in five," was the latest announcement from Officer Odom who continued to organize the troops and finalize the details.

She scurried back into the cabin to grab her pack. First she hugged Melissa, then Sammy. She tried to convince them everything would be alright—she tried to convince herself too. With the clothes left behind by Jason and Larry, she went outside to the dog handlers. The canines registered the scent and whined from their eagerness. On Officer Odom's command, a group of twenty-three people spread out along the woodline. They moved north with three Labradors, a mutt, and a German Shepherd leading the way.

Karen rode on the back of an ATV and her hands straddled the stomach of a man named Vince, who smelled like a musky deodorant. She glanced side to side and observed the people she was responsible for bringing together. Short, tall, thin, heavy; there were the old and the young and everything in between. For the first time since she left the house en route to the cabin, a sense of overreaction gripped her. Had she crossed the boundary of reasonable parental assertiveness? Had she become obsessed with Jason as Melissa suggested?

Every volunteer out there searched for her husband, her son, and a man named Chip. They'd made sacrifices for very little money, if any, and the possibility of getting injured or hurt was real. They did all of this because Karen lied.

She knew the guys were safe—Larry told her so the day before when he sounded so upbeat and happy. *What's the worst-case scenario?* she asked as a small tree branch smacked her helmet. That Larry, with a proven track record of being a phenomenal dad, brought Jason home a day or two later than *she* wanted. So what? They'd have to call Pine View to reschedule the extraction, that was all. Not a big deal. It wasn't the worst thing in the world, only a slight delay. Why couldn't she have more perspective? Why couldn't she have more faith in her husband?

The terrain was bumpy, uneven. While she bounced around the back of the seat, Karen considered the pieces of duct tape she'd found. She had no right to assume how Larry brought Jason to the cabin. Maybe he needed the tape to fix something. Maybe the explanation was that simple. She couldn't trust Pauline or blindly believe the woman's insinuation, she barely knew her. And Chip's wife came across as off-kilter anyway. No. She and Larry must talk. That's where it had to start. He'd at least earned that.

When they encountered Flagler's Hill, the first part of the search was over. Karen disembarked from the ATV and her lower back ached from all the jiggling. She stretched as the rest of the party readied themselves for the steep climb ahead.

With minimal sleep and sparse nutrition, her body revealed its displeasure quickly.

Winded and fatigued, she gasped for air. Her muscles burned at the higher altitude and demanded frequent rests. The backpack felt like an anvil, the hill felt like Mt. Everest. She crawled to combat the treacherous incline and resisted the urge to latch onto the person's foot in front of her. Tree branches and plant roots were used for support. She thought a spin class or weight training session was what she needed and after returning home, she would definitely take one. Why would anyone go hiking for fun? She couldn't understand the appeal.

Upon finally reaching the summit with some dirt irritating one of her eyes, people were sprawled on the ground as if a category five hurricane barreled them over. She wasn't the only one not in mountain climbing shape. But Officer Odom was and it surprised her. He discovered the first physical signs they moved about in the right direction.

Ten yards to the left of where everybody lay, he found an area of tall grass that'd been matted down. The indent suggested a person or animal spent time there in the prone position. He believed it to be a person. When questioned why, he produced a collection of candy bar wrappers. One of the wrappers still had a smidge of fresh chocolate in it.

"Does your husband enjoy candy bars?" he asked Karen.

"Larry eats pretty healthy most of the time. He doesn't eat a lot of candy."

But then she remembered what Pauline told her when they played Yahtzee. Chip's blood sugar level was pre-diabetic, so she stopped buying candy bars because he'd devour the entire bag. Karen felt a blast of excitement. Goosebumps surfaced on her arms. They'd been there! If they traveled that way going up, reason would dictate they travel it again on the way back down.

The probability of intercepting Jason and Larry was likely. It would not only save time and money or mitigate any more hassle, but it kept open the possibility of getting her son home to be picked up by Pine View—even if it meant driving through the night. When she informed Officer Odom of Chip's candy bar habit, he nodded matter-of-factly and spoke to the dog handlers.

Most of the volunteers eventually rose from the ground to enjoy the breathtaking view of the lake below. Many of them stated, "It never gets old," and "I could stare at this forever." But Karen didn't see much of it. She sought treatment for her leg. A sharp rock cut her calf on the ascent and three Band-Aids were required to stem the bleeding after a dousing of hydrogen peroxide.

She watched as everyone drank water and snacked. They chatted effortlessly. The camaraderie of living in a small rural township was evident. Her lower back continued to tighten and she stretched some more, wishing a heating pad was encased around it. But as quickly as she became thrilled about the candy bar wrappers and the likelihood of meeting up with Jason, guilt washed over her.

She felt guilty about spending money for the search, the last the Turners really had. That led to guilt about lying to Officer Odom, which led to guilt about leaving Melissa behind, which led to guilt about not being home when Jason left for the cabin, which led to guilt about lying to her brother to get the money in the first place. As her mind drilled deeper, she couldn't control it. A switch went off. She felt guilt over the girls, guilt about her husband, guilt about her son, and Karen would've continued her self-flagellation as she did daily. But she stopped. And she didn't know how or why.

As she stood gathered among a group of strangers at 10,000 feet atop Flagler's Hill, she experienced a moment of such intense introspection she got woozy. It both elated and frightened her. Feeling guilty was her norm. What started as guilt over Jason had spread to infect her like an insidious disease. She'd become an addict. A guilt addict. She'd grown used to it. She accepted it. But even more disturbing, if it wasn't around, she'd seek it.

On the rare occasions when life ran smoothly, when Jason had a good day or a week and there was no drama, Karen created issues if need be. She'd venture into the past to probe for traumatic memories and exploit mistakes as a way to punish herself, to feel remorse. Subconsciously, Jason's suicide attempts were internalized. Not only was she a bad parent, but by extension, a bad person.

Guilt was so intertwined with her persona that she couldn't live without it. While it made no sense, it made perfect sense. The breeze intensified and the sun hid behind a smattering of clouds. Karen laughed, like the joke had been on her—but it wasn't funny.

Larry pleaded with her over the years to get help and she finally comprehended his meaning. It was so obvious. She was a casualty of her son's unraveling; the collateral damage of a mother. For all the objections to therapy, her attempts to manage the battle alone were a failure. Her system never had a chance. It was like watching a game show, yet she already knew the answers. When her face twisted sheepishly at the insight of what so many people had known, one of the volunteers noticed.

"Are you alright?" they asked, and offered her a bag of peanuts. "You look a little tired."

"I feel a lot tired," Karen said. She removed a water bottle from the backpack and flipped open the lid. There were years of tiredness stored inside her.

Chapter 40

Officer Odom blew a whistle calling everyone back into action. Their break atop Flagler's Hill had ended. The dogs resumed leading the way with their noses to the ground like the miracle machines they were and Karen, still weary from her self-revelation, appreciated that so many people brought them. Why were she and Larry always against getting one? Without the power of the canines' scent, where would the search begin?

The wilderness that encompassed Lake Moonset was vast and open. It stretched uninterrupted in every direction with no obvious right or wrong way. Plucking out three people among thousands of wild acres would be incredibly difficult, and she fell toward the back of the party to concentrate on her breathing.

A painful blister shaved off the skin on her pinky toe. She attempted to remain alert but struggled to find a balance between looking in front of her for safety and glancing at the surroundings. Karen never walked so far in her life.

Up and down. Down and up. The hills went on forever and the sides of the mountains all looked the same. Ravines were scoured, creeks forded. They encountered rocky fields with an abundance of flowers and she lost count of how many snakes were spotted. The same with spiders. Twice she walked through a web where the silk clung to her face. Before she knew it, they'd been on the trail for seven hours. Dusk approached. The shadows of the forest grew longer, darker, making it hard to see.

It would be easy to miss the signs they searched for: a torn piece of clothing, a recently used fire pit, another candy bar wrapper strewn on the ground. When Officer Odom announced the suspension of activities until daylight, she was relieved. They couldn't afford to miss anything.

The tent she erected wouldn't stay up and exhaustion made her abandon it quickly. Karen fell in a mound, her backpack serving as a pillow. Three men approached the officer at the front of the camp. After a brief conversation, she noticed them continue forward in the murky light. It seemed dangerous to send people ahead despite good intentions and the idea of a protest briefly flashed through her mind. Because *she* was responsible for their safety.

The idea, however, lacked conviction. It disintegrated before it took hold. Her eyes closed with the thud of a heavy gate and she was catapulted into sleep land to battle the anguish of incident number three when . . .

Boom! Boom!

Two shotgun blasts echoed through the woods.

Karen jumped to her feet in a panic. Commotion erupted. Officer Odom instructed everyone to stay there while he investigated. She immediately grabbed her flashlight and headed toward the noise. She thought she heard voices. When somebody screamed, her eyes widened and she yelled, "Jason? Larry?"

She stretched out her arms and took longer, more daring strides. A campfire was spotted. Karen tried to run but almost tripped. She yelled their names again. More screams. Maybe an argument. The fire grew brighter, the voices louder, and one of them was recognized. But it wasn't Jason. She could've identified her little boy out of a hundred-person choir singing underwater. Although she only met the man a handful of times over the years, the person who screamed was Chip.

"Get away from me!"—he jabbed a thin, pointy stick in the air—"I didn't do anythin' wrong. The boy said he had to go to the bathroom. It wasn't my fault. You hear? It wasn't my fault."

"Relax," said a man who held a shotgun.

"Nobody said you did anything wrong," Officer Odom added. "We know it's not your fault. Now put the stick down so we can talk."

Chip jabbed the stick several more times and screamed about Larry and his buddy and how he only wanted to help. He cried ferociously. "I'm sorry. It is my fault. If only I'd locked up the gun my son would still be alive, and so would the rest of those kids."—he looked skyward—"Can you forgive me? Can anyone ever forgive me?" The jabs grew weaker as he spun around and around, spiraling himself into the ground where he curled in a ball.

"Chip," Karen said, rushing over to him. "Where are they? Are they nearby? When are they coming back?"

"Easy," Officer Odom said. "Give him some space."

She ignored the command and attempted to pry Chip from the fetal position. "It's me, Karen. Karen Turner. I'm here with the sheriff to help you. Where are Jason and Larry? Can you understand what I'm saying?"

He shook, borderline convulsed, and wailed; a man so filled with regret, his life sentence of pain was evident. She reached out and touched his hand.

"Chip, I need you to focus. Where are they? Are they headed back to the cabin? Are they still at Herrington's Peak?"

"I'm sorry. I . . ."

She helped him sit up and was about to question him further when the officer called her aside.

"They thought they saw a bear," he said. "That's the reason for the gunshots. Everybody is a little on edge right now so let's try to decompress. How well do you know this man? Is he a war vet or something?"

"Not well. Why?"

"Because he's talking about guns and shooting, that type of stuff, like he has PTSD."

"I need to speak with him."

"He's a mess, Karen. We have to let him calm down first. And when you're done with him, you can tell me what you really know. I thought you said he was a friend of the family."

She objected to the officer's demand and put up a fight, but he held firm. So she walked away. For a moment. There were too many answers to be had. She investigated the other tents behind Chip's camp and found sleeping bags plus the rest of the supplies left behind by Larry. The more information she acquired, the more confusing the situation became.

When Karen was finally able to sit next to Chip again with the officer's permission, she dropped an arm over his shoulders. Her tone lightened to that of a reassuring mother.

"You okay?"

"Bein' out in the woods like this . . . Wes and I used to hunt. I never thought he'd hunt people."

"It's alright," she said, shushing him. "It's all behind you. You're safe now. Nobody can hurt you."—she rubbed his arm—"Do you know where they are?"

His body retched but she squeezed him tighter. "You aren't in trouble. We're here to help."

"I'm sorry, Karen, about everythin'. It's been a tough few days. The noise of that gun. God how I hate the noise of guns. Brought it all floodin' back. The images of those kids. So vivid."—he blew his nose in a hanky and looked at her for the first time, a ravage sadness etched in his eyes—"I don't know what to say."

"I think you do."

"How's Pauline?"

"Hard to tell with her."

He nodded.

"Are you ready to do the right thing?" she said.

"If I can."

"Where are they? Did they go to Herrington's Peak?"

Chip hesitated. "They could've. We got separated. Larry said something about a fire tower."

"How'd you get separated?"

"Don't know. Just did."

"Why didn't they bring their sleeping bags or the tents?"

He turned away.

"Where's the fire tower? Did they have a specific destination?"

"Larry talked about a highway. Said he'd keep goin' north."

"What do you mean *he?*"—her brow furrowed—"Weren't they together?"

Chip shook his head no. "He's supposed to come back and get me. I don't wanna be out here no more. I wanna go home, Karen. Can you take me to my wife?"

"Why weren't they together?"—she maneuvered around in front of him and became agitated—"Why won't you tell me what happened? Why won't anyone tell me?"

"I . . . I tried to help. He brought me along to help save him. Like I should've saved Wes. And I messed up again."

"Why were you and Larry really at the cabin? How'd you get Jason from the house? Did you take him? Is that what you did? Did you take my son, Chip?"

"Karen," Officer Odom said with a scowl. "Let him be, for now."

"But he—"

"Can I speak with you for a minute again?"

They stepped away from the fire to the periphery of the camp. "In a few miles, Herrington's Peak splits to the west," he said. "Chip mentioned they went north. Are you sure your husband said they were hiking that Peak?"

"I'm positive. And if Larry said it, that's definitely where they'll be."

"I'll radio Officer Hastings on the other side and tell her to close in on the highway, to check any fire towers. This is a large area we're covering and with conflicting information, and most of their stuff here, the trail could run dry . . . We'll do our best."

"He knows something else, I can feel it."

"Maybe. But the man's on the verge of a nervous breakdown. I can't have that out here. He also could be dangerous not only to us, but himself. Escalating the situation won't help and I think he would've said something if he knew where they were. We'll bring him to your cabin to be held for questioning until I return. You have to keep your head on straight and trust me."

Karen clenched her jaw with her arms folded and gave no response. She walked over to Chip before leaving. "You'd better hope we find them. For your sake, and Pauline."

"I do. Believe me, I do. Everythin' will make sense when you talk to Larry. You need to talk to Larry."

"Oh, I plan to."

"I know you're probably thinkin' that—"

"You have no idea what I'm thinking."

His chin trembled and his voice grew weary. "Just know there ain't a thing in this world you can say to make me feel worse than I do with every breath I take, of every day I'm alive. It's hard livin' when you hate yourself. They went north. So should you. But I don't know where they are. Honest."

As she made her way through the darkness, a darkness that only grew deeper, she heard a voice yell from behind, "You gotta find my buddy! Please, I can't lose another one!"

CHAPTER 41

The stretcher scraped along the ground as the bottom poles dug into the dirt. Jason slowly dragged it behind him and Larry felt like he was in some type of rickshaw, sans the wheels. Rocks of all sizes were scattered across the landscape, particularly the smaller ones. The stretcher constantly wobbled across them.

They circumnavigated fallen tree branches too large to cross and plowed through pockets of dense brush that snapped and cracked around them. Plants, cunning and intelligent in their own survival, scratched, cut, and poked them in self-defense. The temperature was hot, the breezes faded.

There were no well-defined paths one finds on a day hike in a local park. Absent were the symbols attached to trees that guided hikers on long haul treks like the Appalachian and Pacific Rim trails; the colors of blue, yellow, and green showing the way. Larry monitored the compass to stay on course and theoretically the stretcher was a good idea. But like so many things in life, it lacked pragmatism in a real-world environment.

Twice Jason dropped him.

The first time they climbed a hill and his son slipped on a patch of slick leaves. Both of them tumbled backward. Jason crashed into Larry where his foot inadvertently kicked him in the neck. The second spill was the result of too much momentum as they approached the bend on a deceiving little downslope. When the stretcher flipped on its side, Larry's 220-pound frame slammed into the ground with the force of a pro wrestling takedown.

The elder Turner shrieked like a man being tortured to death and the splint twisted off his leg. His head started to bleed with greater ferocity. The constant motion of being dragged through the woods was jarring and bumpy. It instigated an already tumultuous stomach. Several bouts of vomiting occurred and the bile curdled his tongue, the acid burned his throat. On his most recent puking episode, chunks of blood were noticed mixed in with the yellowish mucus.

"You okay back there?" Jason asked, his voice strained.

"Fine, fine," Larry said. "Everything's fine."

In spite of the map displaying the most direct route to the highway in relation to a guesstimate of their location, certain areas were impossible to travel. They couldn't trek up or down anywhere too steep and dry ground was needed so the stretcher wouldn't get stuck. Fast moving creeks were to be avoided. The same with waterfalls and ponds. An alternative had to be devised for the obstacle course that lay ahead.

What should've been twenty minutes in one direction to get from point A to point B wound up being double or triple that because of the zigzag nature and inefficient way of arriving there. At certain spots, Larry had to be removed from the stretcher altogether. Jason was forced to carry him short distances as the only other choice was to backtrack. But as reality set in, the truth became evident. A tipping point had been reached mentally. To backtrack was no longer an option.

Their pace wasn't so much stop and go as it was a sloth-like stop and go then rest. Stop and go then rest. Stop and go then rest. It was mostly at Larry's request. The vibrations of the stretcher combined with the jostling hurt his leg, tore at his head. A constant presence of fresh blood pooled around his wound and kept dripping down his face.

The only time he felt better at all was not being in motion, when he was flat on his back. That's when the dizziness and pain somewhat subsided. And since the gash on his head refused to quit leaking, both of them were now shirtless. A trail of bloody soaked bandages were left behind.

"Pace yourself," he said to his son every time they stopped. "You have to pace yourself."

"We need to keep moving," was always the reply. "We need to get you out of here."

They had plenty of water but nothing to eat, and Larry wondered how much more Jason could endure. He wondered how much more *he* could endure. The stops got longer and the goes got shorter. The rests were harder to end.

At first, they engaged in small talk. Larry asked questions to make conversation and combat his fear, expectantly getting little in return. But as they traveled further into the wild a hardened silence took over. They passed nothing but trees, rocks, bushes, dirt, and leaves. There were inclines and declines, cliff faces taller than buildings. The size of the wilderness expanded as their physical existence shrank. They were a speck of two in an ocean of woods, a flea on a grizzly bear.

Their optimism leaked not like a tire with a nail hole in it, but rather a slash mark. Lake Moonset turned on them, flashing its fangs. The environment they once relished had been reduced to a harsh unforgiving landscape that tormented them along the way.

Larry thought about the woods, about how much he loved being outdoors. If he wasn't injured and they had the right preparations, he and Jason would have a great time hiking and fishing. The irony amused him as he lay on the stretcher with his eyes closed. But only for a minute. Because he was scared. He'd been scared before. Who hadn't?

He was scared when his dad died, and he was scared when Karen had a lump removed from her breast. He was scared when his kids started to drive or money was tight. He was incredibly scared when he almost lost his son to suicide not once, but twice.

His present situation, however, was not the same. It was being scared at a different level, something primal that everyone eventually faced by themselves, regardless of how many people were around or what they said. It was the type of scaredness a person never wanted to think about, but would keep them up in the middle of the night.

To remain calm and give Jason the impression he wasn't scared, that everything was fine, he resorted to something he rarely if ever did. He sang. Not much of a singer with a self-admitted terrible voice, Larry didn't know the words of too many songs. But he did know a little Johnny Cash.

He repeated the first few lines of his favorite song in a soft fragile voice and wasn't sure why he enjoyed it so much. Maybe it was the guitar or the rhythm. Maybe the Man in Black just had something special. When it aggravated his head too much to sing and he couldn't keep his mouth wet no matter how much water he drank, the tune played quietly in his mind.

"Hold on," Larry said when Jason gripped the stretcher again and tilted it up. He raised a hand like one of his students who requested a hall pass to the bathroom. "I need another minute."—his voice had deteriorated, tumbling out dusty and dry—"One more minute."

"We've been stopped for a half-hour. We need to keep moving if we're going to get you home."

"Please. One more."

The salty metal taste of blood intensified. It felt chewy and thick, like he could choke on it. At last check his pulse decreased to the forties. He resorted to long, slow breaths, and it was a struggle to keep the earth around him from spinning. A tiredness he'd never known possible washed through every muscle and bone in his body. How had Edgar Suarez done it? How did the man survive in Yellowstone Park all by himself for so many days in such horrendous conditions? Larry began to question himself.

Why didn't he bring walkie talkies so he could contact Chip? How come they didn't have a flare gun? Why didn't he throw more food in his pack when he went after Jason? Or a tent? Or an extra shirt? He swallowed and grimaced. Why wouldn't the pain stop inside his head? Or the ringing? How the hell did he get the dumb idea to kidnap his son in the first place?

"You ready?" Jason asked. "Let's go."

"Wait," Larry said. He took another breath and held up his hand to request more time.

They started to move again anyway, and plodded in the direction of the highway. At least for a little while. They only made it another ten minutes before Larry couldn't take it anymore. He pleaded with his son in the name of agony. When they finally stopped, their daily total equaled three miles. According to his interpretation of the map, they had eighteen more to go.

CHAPTER

A nice flat spot near a fish-laden creek with berries and edible plants would've been an ideal place to camp for the night. But they settled for what they had: an uneven ground near a tall slab of granite that was eroded at the base. The indentation of the granite formed a cave-like structure and allowed half of their bodies to fit in. The rock also provided the benefit of conduction once they lit a fire. It was an aspect of hiking Larry always found curious from a scientific perspective, how the temperature could change so drastically. Even on a hot sunny day in the middle of July, the mercury would dip into the thirties at night.

Jason searched for food but came up empty, so they drank water for dinner and took in the view of a flowery bush. The sun lost flight behind them as they sat in the shade. Larry shivered. He felt the color drain from his skin. His lips grew cold. He rubbed his arms and blew on his hands, yet still couldn't get warm. If the man got any closer to the fire, he would've been inside it.

"You alright?" Jason asked again.

"I'm fine, I'm fine," Larry said. He tried to smile but couldn't and his teeth started chattering. "As good as I'm gonna be."

The map was spread out between them with one stone fastened to their presumed current location and another at the closest point to the highway. They discussed the best route to take come morning, which not only gave them something to do, but also bestowed a sense of purpose. Larry pressed his fingers against the carotid artery and could feel the blood flow wane. The force inside his vessels weakened, his pulse plummeted. He knew.

"What it is now?" Jason asked, staring at his father.

"It's fine, it's fine," he said, and refused to state the results. The number thirty would be kept to himself. So would the fact that blood began to leak from his ears.

For the countless times he'd hiked in frigid conditions, including a ten-day stint in Alaska with his dad to view the Aurora Borealis, he'd never been so cold in his life. He'd heard seniors talk about the cold, how they could never get comfortably warm sometimes. But Larry was the type of person who kept the house cool all year-round and if anything, he struggled with the heat. He considered the stack of sweaters back home in his closest. He would've killed just to have one of them.

"Tell me," Jason said. "I want to know."

"It's where it needs to be." He started to clear his throat but the pain gripped him.

"I can take it for you so we can keep track. Here, let me have the watch. Let's see what mine is."—Larry handed over the watch and saw Jason take his pulse like an expert—"It's sixty-six."

"That's good. You've got youth on your side. Remember that."

Jason kept the fire roaring as there was no shortage of wood. Larry slept on and off, mostly on, where he whimpered like a dog having a nightmare. Each time when he awoke, he was confused and needed reassurance where he was. He thought they were at the cabin. Jason didn't argue with him after a while, and that's ultimately what he led his father to believe. They were hanging around the fire pit at the cabin and the rest of the family would arrive soon.

The temperature dropped steadily as the constellations rotated across a moonlit sky and the Earth spun on its axis at a thousand miles per hour. Time moved slowly. Their haggard condition made it even slower. There were several more hours until the sun came up and in his moments of clarity, that was Larry's goal—to see the sun come up. Everything is better in daylight, he told himself. The sun makes everything better.

"If you could have anything to eat right now, what would it be?" Jason asked.

"Nothing," Larry said, shaking his head. "I feel sick."

"Mine would be pizza. Like the ones I used to make. That would be my last supper."

"Don't say that. You got plenty more suppers ahead of you."

Larry coughed and droplets of blood splatted into his hand. He'd grown tired of Jason's random questions but understood what the boy did. It was a standard survival practice to keep an injured party engaged, particularly with a head wound.

"What if you could see any basketball game you wanted right now? Pro or college. With any seat."

"My bed. The only thing I want to see is my bed."

"I'd see a Warriors game."

"Morell Park?"

"Golden State."

More coughing, this time a coughing fit. Larry spit on the ground and grunted. He drooled on himself. They looked at one another as he wiped his chin, an intense understanding between them.

Jason unzipped the bottom of his pant leg and removed it. He handed it over. "Here, for your lips. To clean them."

Larry waved him off. He wiped his chin again, this time with his forearm, and smeared blood across his cheeks. "You need heat to survive."

"Right now, you need it more. Come on, take it. And if you want, I could . . . I could help."

"You are helping. More than you know."—Larry accepted the cloth and dabbed the stains on his face—"I'm in a rough one, Son, aren't I?"

Jason nodded.

"It's not good, is it?"

Another nod. Jason's jaw quivered a bit. "Are you scared of dying?"

Larry glanced at him and sighed. He leaned forward. "What kind of question is that to ask your father?"

"The kind adults never talk about."

A long silence ensued. The hiss of the flames and the crackling of wood filled the cool air. Larry's goal was to be strong for his son to the end, to be tough. He wanted to show that he wasn't scared, but he also wanted to be honest.

"Yeah, I'm scared," he said. "I think everybody is when it gets right down to it. It's easy to say you aren't when it's only talk, when you feel healthy. Seeing it come straight at you, that's something different."

"But how? You always go to church and tell me I should pray. You're religious."

"You should pray. It's powerful. Body, mind, and spirit. That's what I tried to teach. But it doesn't mean you can't be scared because nobody knows what will definitely happen. You think you *might* know, and you hope, but you really don't. The only thing we have for sure is our faith."—he removed the saturated bandage from his head and threw it in the fire—"Are you scared too?"

"Yeah. At least most of the time."

"Then why do you want to do it so bad?"

Jason nibbled his lower lip and the fire reflected in his watery eyes. He poked the coals with a stick. "This is so freaking hard for me to talk about. I'm embarrassed, like I did something wrong. I'm supposed to be a man. Look how big I am. But I usually feel weak and small."

"There's nothing to be embarrassed about."—Larry coughed and gagged for a moment. It took a minute to compose himself—"Would you feel the same if you had a heart or kidney condition?"

"No."

"Then what's the difference? The brain is just another part of the body."

"But there's a stigma attached to the brain. It means you're a screw-up. That's what everybody thinks. That's what I think most of the time. I know it's illogical, but . . . Are you ashamed of me? For how I am."

"Not for a second. I'm proud of you, Jason. You're my only son, and I wouldn't change that for anything."

"What about Karen?"

"Never."

"Why won't this thing go away? What did I do to deserve this misery?"

"You did nothing wrong. What's happened can't be explained. Sometimes in life it . . . It just is."

Jason threw a log on the fire. "It beats me up, you know, like a bully. I can't think of any other—"

"Dying isn't the answer. You have to know that by now. It affects all the people who care about you and will ruin so many lives."

"But we're all gonna die someday. In the long run, does it really matter what we do?"

Larry hung his head and took some deep breaths. He touched the ground to avoid toppling over. "What if dying isn't what you think? What if the afterlife is worse because the way you went about it? Have you really thought about what comes next?"

"You're only saying that because of your religion."

"I say that because what you tried to do is unnatural. It's wrong. Our job is to live as long as we can and do our best while we're here. We cannot die of our own hand. It's not our decision to make."

It was quiet for a minute before Jason said, "I . . . I don't want to do it all the time. But sometimes the thoughts come so hard. They back me down. I can't seem to shake them."

"Life is special and mysterious. We make of it what we will and at some point, there are no excuses. But children are supposed to outlive their parents. It's the universal law of our species, of how we function."—he scraped up a handful of dirt—"You aren't supposed to die before me."

"Stop it, Larry. You aren't gonna die. Understand? Once the sun comes up we're gonna get you out of here. You're gonna see Karen and the girls again. I'll carry you all the way back if I have to. Enough."—Jason sniffled and looked away from his father—"If you could meet any celebrity, who would it be?"

Larry closed his eyes. He didn't answer. For the next several hours he drifted off to sleep and began to sweat as he shivered. When he woke, he asked why they weren't at the cabin.

"We'll be there soon," Jason said.

"Good, good. Tell Pops we're going fishing. But we need to use live bait this time."

"I'll tell him."

Larry refused to drink more water when it was offered. "I'm done wetting myself and I'm not thirsty. Now tell your mother I don't like lamb chops. She won't listen to me. Keeps trying to serve me lamb chops."

"She knows. She'll make something else."

"Good, good. She listens to you. You're her favorite." He didn't feel cold anymore and his gash nor leg no longer hurt. His head felt detached from his body, like it floated in space. A reassuring peacefulness wrapped around him. He was on the slide at a playground, slipping one way to the end. The worlds of his existence were colliding.

"If we play man to man, I think we can win the states this year."

"It's a smart strategy," Jason said. "We'll work on it."

"The Smolinski boys are good, but you're better."

"I know."

"Make sure you get Christmas presents for Pops and Grandma. They do a lot for you."

"I will."

"Jason?" Larry asked. "Jason, is that you?"

"I'm right here."

"You aren't gonna leave me?"

"No way, I'm staying."

"Good, good. I never want you to leave me. I wish we could do it all over again . . . I'm sorry about the sheet in your room."

"No worries. Save your strength."

Larry rubbed his eyes. "How'd we get here?"

"We walked."

"Me and you? From the house?"

"Yes."

"We did walk, didn't we?"—Larry grinned and reached out his hands—"You're a good boy, you know that?"

Jason got up and sat next to his father. He put an arm around him. "Everything's going to be okay. I'll take care of it."

"I know. And I love you, Son. Always have. Always will."

"Love you too . . . Dad."

They sat like that for another hour, Larry fading in and out of consciousness. There was nothing that could be done as Jason listened to whatever his father had to say.

"Where's Chip?" Larry asked.

"Back at the camp."

"Good, good. Be sure and thank him for me. I never would've made it all these years without him."

"I will, Dad."

"Tell the girls I want meatloaf for my birthday. And chocolate ice cream. They asked me the other day."—Larry looked down at his bare chest—"Where'd our shirts go?"

"We gave them to some homeless kids."

"That's good. It's important to help people."

Larry's breath labored and he wheezed. Blood now covered his teeth and lips, his nose and ears.

"Feeling tired," he whispered. "Gonna sleep like there's no tomorrow."

"Me too."

"I only need one thing." Larry took his time and concentrated all the strength left for his final request. He spoke slow. He tried not to slur. "Promise me you'll stop killing your mother. Fight this. You know how to win."

Jason squeezed his father tightly as the last gasp was near. Giant tears raced down his face. For the first time in five years, Jason Turner cried for somebody other than himself.

"I will," Jason said, trembling. "I promise. I'm sorry, Dad. I'm sorry. I'm sorry."

"Stop killing your mother," Larry repeated. "Go find her. Fight. Don't stay here with me. Stop killing her . . . Stop . . . Please . . . Fight." With one final shallow breath he said, "Go," and his eyes closed. His head fell to the side. The plan to save his son, to save his family, was officially over.

Chapter

Base camp at Herrington's Peak was a cluster of tents on a steep slope mixed in among the cedar and bristlecone pine trees. Makeshift clotheslines were hung up for drying and small charred fire pits littered the landscape. Karen crawled from her tent that'd collapsed on one side. She threw sticks on the fire, then blew on the coals. The wind calmed to a peaceful breeze and she winced, catching a whiff of her body odor.

Day five of the search began like day four. Participants were intent on leaving. Supplies had grown lean and there'd been no sign of the Turner men, no more breadcrumbs to indicate the volunteers were being led on the right path. Morale plummeted. She noticed some people on the edge of camp with their gear packed. They appeared ready to head back down the mountain, not up.

She'd heard rumors that to climb even rougher ground would be the remaining party's last effort. It was becoming too dangerous. Whispers spread that the search and rescue mission had devolved into a search and recovery. The two lost souls had simply been gone too long. Lake Moonset claimed them. But Karen refused to believe it. She knew Jason and Larry were still out there. She also knew they were running out of time.

The blisters on her feet were raw and bloody. They wouldn't heal properly until she stopped walking. After changing the bandages and wishing for a clean pair of socks, she gazed at the imposing summit ahead. It resembled a photo from *National Geographic* with a thin layer of mist on top. Only people with experience were to make the challenging ascent and she was not to come along—that's what she'd been told. But she planned to go anyway, to be at the vanguard. Neither words or sore feet could thwart her.

Officer Odom reviewed a map with his tent unzipped and the front flap open when Karen limped over. An LED lantern lit everything brightly.

"The weather is good," she said. "You want to blow the whistle, set it in motion? We need to leave before we lose anybody else."

"Good morning to you too," he said. "How about letting these folks eat breakfast and get warmed up first? We got all day to make the ascent. If people want to quit, they can. We pushed kinda hard already."

"But we're almost there and I know they're waiting. I can feel it. So let's not waste any time."

He called her closer with a flick of his hand and pointed to the map. "You see that outline? That's the area we've covered. I've got some very experienced woodsmen out there who know these parts and we still haven't found any evidence your husband traveled this way. If we don't find them soon, well, I can only conclude one thing . . . They were never here."

"But this is where he said they were going. How could we not see them?"

"Are you sure you heard him right, that it was Herrington's Peak?"

Karen thought she was sure but her mind was frazzled that day when speaking to Larry. She was upset with him for taking Jason and worried about them getting home in time for Pine View. Could she have heard him wrong? Perhaps the names of the peaks got confused. But it wasn't like her to mess up such a crucial detail—especially involving her son. No. She definitely heard Larry right. She'd bet her life on it. So why would he tell her one thing and then do another?

"Yes, I'm sure," she said, defensively. "You already asked me that. And if for some reason we don't find them today, even though we will, maybe another course should be charted."

He shook his head. "Can't do it, Karen. Too late. This thing needs to get wrapped up."

"You see, when they hiked in the past, it was usually to the south. That's Larry's favorite area. It's not so steep over there for Jason and there are plenty of trails. Maybe they lost their phones and couldn't tell me, but decided to forget going this way. It's too rugged. So they changed—"

"That's not gonna happen."

"South would definitely make more sense when you think about it. Where else could they be?"

"Today is it. These people have tried their best, and so have we."

"What does that mean? Because I can get more money. I'll find a way to increase their rate if that's what it takes."

"This has to be over," he said, slipping on a fleece jacket before he left the tent. She was right behind and badgered him further about blowing the whistle when his cell phone rang.

Officer Odom nodded several times when he answered and Karen heard a woman's voice on the other end. It sounded official. She stayed close as he tried to move away but she couldn't make out what they said.

"What's going on?" she asked. An uneasy feeling swirled in her stomach.

He covered the phone and turned to her. "I need a minute. Go back to the camp and I'll meet you."

"Is this related to the search? Is this about—"

"It's not a request, Karen. Please go."

She hesitated, trying to read his uncertain eyes, then edged her way down the slope. The swirling in her stomach intensified to a painful knot, and she stopped to look back. She picked up a pinecone and threw it. The second he was off the phone, she'd confront him again.

A few more people were spotted deserting the camp and she hurried toward them. "You can't just leave," she said. "One more day. It's all I ask. I know we'll find them soon."

"We're ready to go home, Mrs. Turner. They ain't up here."

"But this is my son we're talking about. Just a little bit further. I can pay more." She continued to plead her case until seeing Officer Odom stand near a fallen oak tree with the trunk split in half. He stared at the ground with a hand on his hip, then looked at her. She waved, but he didn't wave back, and she rushed over.

"What did the woman say?" she asked, trying to catch her breath. "What was it about?"

He gently grabbed her elbow and directed his focus far above her head. Beads of sweat clung to his skin despite the cool weather. "The call was from Officer Hastings of Portersville. She's on the other side of the mountain. She said they, uh . . . They found something Karen. They found . . ."

All the moisture in her mouth evaporated, like she'd eaten a spoonful of sand. She gazed up at him, her mind a glass pane waiting to shatter.

"They found two bodies. One of them—"

"No!" she screamed. "Don't say it!"

He redirected his eyes to look right at her. "I'm sorry, they found two—"

She shrieked and crumbled onto the ground, covering her ears like a child having a tantrum. She didn't want to hear any more. The worse had been expected not only for that day or that week, but the last several years combined. The conclusion to her situation seemed obvious, almost inevitable. Now it was here—hope was gone. The tone of the messenger's unsteady voice combined with his appearance told her everything. Jason and Larry had been found. And the word *bodies* was used.

Karen wanted to run, to distance herself from the past and the present and future. But she had nowhere to go and no way to get there. It all led back to the same point from when it started anyway. Regardless of how hard or how much she tried, an escape would never be possible. The fence was too tall, the maze too confining, and she knew. She always knew. So she rocked back and forth and cried.

A crowd gathered around to witness the scene and people spoke quietly among themselves. Officer Odom ordered everyone back to their tents, to prepare for the day as usual. He'd be with them soon. Reluctantly, the group dispersed.

He sat down next to her and gripped her shaky hand. After a long, hysterical sob, she whispered, "I'm ready."

"I'm sorry, Karen. One of the bodies seems to be that of your husband. My condolences. He's passed away."

"And the other?" she asked, her eyes bulging from the darkened sockets. The future of her mental stability rode on the answer.

"He's alive and—"

She hugged Officer Odom, squeezing with all the strength she had left. "Thank God," she said as the tears leaked onto his jacket and her chest heaved. "Thank you so much dear heavenly Father."

"He's in rough shape. But his vitals appear to be stable. There was no ID on him either, but given his age and the physical description you gave, we can be ninety-nine percent sure it's your son."

"Can he talk? Can he move? Is he paralyzed? Is he—"

"We're gonna get you over to the hospital ASAP. They say he'll make it. That's all I know. I called in a favor and the medevac chopper is coming back for us after they drop him off."

The sun rose higher and warmed the air as the dew burned off. He draped a blanket across her back before walking to the top of the camp. He blew the whistle. "Alright everybody, listen up. I have an announcement to make. The men we're looking for have been located by Officer Terry Hastings over near Cutter's Creek."

Cheers erupted and Karen heard the stir of commotion, but it sounded muffled like it was far away. She felt numb inside and couldn't stop trembling. Was Larry really gone? How was that possible? Was Jason truly okay? For a second she expected to wake up in the tent and start the day again.

"I'm sorry to have to tell you this," the officer continued, "but of the missing men, only one survived. We presume that it was Jason, the youngest. As of now those are the only details I've received. I need you to all head back to the Turners' cabin. I'll go forward via the air. Vince knows these woods better than anyone and will lead you home safely. Thank you for doing such a tremendous job. I'm honored to be your servant."

As quickly as the cheers erupted they vanished. Mrs. Turner's husband was dead. The boy's father was dead. A pall spread across the mountain like a tide of wretchedness rippling across a pond. The troops packed up their tents and supplies with minimal conversation, then set out down the side of the mountain. Karen sat unmoved on the cold, hard ground. She was disheveled and dirty and her body was spent—as was her mind.

She pulled her knees to her chest and wrapped her arms around them. Metal jingled, boots stomped, and the friction of clothing could be heard from behind. She sobbed a little harder each time a volunteer stopped and stroked her arm or touched a shoulder and said, "My condolences about your husband, Mrs. Turner," or "It's a miracle about your son, Karen."

She didn't know how to balance her emotions or where to begin. One minute she was high with relief about Jason and the next she was grief-stricken over Larry. She noticed the discolored band of skin on her ring finger that would now be permanent. A helplessness inflicted her spirit as if the universe had slipped her a drug. The world appeared different. How much time had elapsed since Jason's unraveling? The months seemed like years and the years seemed like decades. Karen had been forced to handle so much. She stared at the clouds drifting above and wondered if Larry was already up there, watching over her, protecting her. From that moment forward, she'd be forced to handle so much more.

The wind stopped, the barking of dogs receded. The camp that was usually loud with chatter and movement and instructions getting shouted became quiet. Eerily quiet. And she hated it. For that's what awaited her at home when the shock dissipated and the daily routine of life resumed. More quiet. The silence of a widow. She felt dizzy and laid back, staring at the clouds once more. She and Officer Odom were the only ones left.

"The chopper should be here within the hour," he said. "After I leave the hospital I'll go to the cabin and meet with Chip, to hear what he has to say. We'll need to get a statement."

Karen wiped her face with the blanket and turned to him. "Can you tell me what was said on the phone? How were they found?"

"It's not important how we found them, just that we did."

"I think it could help."

Officer Odom scratched his jaw, then rubbed his chin. When he spoke, he did so lightly. "A male figure approximately in his early twenties had been located less than a quarter mile off of highway 40 near Cutter's Creek. He was in a drainage ditch. Face down. No shirt. Pants torn to shreds. Insect bites and . . . I don't want—"

"Go on. Please."

"Insect bites and bloody scabs covered his entire body. Second degree sunburn. He was severely malnourished with lots of bruises, but he had a pulse and was breathing."

"And Larry?"

"An older male, age not determined, was found next to your son on some type of stretcher contraption. He'd been dead for a while. Serious decomposition and insect manifestation had set in. Head trauma. Foot injury. They'll do an autopsy to determine the cause of death."

The details of her husband's demise only led to more questions and there were so many answers she wanted to know, but probably never would. Whatever happened out in that wilderness, Larry deserved better. If only Pauline had contacted her earlier, maybe she could've prevented it.

They remained like that in the stillness, in the somberness, and waited for the chopper to arrive. At the base of Herrington's Peak. The last of the *Moonset Seven*.

"Please know that I'm thankful for you," she said. "Can't thank you enough, sir. For all that you've done."

"Just doing my job, Karen. We did it together . . . Once again, my condolences about your husband."—he stood as the sound of a helicopter rumbled up from the floor of the valley—"You gonna be alright?"

She shook her head no, then sat up and shrugged. "I guess I have to be. For my son. He'll need me now more than ever."—she held out a hand to block the sun's glare—"And of course, for my daughters too."

CHAPTER 44

A vehicle pulled into the driveway and the brakes squealed when it stopped. The engine idled as Karen dashed to the living room window. She peered through the blinds and watched Jason climb from the passenger's side of Chip's truck. He raised a foot on top of the running board while they chatted.

It took them a month to finish painting Principal Smith's house, even though Larry had most of the project completed beforehand. Today was to be the final day. Karen was excited about that. Maybe now her son would cease spending so much time with that man.

Earlier that afternoon, she received a phone call from Larry's former colleague to say how proud he was of Jason—that her husband would be proud too. Principal Smith also said he put a little extra money in the check as a bonus, as a way to say thanks.

The praise of her son poured in like the steady stream of a garden hose since Larry's death. It was hard for her to believe. She received letters from former teammates, emails from neighbors, and phone calls from people she hadn't spoken to in years.

After Larry passed, when Jason was alone in the woods, he hauled his father's body across thirty miles of rugged countryside by himself. Both shoulders suffered structural damage from the journey, one of them required surgery. Weeks of physical therapy were needed but the cuts healed fast and the bruises faded. The now twenty-two-year-old made a splendid and full recovery. Because he should have. Because as Larry and Karen always told him, he had youth on his side. There was nothing in life more precious.

She blew a strand of hair off her face and moved from the window as Jason and Chip continued to talk. Karen didn't approve of them working together. It left a revolting taste in her mouth and at first she protested, until realizing she had no say. The choice wasn't hers. But what bothered her more than their work relationship was their personal one. They hung out socially. It didn't seem right.

She cringed when Jason went to Chip's RV for dinner or they took a scenic ride into the mountains. The Waltzers were despised for what they'd done and unwelcome in the Turners' home. She believed they should both be in jail. The one time Chip wormed his way inside the house to use the bathroom after dropping off Jason, she threatened to call the police. And when Pauline sent her a monogrammed scarf as a perceived peace offering, Karen promptly threw it away.

"So, let me see it," she said with a big smile when Jason walked through the front door. A puppy named Lia ran toward him and jumped on his leg. "I talked to Principal Smith and he told me about the check. Congratulations. Pick up the dog and I'll take a picture."

Jason removed his paint stained sneakers and played with the puppy, a Labradoodle that already weighed thirty pounds. He posed for the picture as instructed then went into the kitchen. Karen followed.

"Any idea what you'll do with the money?" she asked. "A down payment on a new car would be nice. Something spacious. How about an SUV? Or it could always be used to buy books for college, you know, if you decide to go."

"I'm not sure. I haven't even cashed the check yet."—he grabbed a diet soda from the fridge—"Maybe I'll become a house painter like Dad, buy some updated tools. Maybe I'll start coaching."

She offered further suggestions about the money when a timer beeped. Karen bent over to check on dinner and removed a bubbling pan of lasagna from the oven. When she turned back around, Jason was gone. His footsteps were heard going up the stairs.

It was only the two of them now. Sarah transferred to that college in Texas and left the day after Larry's funeral, taking the train. She declared to never set foot inside the house again or return to California. The details of her father's death were twisted around to suit her agenda and she blamed her mother for everything. Although Karen fully expected it, she cried herself to sleep for several nights afterward.

Melissa moved out quickly as well. There were too many memories, she'd said, and staying at Sammy's until graduation would be much easier. She visited her mother twice a week near the museum for coffee. They discussed the possibility of going shopping or to the movies, but neither of those happened.

Karen leaned against the counter with a red apron on. She sorted through a stack of mail while the lasagna cooled. Another hospital bill was received and the total so far for Jason's surgery and recovery equaled the cost of sending him to Pine View in the first place. She paid what she could and was put on a payment plan for the rest of the fees not covered by their insurance.

Jason never went to Pine View, never set a toe or a foot anywhere near the facility. But due to insufficient notice, the Turners forfeited their deposit. She complained at first to the management that it wasn't fair and their policy should accommodate extenuating circumstances. The week after her son's rescue and Larry's death had been chaotic. Couldn't they make an exception?

But maturity prevailed and she came to her senses. The paperwork had been properly explained, signed, and the terms were quite clear. Because after all, she asked herself, what in life was fair? The answer was nothing.

Money was no longer as worrisome with Larry's life insurance policy resolving a good portion of their debt. But like everyone else she knew, she feared not having enough of it. The loan from her brother was paid back in full, with interest, and she erased one of their mortgages. Jason's medical bills from incident number one and two had been wiped out and she paid twenty sessions in advance with Dr. Baker for him. Both girls' college funds were replenished to the fullest.

She grabbed the lettuce from the fridge to make a salad and the years of clutter on the door had been removed. The surface was now covered exclusively with photos of Larry. The shrine was added to first on a daily basis, then weekly, then monthly before it petered out. Karen still pulled over a chair every few days and would stare at the pictures for hours. The snapshots of their life together were reflected upon.

It seemed like only yesterday Larry brought her on a romantic vacation, caught his first prized fish, or coached his team to a regional championship. There were photos of Larry and the kids; Larry and his parents; Larry and her at the beach. She'd captured his image at anniversary parties, birthday parties, and all the holidays. Larry as Santa; Larry as the Easter Bunny; Larry in his favorite brown suit, the one he wore every year for the first day of school, his Mighty Warriors pin stuck to the lapel. That's how he wanted to be remembered, he once told her. As a teacher before a coach, and as a father over both of them. A loving husband was always atop his list.

Karen thought of him often and missed him more than she ever dreamed possible. At least one morning a week she reached for his warm body in bed. When she closed her eyes she could hear him, at times even smell him. She half expected him to walk into the house someday like nothing happened and ask what's for dinner, then go check on Jason.

Why did she take him for granted? How could he be gone? She assumed he'd always be there and criticized herself for not being warmer or more understanding—especially toward the end. It was a new kind of guilt she'd have to adjust to, adding to the list. Perhaps she'd work through it in her next therapy session. She'd gone three times already and while it still made her uncomfortable, she planned to go back. For him. Karen would do anything for *him* now.

She set the table and continued to sift through the mail when an envelope addressed to Jason appeared. It was from Zack Smolinski, her son's former teammate and friend. She glanced over her shoulder like she had something to hide, then opened it. Karen opened all his mail and rationalized she did so to keep him focused on the right mental track. Inside were tickets for a college basketball game in January. She approved of the positive opportunity the tickets provided and decided to forward them along.

The dog barked and she put it outside before summoning her son for dinner. Music played softly as they ate, a suggestion from Dr. Baker. Jason was allowed to pick whatever he wanted and once more, he chose country-western.

"Thanks," he said when finished. He scrunched up a napkin and dropped it onto his plate. "It was good."

"There'll be plenty of leftovers in case you get hungry later. And I'm making cookies after I do the dishes. Your favorites. You want me to bring you some?"

"No thanks. If I want any I'll come down."—he stood and yawned—"I think I'll take a nap."

She pulled back her blouse and turned up her wrist, glancing at a new watch. "But it's only six o'clock. Don't you want to go do something? Maybe go to the park or hang out with some kids your own age."

"Been working all day and my shoulders ache. It's hard. Some other time."

Karen swallowed like a bone got caught in her throat. She forced an awkward smile, and told herself to go easy. Relax. But she'd lost too much already. She wouldn't lose him again.

"That's the second time this week you've taken a nap. Everything is okay, Jason, isn't it?" The *isn't it* part of her question came off as desperate and she scolded herself for sounding too eager. "Is there anything you want to talk about? Have you been taking your vitamins? How about your meds? Are you sure you don't want more to eat?"

He pushed in his chair. "I'm tired. That's all . . . I've had enough." He walked to the back deck and retrieved the dog without another word.

After making a batch of peanut butter cookies and putting on a fresh pot of coffee, Karen went to the living room and sat on the couch. There was a magazine in her hand she had no interest in reading. She glanced up at Jason's room.

Her mind scrolled through a list of excuses as if searching through a rolodex, and it didn't take long to select one. Did the tile near the stairway seem cracked? Was the baseboard buckling because of it? The problem had to be investigated immediately, and before Karen knew what transpired, she made it to step number three. Her fingers tapped anxiously on the bannister.

She looked at Jason's door and second-guessed her decision to put it back on the hinges. They both agreed that he'd earned it, and Dr. Baker approved, but . . . The area atop the hallway was always so dark. The only light in his room came from the glow of a TV. *Why are there never any lights on up there?* she asked herself. *Why does a boy his age need a nap?*

She lingered on the stairs until cautiously taking another step. That was followed by one more. Slowly, Karen inched her way forward hoping to hear Jason converse on the phone with a friend. Maybe he'd play one of the motivational CDs she'd bought him or lift weights again like in high school. She wanted to hear him do something, anything, but the only noise came from the TV. It was always on, all the time, and remained fixed to either the science or nature channel. That's all her son watched since getting home from the hospital.

Karen slumped against the wall and slid onto the floor. It reminded her the carpet was due for a steam clean. She wondered if Jason was truly alright. Could he simply be faking? Perhaps she needed to be around more often to find out. Maybe she'd returned full-time at the museum too early.

A good mother should be home to take care of her children, to see what's happening. That included access to them when necessary. Maybe putting the door back up gave him too much freedom and privacy. Maybe, as initially suspected, her little boy needed her more than she knew.

She closed her eyes and lowered her head, covering her face with a hand.

Jason seemed dramatically changed by Larry's death, especially at first. Glimpses of his old self made rare but pleasant appearances. He was more mature since getting saved, more self-aware. Although she tried to pry, dig, and scrape, he never talked about any specifics of his ordeal. Not the woods or the duct tape or the cabin or the rescue. At least not to her. But he did give a statement to Officer Odom.

"I went with my dad and his good friend Chip to the cabin, to help fix it. We got lost hiking, then got separated. We were on the way to Herrington's Peak. My father tripped going down an embankment and hit his head. It's as simple as that." And so it was.

Lately, however, Karen started to notice things. Small things. Jason frequently appeared exhausted and while his sleep increased, she questioned if a full ten hours every night were really needed. He also didn't talk as much, becoming laconic. Their conversations dwindled in both strength and stamina.

While he continued to eat better than before and gained twenty pounds, he no longer filled his plate with seconds or requested dessert. His attitude with her also changed. He turned super polite, almost robotic in their interactions. Was that how it happened the first time? Subtly, gradually. Did his personality disintegrate until it was too late? How did they never notice? How did they miss the signs? Was he backsliding again? Was incident number three on the horizon? Could it be predicted? The only person Jason socialized with was Chip, and what kind of person is that for a boy to spend time with? What kind of . . .

Stop it, she said and forced herself up. She stared at his door before taking a few additional steps. There were plenty more sheets in the linen closet and it would be easy to remove the wooden barrier and replace it with cloth. Maybe go with yellow or blue this time instead of green. On a temporary basis. For his own protection. For her peace of mind.

Let him be, she told herself, now standing right outside his room. *He's doing good and you have to let him be.* Intellectually she understood the concept. She was smart. But Karen Turner couldn't help herself. When it came to her son, she was incapable of letting him be. She'd been damaged too far and too deep for too long. So she brushed the thoughts aside and knocked on the door anyway.

"Jason, are you okay in there?"

Silence.

She counted to ten quietly and knocked louder. "Jason, I asked if you're alright?"

A long pause ensued. Her chest thumped as her mind began to spin. She gripped the knob with a sweaty palm and was about to turn it, when a voice called out, "Everything's fine, Karen. Everything will be fine . . . I promised."

Everything's fine, she whispered, and rested her head on the door. It never got any easier. And the next night she'd do it again.

She went downstairs to finish cleaning the kitchen. A photo of Larry was removed from the fridge. It was her favorite, the one taken in black and white. She kissed her husband as a tear rolled over her cheek.

Because everything's fine.

Everything was always fine.

THE END

ABOUT THE AUTHOR

Daniel Pare grew up in the northeast, lives in the south, and has traveled extensively out west. *No Matter The Price* is his debut novel. He is currently at work on his next novel and a collection of short stories, and is a member of the Florida Writers Association.

Visit www.danielparebooks.com for all ways to connect.

NOTE FROM THE AUTHOR

Word-of-mouth is crucial for any author to succeed. If you enjoyed *No Matter the Price*, please leave a review online—anywhere you are able. Even if it's just a sentence or two. It would make all the difference and would be very much appreciated.

Thanks!
Daniel Pare

Thank you so much for checking out one of our **Literary Fiction** novels. If you enjoy this book, please check out our recommended title for your next great read!

The Five Wishes of Mr. Murray McBride by Joe Siple

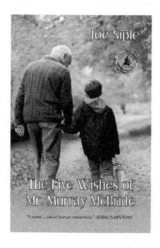

2018 Maxy Award "Book of the Year"

"A sweet...tale of human connection...will feel familiar to fans of Hallmark movies." *–KIRKUS REVIEWS*

"An emotional story that will leave readers meditating on the life-saving magic of kindness." *–IndieReader*

CPSIA information can be obtained
at www.ICGtesting.com
Printed in the USA
FSHW010158060821
83663FS